The Coming of the Lord

The Coming of
of the
Lord

Angela Murphy Murder Mysteries Book 2

Elly Grant

Published 2017 by Creativia
Book design by Creativia (www.creativia.org)
Cover art by http://www.thecovercollection.com/

For more information and to buy copies, you can link to Elly author page on Amazon at
http://www.amazon.com/Elly-Grant/e/B008DGF83W/
or http://www.amazon.co.uk/Elly-Grant/e/B008DGF83W/
or visit her website at http://ellygrant.wix.com/ellygrant

Books by the Author

Death in the Pyrenees series:

- Palm Trees in the Pyrenees
- Grass Grows in the Pyrenees
- Red Light in the Pyrenees
- Dead End in the Pyrenees
- Deadly Degrees in the Pyrenees

Angela Murphy series:

- The Unravelling of Thomas Malone
- The Coming of the Lord

Also by Elly Grant

- Never Ever Leave Me
- Death at Presley Park
- But Billy Can't Fly
- Twists and Turns

Chapter 1

Rachel Stone was singing along with a song on Radio 2 as she washed the breakfast dishes in the kitchen sink. It was a bright, Spring morning and she was enjoying watching the birds eating the scraps of food she'd put out on the bird table. She pushed back hair from her eyes with a soapy, Marigold-gloved hand, leaving a wet streak on her forehead. Drat, she thought, and reached for the dish towel to dry her face. Rachel was a short, plump woman with a round, rosy-cheeked face, framed by soft, golden curls and she was proud that she looked young for her age. Alan, her husband of thirty years, had left for work and she loved having this time of the day for herself.

"You've got a nice voice you should sing hymns in church. Jesus would like that."

A startled Rachel turned towards the voice and saw a large, scruffy-looking, black man standing by the kitchen door. He looked unkempt, his coat was mud-stained and on his sockless feet were sandals. His face had a broad, flat nose and wiry whiskers sprouted from his chin. It took Rachel only a moment to realise that he was unfamiliar and she knew his rough, Glasgow accent with its African twang, typified a less affluent area.

"Who are you? How did you get in here?" She demanded.

"The front door was unlocked," he replied, as if surprised by the question. "Surely you expected me, lady? You led me to your door."

"I don't know who you are or what you're doing here, but I want you to leave my house, now."

The man stood his ground and a slow smile crept over his face. "I am the voice of one crying out in the wilderness," he said. "Repent your sins. The kingdom of heaven is close at hand."

The hairs on the back of Rachel's neck prickled. This man is nuts, she thought. I've got to get him out of my house.

"Do you want some money?" she asked. "I could give you ten pounds. You could get a bus or a taxi. You can't stay here," she added meeting the man's gaze.

"You are a sinner, lady, and sinners must be punished."

"This is ridiculous," Rachel replied, raw fear giving her voice strength. "You will leave my house now or I'll call the police. Is that what you want? Do you want me to call the police?"

"You're going to call the police, on this telephone?" The man's deep voice resonated. Then laughing, he wrenched the phone from the wall and smashed it on the floor. "I don't think so, lady, I don't think so."

Rachel was terrified. She felt her knees go weak and she gripped the edge of the sink for support. She began to shake, her skin felt damp with perspiration, tears welled up in her eyes and her teeth chattered.

"Take whatever you want and leave me alone. My husband will be home any minute. He's just gone to the shops."

"Oh dear, lady, a liar and a thief, do you think the Lord will forgive you? I know your man is at work. I saw him leave in the car."

He's mixing me up with someone else Rachel thought. He must be. She said to him, "I'm not a thief. I've never stolen anything in my life."

"You took the money," he insisted. "I saw you. You are a thief. The money wasn't yours but you put it in your pocket. It's still there."

"What are you talking about? What money? I don't have your money. You must be mistaking me for another person."

"No," the man answered vehemently. "You took the money. I saw you."

Rachel was scared. She couldn't get past the man to escape from the kitchen. "What's your name?" She asked trying a different tactic. She wanted to distract him.

"You know me, lady," he said. "I am John, John the Baptist. I put the coin on the step in front of your door. The coin you picked up and placed in your pocket."

A memory of finding a coin when she went to put out the bin earlier slowly came back to her. She'd put it in her apron pocket and thought no more about it. No normal person would leave a coin lying on the doorstep. Rachel stared at the man, his hands were clasped in front of him and he was praying.

"Accept this sinner, Oh Lord. She is ready to repent." John turned to Rachel. "I am announcing the coming of Jesus. Accept him into your heart. Are you ready to meet him? Are you prepared to meet our Lord?"

Oh, God, she thought, I'm trapped in my house with a maniac. She wanted to shout for help, but the words were frozen in her throat and she could barely swallow.

As John stepped forward towards Rachel, he reached over to the worktop and lifted a knife from the block. His eyes gleamed with madness.

"No," Rachel shrieked finding her voice as she scrambled about in the sink trying to grasp something, anything, to defend herself. "Keep away from me. Don't touch me."

Unblinking, John strode over to her. The large man towered above her. Reaching out, he grabbed her by the hair. A sour stench engulfed her and she could taste his body odour. With his large, meaty hand, John forced her face into the sink of soapy water and held her down.

"I baptise you in the name of the Father," he began.

Rachel spluttered and struggled against his grip.

"The Son."

Hot urine ran down her legs as she desperately clawed at the air.

"And the Holy Spirit."

Finally, John dragged the drowning woman's face out of the sink.

Rachel coughed and choked, mucus streamed from her nose.

Then, as John held her face inches from the radio, she heard a newsreader say, "Do not approach this man. John Baptiste escaped from a high security hospital..."

Rachel gazed into the protruding eyes of the madman and she realised there was no escape. A terrible sadness engulfed her. She knew she was going to die.

"Gather this lost sheep back into the fold, Father. Forgive her, Oh Lord. She knows not what she's done."

Terror stricken and powerless to move only Rachel's eyes could follow the curve of his arm, as the knife plunged into her throat. As she gurgled her last breath the crackling voice of the news reader stressed, "I repeat, do not approach this man."

John slowly lowered Rachel's body. He was exhausted, completely spent. He sat on the kitchen floor beside her, bent his knees and held his head in his hands. Gradually, the tight band that encircled his skull eased and he relaxed. It had been several days since he'd stopped taking his medication. Days of worry and stress, wondering how he would save this soul for the Lord. The coin on the step was a brainwave, a perfect test for a sinner, and he hadn't been disappointed. Now this woman was at peace and he could rest a while. He shut his eyes.

* * *

It had been over twenty-five years since John had been at this house. He'd been about eight or nine years old when his mother had said they were going to visit Granny. He remembered clearly walking down the avenue and looking into the pretty gardens. The street had been incredibly clean, not at all like the area he'd called home. The white painted stonework of the bungalows reflected the sunlight and it had dazzled him. In his mind, there was a vision of his mother smiling. It had been a rare occurrence. Her skinny frame had been wrapped in a threadbare cardigan and her poor battered face was full of hope. She had rung the doorbell and they'd waited, listening, as footsteps approached, but instead of the welcome they'd expected, they were faced with Granny's stern, unrelenting coldness. This impression had shocked John and it had stayed with him all his life.

"Take your black, bastard son and leave here," the older woman had said. "You made your bed now you can lie in it. You've brought me nothing but shame and hurt."

"My son is not a bastard," John's mother had hissed. "I'm married. How dare you say that? He's your grandson and he's just a wee boy. Have you no compassion? Look at my face Mum. Look at me. He'll kill me if I go back to him. He'll kill me."

The older woman stood perfectly still with her arms crossed obstinately over her chest. She blocked the doorway with her body.

"He's not my Grandson. I don't have any coloured people in my family. I warned you when you left that I wouldn't have you back. Now go away before I call the police. I don't want you here."

"But Mum," John's mother beseeched, "Look at me. I'm begging you. Help me Mum or he'll kill me."

John's Grandmother retreated inside the house and slammed the door shut. His mother sank down onto the step and sobbed.

"Mum, Mum, what's wrong? Who's going to kill you?" Alarmed, John tugged at his mother's sleeve.

She raised her head, her face a picture of defeat and stared at her son with sad eyes.

"We're going home now, John. Don't worry, everything will be okay."

John's mother took him by the hand and they walked down the path. She carefully shut the gate. Every so often, as they walked along the road, they glanced back at Granny's house. It was the last time his mother would ever see it.

John didn't know if the dead woman by his side was his Grandmother, he couldn't recollect what she looked like after all these years, but he did remember the street and the house. He could only hope and pray that it was her and she was finally reunited with his mother in heaven.

John's head began to nod with tiredness. He slapped his face hard with his open palms because he couldn't risk falling asleep and being discovered here. Holding onto the work top he hauled himself up and rocked slightly on his feet. There was blood everywhere. Great spatters of arterial blood had sprayed the walls and puddles of the sticky redness covered the floor. John distractedly dipped his fingers in a pool on the worktop and began to draw crosses on the wall behind him. He prayed.

After a while he stripped off his bloody garments, dropping them onto the floor, and went in search of a bathroom. Once showered, John took a razor from the medicine cabinet and shaved off his hair and his whiskers. Then he wrapped himself in a towelling robe, which was hanging from a hook on the door, and began searching the house for clothes and anything else he could use. In the smaller bedroom, he found a sweatshirt and sweatpants hanging in the wardrobe. They obviously belonged to a big man because they fit John like a glove. He liked the feel of the soft fabric against his skin. He also helped himself to a Regatta jacket, but the footwear, which would have completed the outfit, were a size too big and his feet slipped out of them when he tried to walk. Next, John searched the master bedroom and was delighted to find Adidas trainers discarded on the floor beside the window. They weren't the same quality as the Reeboks he'd rejected, but they did fit him, so the Reeboks would have to do. He pulled out the drawers from the chest and selected a few pairs of socks and some underpants. Lifting a holdall from the top of the wardrobe, John quickly filled it with his loot before returning downstairs.

He hadn't noticed Rachel's book, a romantic novel, which lay on the bedside cabinet or her reading glasses, or the pretty little knick-knacks which decorated the room, or Alan's dish where he threw his loose change when he undressed at night. None of the trappings of normal family life touched John's consciousness because he'd no experience of it.

The house was covered in blood. It had been trampled through the hall and up the stairs. John didn't want to spoil his new clothes, but he needed to find money because he'd almost used up what he had. Searching the living room, he discovered Rachel's handbag lying on the sofa. Tipping the contents onto the coffee table, John took Rachel's wallet and placed it in his jacket pocket. Then he found her mobile phone and quickly located her bank card PIN number. The nurse he'd killed when he'd escaped from the hospital had kept her PIN number on her phone. How careless, he thought.

John slung the holdall over his shoulder. He lifted a pair of Ray Ban sunglasses off the hall table and put them on, stopping only for a moment to admire his reflection in the mirror, before leaving the house the same way he'd entered three hours earlier. He carefully closed the door and whistled to himself as he made his way along the pretty avenue with its perfect gardens and white painted bungalows. John felt free, his step had a spring in it and he broke into song.

"Mine eyes have seen the glory of the coming of the Lord," his deep voice resonated. "His truth is marching on."

Chapter 2

After leaving Rachel's house John walked to the main road and headed south, away from the city. He strode along the pavement passing some very substantial, red-sandstone villas until he reached a roundabout with roads going off in several directions. John noticed that one of the roads had shops on either side and, as he was looking for a bank to withdraw money from Rachel's account, he chose that route.

There was the usual mix of estate agents, charity shops, coffee shops and bistros which could be found in most suburban shopping areas, with a baker, fruit shop and a Tesco Metro thrown in for good measure. John quickly located the bank and, using Rachel's card and PIN number, withdrew three hundred pounds. He didn't dare try to take out any more money in case he drew attention to himself. As it was, John felt rather uncomfortable being the only black face in this wealthy area. He was sure there must be other black people living in the district, but he didn't see any. His Granny's cruel words came flooding back to him and he realised then why she didn't want him in her family.

With money in his pocket, he treated himself to a sausage roll from the baker's and wolfed it down, wiping the sticky crumbs from his mouth with his sleeve. Then he went to browse the charity shops, dropping Rachel's bank card in a post box as he passed by. He knew he couldn't risk using it again because the police could trace him by it. John reasoned, by posting it instead of throwing it in a bin, he was doing the right thing. It was the property of the bank after all and now it would be returned to them.

When he entered the first shop, which was run by OXFAM, he was aware of the staff staring at him. They spoke in whispers to each other, with hands held in front of their mouths, but John knew they were talking about him as they kept glancing his way. It made him feel very uncomfortable so he left the shop without having a proper look around. The next shop was a different story, it was empty, but for a large, pretty lady with a smiling face.

"Are you looking for anything in particular?" she asked. "If you need a hand with sizes, or if you want to try on anything, just let me know."

"Thank you, lady," John said returning her smile shyly.

"I haven't seen you before," she continued. "Are you new to the area?"

"I am a minister of God. I'm visiting churches."

"Evangelical or Church of Scotland? The one up the hill or the one round the corner? I'm a member of the Church of Scotland myself, but I'm sure the Evangelical Church is nice too. My name's Libby, short for Elizabeth. What's your name?"

"I'm John," he replied nervously. He wasn't sure how much to say to this lady, although she seemed friendly.

Libby watched John fingering the hangers on the rail holding gent's suits and jackets.

"There's a Hugo Boss in your size on that rail, I think," she said. "It's a lovely suit, very well cut, previously owned by a bank manager. Would you like to try it on?"

"No thank you," John replied. "I have to go now. I'm due at the church in five minutes. The Evangelical Church," he stressed.

"Oh well, nice to meet you John, perhaps I'll see you again soon," Libby replied.

John nodded and made for the door. "I don't think so lady," he muttered under his breath. "I don't think so."

John headed for the Church of Scotland he needed to pray and he wanted to feel embraced by the sanctity of the church. It was a beautiful building, set in tranquil gardens filled with pink blossoming cherry trees. What a lovely way to honour the Lord, John thought approvingly. He went to the front door and tried the handle, it was locked. This can't be right. A church is for the people. It can't be locked. He banged on the door, but nobody came to let him in. He could feel his temper rising.

"I am announcing the coming of Jesus let me enter my father's house," he shouted at the door. Bang, bang, bang he thumped on the wood with all his might. It vibrated under the force. "Let me enter the Lord's house. Open these doors for me," he demanded. Sweat broke out on his brow and his head began to ache. He had to get inside.

John walked round to the side of the church, surely there was another way in, he thought. He reached a small annex which was attached to the building. A sign identified it as the church warden's house. This is the home of the sinner who locked the church, he thought angrily, the man who denied me entrance to my father's house. John hammered on the door.

"Hold your horses," a voice from within called. "I'm coming, I'm coming."

The wooden door opened with a creak to reveal a short, balding man wearing a black suit.

"What can I do for you?" he asked. His face was bland and unsmiling.

"I want to get into the church to pray, but it's locked," John replied.

"The church is always locked unless a service is taking place. We can't leave it open for just anyone to come in. Haven't you heard about the burglaries and the vandalism? They're rife you know."

"But I am not a thief or a vandal. I am a man who wants to pray."

"I'm sure that's the case, but you still can't come in. You'll have to come back when the service is on. Now, I'm sorry, but you must be on your way. I've got work to do."

Mr Gordon, the church warden, hit the floor with a thud. He hadn't seen the punch coming. It hit him full in the face, breaking his nose and immediately rendering him unconscious.

"Now you will know the wrath of God," John spat. "How dare you lock our Father's house? How dare you choose who enters and who does not?"

John stepped over his comatose victim and entered the house. Once inside, he dragged the man clear of the door and shut it. He searched the front room, tipping out drawers, ransacking it, until he found a set of keys. Then he left Mr Gordon lying on the cold, stone floor and made his way back round the pathway to the church entrance.

It took John only seconds to identify the correct key, unlock the large, timber door and step inside. Once there, he stared at his surroundings then looked up, open-mouthed, at the magnificent vaulted ceiling. The stained glass windows depicted biblical scenes, the wooden pews were highly polished and everything smelled very clean. John climbed the stairs and stood at the lectern. He became calmer. He liked the way his voice resonated, echoing around the building as he preached to his invisible congregation. When he'd finished his sermon, he walked down the aisle towards the front door, occasionally stopping to talk to the imaginary people who filled his church. Thanking them for attending his service, praying for their mortal souls and blessing their children.

When he left the building and stepped into the sunshine, he felt reborn and uplifted. My work is done here, he thought. It's time to leave this place and move on, time to spread the Lord's words somewhere else. John made his way back to the main road and stood at a bus stop. He decided he would get on the first bus heading towards the city and see where it led him. The Lord would guide him, he reasoned, he always had.

Chapter 3

"Fuck, fuck, fuck, I've been here all day and now it looks like I'll be at the job half the fucking night," Detective Inspector Frank Martin's voice boomed out from his room at the end of the main office. DC Angela Murphy and her recently promoted colleague, DS Paul Costello, exchanged glances.

"Please let something, anything, take us out of the office. I've been pushing paper all day and I'm getting stir crazy," Paul said sitting up.

"The Boss has been working for nine hours. He should have been away home by now. It must be serious if he thinks it'll take half the night," Angela commented.

"I don't know what the old bastard's been doing for nine hours," Paul said. "I've been here half that time and I'm bored out of my tiny mind."

"Murphy, Costello, my office, now."

"Oh well, here we go," Paul said as he and Angela rose from their chairs and made for the big man's room.

Considering Frank's fastidiousness about his appearance, his office in contrast, was a complete shambles. Angela and Paul negotiated their way around boxes and piles of debris, climbing over heaps of files which were precariously stacked against the walls.

"Sit," Frank commanded. "Sorry about the mess. I'm waiting for a new filing cabinet," he added by way of explanation.

Angela stared at the discarded open pizza box with a half-chewed, single, greasy slice, sitting inside and the three crushed cola cans, one of which had drizzled sugary liquid onto the desk. The files were the least of his worries, she thought.

"We've got a murder," Frank began.

"Yes," Paul exclaimed slapping his knee with his hand.

Frank drew him a dark look. Chastised, Paul help up his hands.

"Sorry, boss, I'm just a bit crazy from handling hours of paperwork. Of course I'm not happy about a murder."

Angela felt a shudder of excitement. Although any death was upsetting, particularly murder, she knew this was the sort of job that could fast track her career. She'd already made a name for herself, by being part of the team responsible for catching a dangerous serial killer. It had been her first ever case as a detective. Now, only eighteen months on, another juicy morsel was landing in her lap.

"The victim is named Rachel Stone, murdered in her own home, no sign of forced entry. Husband came home from work and found her dead. Forensics is at the scene and we're going there now. Victim lived in Clarkston," Frank added looking at Angela for a reaction. She didn't let him down.

"Clarkston, that's next door to where I live."

"What's the matter Murphy? Do you think people don't get murdered in posh areas?"

"There was a boy called Harvey Stone at my school," Angela continued. "Big, handsome lad, good at sport and super smart, all the girls fancied him. He won the National Maths Challenge."

"Yadda, yadda, yadda, can we stick to Rachel Stone please? Can you stop being such a girl, Murphy?"

Paul chuckled.

"Sorry, boss," Angela said.

"I've been informed that the family's rabbi is at the scene and he's making a nuisance of himself. Complaining about this and that, he doesn't want a post mortem carried out or the body to be washed, that sort of thing. We'll have to handle the situation with kid gloves or we'll be accused of racism."

"Harvey Stone was Jewish," Angela said. "I wonder if he's related. He must be related. There can't be many Jewish families called Stone living in Clarkston."

"Old boyfriend, was he?" Paul asked teasingly.

"I wish. He was gorgeous and very sweet too. I wasn't in his league."

"Enough about Harvey Stone please. Gather up your stuff, we need to get moving or we'll be there all night. Take your own cars because we won't be coming back to the office. I want you two in here, bright eyed and bushy tailed in the morning. This is our case now. Somebody else will cover the shifts."

They all rose to leave. “Oh, and Murphy,” Frank began. “You’re not going to go all soft on me if the corpse turns out to be Harvey’s Mum, are you?”

“Of course not, boss. Don’t be ridiculous. I hardly knew the guy.”

“But you wanted to,” Paul muttered under his breath.

Angela prodded him hard in the ribs, “Don’t start, Costello. At least I was choosey. You went after anything in a skirt.”

“I’ll have you know I’m a happily married man,” Paul protested.

“With five kids,” Angela replied, “Five that you know about.”

“Stop bickering children. You’re driving me to the scene Murphy, and you’ll be taking me home Costello. I don’t have my car with me today.”

Paul and Angela exchanged glances. The boss never had a car with him these days because he had a problem with alcohol. Although most of the time he managed to keep it under control. Nobody spoke about it, but Angela hadn’t missed the bottle of whisky and empty glass on the floor beside his desk.

When they arrived at the scene Frank walked over to a uniformed officer who was standing at the garden gate.

“Well, hello there, Jim. How’s it going?” he asked.

“Hi Frank, yeah, yeah, going good. Denny’s due to begin his shift so I’ll be leaving in about five minutes,” he replied. “Corpse is in the kitchen. Husband’s bro lives next door. He’s a rabbi and a right royal pain in the arse. The family solicitor is Donatello and he’s already here. The brother called him immediately after he called us. They’re all in the brother’s house.”

“Donatello, eh? I can’t stand that wee ninja turtle. He’s a pernickety wee bastard. You can keep him busy Costello while Murphy and I talk to the husband and the rabbi.”

“But won’t he insist on being present when we interview Mr Stone?” Angela asked.

“Probably, but we’re not formally interviewing the husband yet. We’re just going to give our condolences, right?”

“Yes, boss. I get it. Do you want me to take the husband or the brother?”

“Play it by ear. We’ll see how the land lies when we get inside. First we’ll have a quick look at the scene before the corpse is moved.”

As they headed through the gate Jim, the uniformed officer, said to Frank, “Kitchen’s a blood bath. Corpse is nearly decapitated. The rabbi chucked up in the hallway. I see Denny’s arrived now, so I’m going home for my dinner. Good luck, Mate. I think you’re in for a long night.”

Frank and Angela were handed sterile suits at the front door which they quickly pulled on before entering the house.

"I can't stand vomit," Frank observed as they walked through the hall. "Whenever I see sick, it makes me want to throw up. Blood, guts, maggots, no problem, but I really hate sick."

They entered the kitchen. It was a gruesome sight with blood everywhere. Rachel Stone's body was grey from loss of blood. Her head, which was almost separated from her body, rested on her shoulder. Her eyes staring lifelessly at the floor. Frank talked to the forensics girl while Angela made some notes.

"If the person who did this has got any kind of a record, we should find out who he is quite quickly because his prints and DNA are everywhere," the girl said. "He even had a shave in the bathroom. He must be a real psycho to do this," she added, with a sweep of her arm towards the corpse. "Then afterwards, to calmly have a shower and a shave."

Frank and Angela took their time observing the kitchen, both shocked by the savagery they faced, before walking around the rest of the house. When they entered the lounge Angela pointed to a photograph of a tall, athletic looking young man.

"That's Harvey Stone. The body must be his Mum right enough," she said sadly. "What did you make of all the crosses on the kitchen wall, boss?" she asked. "Do you think this is a race crime?"

"I hope not, Murphy. I hope it's just some religious nutter. If it's anything else the press will have a field day and we'll have all the shit-stirrers doing what they do best and panicking people. It would be much better if the murderer was sociopath or a psychopath." Frank rubbed his eyes with his chubby fingers. "I can't believe I just said that," he said. "Imagine preferring to have a dangerous maniac wandering the streets, than some racist supporter of the BNP."

They spent another thirty minutes looking around, taking in everything, searching for anything that could give them a lead. Then Frank spoke to the forensics people once again.

"We're going next door now. We'll come back tomorrow when you're done here. Try to put a name to the fingerprints as soon as you can please. I have an awful feeling in my gut, that if we don't find this fucker quickly, more bodies will start to turn up. Somebody very dangerous did this and we need to stop him."

Angela felt unnerved. This murder had happened right on her doorstep. Houses cost a fortune in this district. It was considered a great place to live. If it hadn't been for an inheritance, Angela and her husband Bobby could never have afforded to buy in such a prestigious area. She'd always felt safe here, but after what she'd just witnessed, she wondered if she would ever feel the same way about it again. Maybe it was naivety, but even doing the job she did and coming into contact with all manner of bad boys and girls, she'd never felt frightened. Would she be able to walk these leafy avenues without looking over her shoulder now?

The three detectives made their way to the adjoining bungalow. The porch door was lying open and, as they walked up the stone-chipped path, their feet crunched beneath them. They were stopped at the front door by a tall skinny boy of about fifteen who introduced himself as Gary Stone, the rabbi's son.

"Please wash your hands," the young man said indicating to a large jug of water and a bowl which had been placed on a side table just inside the porch. "You cannot enter this house after being with the corpse without washing your hands," he explained.

Not wishing to cause offence the detectives did as they were asked then they entered the house. Rabbi Stone stood in the hallway.

"I am very sorry for the intrusion, Sir," Frank said. He didn't extend his hand for the rabbi to shake because he didn't know what the protocol was. The rabbi was dressed in a black formal suit and wore a large, black yarmulke on his head. Like his son, he was tall and skinny. His pale complexion looked as if it had never seen the sun and his face had a tired, gaunt look. His eyes were sunken and his cheeks hollow.

"It's a terrible business, terrible," he said. "Who would do such a thing? Rachel was such a gentle person. In all the years I've known her, I've never heard her raise her voice in anger. She was a good wife and mother and a pious woman. Did you see the crosses on the kitchen wall? Was it a racist who did this terrible thing, perhaps to terrorise us?"

"I'm sorry Rabbi, but I don't have the answers yet. I can tell you that the forensic people are working tirelessly to gather clues. They have lifted a number of fingerprints, so with a bit of luck the killer will be in the system and we'll be able to identify him. But for the moment, we are just as in the dark as you are."

The rabbi hung his head. "I know you'll do everything you can. I can tell you're a caring person. Please help us detective, my brother is devastated by his loss. Doctor Jacobson is with him now, but you can go through and talk to him." Rabbi Stone indicated to a door on the left.

"Where is Mr Donatello?" Frank asked. "My colleague, DS Costello would like a word with him, if you don't mind." Frank winked at Paul who nodded back.

"He's in my study," the Rabbi replied. "Follow me and I'll show you where it is. His partner Saul Greenberg is actually our lawyer, but we were told that Mr Donatello has more experience of dealing with the police, so that's why he's here instead of Saul."

Paul walked after Rabbi Stone. They headed off to the left, round a corner beyond the door leading to the front room. Frank and Angela entered the lounge, the curtains were closed over and the room was very dim. A single small lamp in the corner gave out the only light. Alan Stone sat on a low chair and held his head in his hands. Doctor Jacobson knelt beside him, resting his hand on the other man's shoulder and talking softly to him. He stood up when the detectives approached. The doctor drew Frank to one side.

"Mr Stone is very shocked, I've had to sedate him and I may yet have to send him to the hospital. You can, of course, talk to him, but tread gently. He might be a bit confused because of the drug I've administered. If I see him becoming agitated, I'll have to stop you."

Frank exhaled deeply and nodded to the doctor, "I understand, Sir," he said. "I'll be careful not to distress him. But we are trying to catch his wife's killer. I'm not here to cause him any more grief. Anything he can tell us might help us to apprehend the murderer."

Damn, Frank thought to himself this could be a complete waste of time. He pulled over a couple of chairs so he and Angela could sit beside Alan Stone. He thought they would seem less intimidating if they were all facing each other at the same level. Doctor Jacobson sat on a chair discreetly placed in the corner of the room.

Angela spoke first. "Mr Stone, Mr Stone," she said gently. "I'm Detective Murphy, Angela. I went to school with your son Harvey."

"Is Harvey here?" Alan Stone asked lifting his head from his hands.

"He's on his way," the doctor called over. "A friend is driving him up from Manchester. He should be here in a few hours."

Alan Stone stared at Angela, "You're not Jewish, are you?" he asked.

"No Sir," she replied. "But I live locally. Just down the road, in Netherlee."

"You've been to my house? You've seen what he did to my Rachel?" Alan began to sob. Angela pulled a clean tissue from her pocket and handed it to him. He swept at his eyes and loudly blew his nose. "Thank you, you are very kind."

"Did anything unusual happen today?" she probed. "Did you see anyone hanging around in the street? Or have you received any unexpected mail or telephone calls?"

"Nothing was different. Rachel was in the kitchen, as usual. I kissed her when I left for work at eight-forty-five, as usual. I drove to work, as usual. But when I came home… when I came home," his voice trailed off and he began to sob loudly.

Doctor Jacobson rushed forward, "I think that's enough now. Please leave, he can't take any more."

Frank and Angela stood up from their chairs. They shook hands with the doctor, made apologies to Mr Stone and headed back into the hallway.

"Poor sod knows nothing," Frank said. "Normal home, normal day, then bang, he's part of a nightmare and he can't wake up."

"It's awful, really awful, poor Harvey coming home to this."

"Never mind poor Harvey. What about poor Rachel? We have to catch this bastard before the psycho fucker does someone else."

Angela shuddered, the same thought had occurred to her. She lived only a few minutes away from the crime scene and she was scared. After a moment or two they were met in the hall by the rabbi, Mr Donatello and Paul.

"When did you get here?" Donatello asked, staring at Frank. His face was like thunder. "I hope you haven't been talking to my client. You know he's been sedated and you can't use anything he's said. I thought DS Costello was going to question Mr Stone, that's why I'm here to accompany him. What's going on? I demand you tell me what you're up to."

The expression on Frank's face was grim. He leaned in close to Donatello's face until their noses were practically touching.

"I do not need your permission to speak to the victim's husband. I do not need your permission to be in this house. There's a fucking psychopath out there and I need to get information so I can catch him. Do I make myself clear, Mr Donatello?" Frank hissed.

Nobody moved an inch. It was as if time stood still. "Crystal," Donatello replied barely able to control his anger.

"I'd like to speak to you, now, Rabbi, if I may," Frank said. "Is there another room we can use? I don't want to disturb your brother any more than I have to."

Rabbi Stone led the group into the other front room which was laid out as a formal dining room.

"Please take a seat. I'll ask my wife to bring in some tea," he said, and within a few minutes, they were all seated at the table enjoying strong tea and biscuits. Even the normally twitchy Donatello began to relax.

"I'd like to establish a time line, if I may, Sir," Frank began. "You said that you went to your brother's house at about five forty-five because you heard him screaming. Is that correct?"

"Yes, that's right. It was a terrible sound. He was screaming over and over again. I could hear it through the walls of the house, so I immediately ran next door. That's when I found him and Rachel."

"Did you hear or see anything unusual during the day?"

"We were out all day. I left this house with my family at about eight-fifteen. Alan was still home because I saw his car in the driveway. I dropped my son at his friend's house so they could walk to school together. Then I drove my daughters to university. Leah's at The Cally studying nursing. Ruth's at Strathclyde doing business studies. I dropped them both off at the top of High Street at about eight forty-five. Then my wife and I drove to Glasgow University for a seminar on 'Religion in the Modern World.' The seminar began at nine-thirty and included lunch. Then there was a group discussion so we didn't get back here until about four-thirty. My son went home with his friend to study and he returned home at about five. The girls travelled back on the bus. They got in about ten minutes after Gary."

"So we can assume that Rachel was killed sometime between eight-fifteen and four-thirty," Frank said.

"I hope you're not suggesting that my client had anything to do with his wife's murder. He told me he left for work at about eight forty-five. So your time line should begin then."

Frank glared at Donatello, "Don't tell me how to do my job Mr Donatello. You're only sitting in this room because I've allowed you to be here. If you can't keep your mouth shut then I'll have to ask you to leave. Do you understand?"

Donatello was livid, his face was purple with anger.

"Now calm down before you have a stroke," Frank added.

It was the last straw. Donatello stormed out of the room.

"I'm sorry about that, Rabbi. I'll have to confirm everything you've told me with your wife and children, if that's all right. Detective Murphy will talk to the women and Detective Costello will speak to your son."

"The girls are in the kitchen. Please feel free to go there," Rabbi Stone said. "I'll fetch Gary from his room."

The detectives quickly confirmed the details, said their goodbyes and left the rabbi's house. When they stepped outside Paul and Frank headed for Paul's car.

"Assume we'll meet in the office first thing, Murphy," Frank called out. "I'll phone you if anything changes."

Angela inhaled deeply, pulled out her mobile and rang her husband, Bobby.

"Don't open the door unless you know who's there and make sure the downstairs windows are all locked," she instructed. "Oh, and leave the outside light on for me please. I'll be home soon, Pet. It's been a shitty day, a truly horrible day."

Chapter 4

When Angela climbed into her car she immediately locked the doors then quickly looked behind her to make sure no one was sitting on the back seat. Her hands were shaking and she felt unnerved. She didn't know why she was so frightened. After all, she came into contact with mindless violence every working day, but something about the situation she'd just witnessed shocked her to the core. Perhaps it was because the crime scene was right on her doorstep, or maybe it was that she knew the family of the victim, Angela couldn't be sure. She couldn't put her finger on what was different about this case.

She turned the key in the ignition and pulled away from the kerb. The street was busy with people going about their business, mothers ferrying children to various activities scurried along the pavements, couples chatting as they headed for the local pub or to the cinema, tired looking office workers trudging home laden with shopping from the nearby supermarket, everything looked normal. Was the killer still here, Angela wondered? Hiding in a garden or maybe walking along the street heading God knows where?

The journey home took Angela less than five minutes and when she arrived she pulled in under a street light at the side of her house. It wasn't yet fully dark, but she didn't want to park in the garage because it would mean walking through the back lane. She looked about her before unlocking the door then she jumped out of the car, slammed the door closed behind her, pressed the button on the key to lock it, and ran up the path. When she entered her home it felt warm. Music was playing and delicious smells from cooked food filled the air. Bobby came out of the kitchen to greet her.

"I'm so glad you're home. I've been worried about you. You sounded so upset on the phone. What's happened?"

Relief overwhelmed her and Angela promptly burst into tears. She allowed Bobby to help her out of her jacket, lead her into the lounge and sit her down on her favourite armchair. He walked over to the sideboard, took a bottle of whisky from it and poured them both a glass.

"Sip this," he ordered. "It will steady you. Then you can tell me what's upset you."

Angela took a gulp of the golden liquid. It burned her throat as she swallowed. After a couple of minutes her hands stopped shaking. Bobby waited patiently for her to speak.

"There's been a terrible murder," she began. "The scene was very bloody. I think it's the work of an absolute psycho and it happened only minutes away from here, in Clarkston. I went to school with the victim's son. Someone killed her while she was washing dishes at the kitchen sink. They came into her home and murdered her while she was washing the dishes."

Bobby blew out his breath with a low whistle. "Do you think it's someone local? Could we walk past this man in the street? Could it be a neighbour?"

Bobby's questions made Angela realise what had frightened her so much. The killer was just as likely to be someone she knew as a stranger. He might very well be living beside them. The problem with maniacs was that they usually looked like everyone else. The case of Thomas Malone, her first encounter with a madman, was the perfect example of this. People thought he was a quiet, shy young man, yet his mind unravelled in the most deadly of ways.

"He could be anyone, Bobby, and he could be anywhere. We should find out quite quickly if he's known to us because his fingerprints and DNA were everywhere. The guy is some kind of religious nut. He drew crosses all over the wall with the victim's blood, but I don't think this is a race crime. The victim's family are Jewish and her brother-in-law is a rabbi, but I don't feel they were specifically targeted because of their religion."

"No wonder you were shaken. It all sounds horrible," Bobby replied. "I don't suppose you'll want dinner after that. I've made your favourite, Italian beef stew, but it'll keep for tomorrow if you don't feel like eating."

"I'm feeling better now I'm home," Angela replied. "Just give me a few minutes to get changed then I'll be able to eat. We can have that bottle of Hardy's red wine. I'll be ready for another drink."

Angela climbed the stairs to her bedroom, but as she ascended she had to fight the urge to look behind her. She ran up the last few steps as if the devil himself were at her heels.

When she left the room Bobby phoned his friend and business partner, Jake. They'd planned to get together after dinner to discuss their strategy for dealing with a new supplier, but Bobby didn't feel he could leave Angela alone and neither did he think she could cope with having Jake in the house this evening. She didn't like Jake, a serial womaniser, and had little time for his wife, Miranda, who put up with his dalliances, but exploded dramatically from time to time whenever she caught him out. It meant that socialising with the other couple had now become a rare occurrence as they never knew when things would kick off. Angela did, however, fully approve of Bobby and Jake being in business together. Jake had taken Bobby in as a junior partner of his firm over a year ago and the company had grown from strength to strength. Her husband was so much happier since he'd changed career and no longer worked as a teacher, and the money he earned, together with Angela's salary, afforded them a very comfortable lifestyle.

The phone rang four times before being answered by Miranda who informed him that Jake was in the shower.

"Would you please let him know I won't be over tonight," Bobby said and he explained about the day Angela had had.

"I've just heard all about it on the news," Miranda replied. "It's an awful business. Why don't you both come round after your meal? You and Jake can talk shop and Angela and I can have a few drinks. It might take her mind off things."

"I'm sorry Miranda, but I don't think she's up to socialising. We're planning to have an early night, Angela's exhausted. Tell Jake I'll call him in the morning."

"Oh well, if you're sure."

Bobby was hanging up the phone when Angela re-entered the room.

"Who was on the phone?" she asked.

"Miranda, she invited us round."

Angela pulled a face. "I think I've had enough drama for one day," she replied, "Don't you?"

* * *

Within a few minutes of Paul driving off, Frank had fallen asleep. His pudgy cheeks sagged and his pallor paled, his skin was shiny and sweaty giving him the appearance of a pork sausage. He began to snore loudly. He's as bad as my baby, Paul thought, two minutes in a car and he's nodded off. Oh, well, at least I don't have to listen to him whining, or be forced to make conversation with the old bastard.

The traffic was heavy and Paul too, felt tired. He opened his window for some fresh air and the overpowering smell of exhaust fumes from the bus in front of him made him nauseous. That bus should be off the road, he thought. It would never pass an emissions test. He didn't risk turning on the radio in case it woke Frank, better being poisoned by fumes than blasted by expletives. Using the hands free he called home to talk to his wife, speaking softly so as not to disturb Frank. His middle daughter, Grace, answered the phone.

"Can I speak to Mummy, Pet?" he asked.

"Probably not," she replied.

"What do you mean, probably not? Where is she?"

"At the doctor with Michaela."

Paul felt a wave of panic, "What's happened? Is Michaela hurt? Who's looking after you all?" His voice rose, waking Frank.

"Mrs Callander from next door is here. She's changing the baby's nappy, but she's not very good at it. I offered to show her what to do, but she said she could manage. The dog ate half a packet of raw bacon and he's throwing up all over the lounge, but I'm not cleaning it up because I didn't give him the bacon in the first place. Michaela put a saucepan on her head and let the baby hit her with a wooden spoon. It made the baby laugh. You should have heard him giggling it was very funny. He got hiccups."

Now he was fully awake and hearing the conversation over the hands free, Frank began to laugh. Paul threw him a black look.

"I'm glad you're finding this amusing," Paul said frowning. "My child is hurt and she's at the doctor's and you think it's funny."

"Sorry, I'm sorry," Frank said, coughing to stifle a chortle.

"Michaela's not really injured, Dada, but her ears are folded over and Mummy couldn't get the pot off her head. Then she started to cry and told Mummy she had earache so Mummy phoned the doctor and he said to bring her into the surgery. Mrs Callander is asking when you'll be home." Grace's words came tumbling out. The child barely drew breath. "Oh, dear, Toto's done a poo on the carpet now and I'm not cleaning that either," she added vehemently.

Paul sighed resignedly, "Tell Mrs Callander I'll be about fifteen minutes. I'm dropping off Inspector Martin and I'm just pulling in at his house."

"Oh, no, Dada, Poppy's just stepped on the poo. Oh yuck, get away from me Poppy," she cried. Then the phone went dead.

"No wonder you're always volunteering to take on extra shifts," Frank said. "I don't know how you manage with five kids. Is it always like that? I don't think I could cope. Give me a thug or a rogue any day."

Paul looked tired and strained. Yeah, me too, he thought.

Frank opened the car door. "Anyway, thanks for the lift. I'm going in to have a nice home-cooked meal with my wife in peace and quiet. Then I'll stretch out on the 'Layzee Boy' and have a wee nap in front of the telly. I'll see you at seven-thirty, sharp, tomorrow morning. Have fun," he added chuckling.

Frank slammed the car door leaving Paul scowling in his wake.

"I hope you choke, you smug fuck," Paul muttered, but he knew it was just sour grapes. He dreaded what waited for him at home. He was pretty sure it wouldn't be a home-cooked meal.

When he eventually pulled up outside his house Paul sat for a couple of minutes. Still gripping the steering wheel, he rested his forehead on his hands. He was under tremendous pressure at the moment. There was no question that he loved his wife and they'd always planned to have a big family, but with seven people in the house, not to mention the dog, the hamster and a tank of goldfish, it had become far too small for them. His promotion to detective sergeant came with a salary increase, but he seemed to be working much longer hours just to stand still. He'd managed to identify an affordable house that was currently for sale and which would give them two extra rooms, and one of the uniformed officers from Ayrshire, who was relocating to Glasgow, had made a good offer to buy their house, so a move was possible. But the new house wasn't in the school catchment area they would have preferred. And a bigger house would mean bigger bills and they were already stretched to the limit.

Paul felt like crying. He didn't want to worry his wife, he'd always provided for his family and taken care of them, but he was scared. What if he took ill or was injured and couldn't work? They had no cushion, nothing saved for a rainy day. Seeing what had happened to Rachel Stone, murdered as she washed the dishes, made him realise just how quickly and unexpectedly things could go wrong.

* * *

DI Frank Martin was an alcoholic and he battled with his problem every day. He rarely got drunk now, but he couldn't trust himself not to reach for a bottle in times of crisis. If it hadn't been for his junior officers, he would have lost his job over a year ago. They closed ranks, supported him, and saved him from himself. Now he kept a full whisky bottle and an empty glass beside his desk to prove to them he was in control. He could see them glancing at it to check the level of the liquid every time they came into his office. Only he knew that the whisky was long gone and the bottle was filled with nothing more than weak tea. His real stash was in a vacuum flask in his desk drawer and he'd now switched to drinking vodka because it had less of a smell. The tell-tale mints had disappeared too and instead, after imbibing, he sucked scented wine gums. Frank wasn't stupid. He understood the philosophy of taking his sobriety one day at a time, but when should he start that first day? Now there lay the problem.

At the beginning his wife was supportive. She thought she could save him. Gradually, however, she realised that he was the only person who could fix his problem and he wouldn't discuss it with her or anyone else. He'd attended a couple of AA meetings over a year ago, and he kept a contact number for support in his wallet, but that's as far as it went. His wife had now given up trying and they simply didn't talk about it anymore. Frank knew that when they sat down to dine and he opened a bottle of wine to accompany the meal, she would join him and drink with him. They would act as if everything was normal, and to them, it was.

As he turned the key in the lock and opened the front door he called out, "Hi, honey, I'm home. Dinner smells great."

The truth was, he didn't care what was on the menu. He was so tired and hungry he could eat anything, just so long as it had stopped moving.

Chapter 5

When John got on the bus he sat near the front because he wanted to be able to get off quickly when God sent him a sign. The journey was slow as at every stop on the way, somebody got on or off. John wasn't used to being in contact with so many people. They fascinated him. As the bus continued past Muirend, then Cathcart, he stared out of the window at the streets full of tenements. The buildings seemed cleaner than he'd remembered. In the years while he'd been away they'd been stone-cleaned and refurbished and now, instead of the sooty black caused by decades of smoke and grime, the sandstone was a warm red.

As the bus passed Queen's Park and turned into Victoria Road, John suddenly saw the sign he'd been waiting for. Walking along the street were two nuns. They stopped to speak to a woman and her child.

"Thank you, Lord," John muttered. "Thank you for sending the sisters to guide me." He jumped to his feet, pressed the bell to alert the driver that he wanted to get off then made his way to the exit. When the driver stopped the vehicle and opened the door for him, John stepped down, calling out, "Thank you, Brother," as he alighted. Once on the pavement, he immediately looked back along the street, but the nuns had gone. He peered round in each direction, but they were nowhere to be seen. However, he did notice a man who seemed to be searching for something. His expression was serious and he looked agitated and upset. John walked towards him, ready to offer him his help.

Peter James was practically on his knees, patting the ground, searching for his keys which had slipped from his grasp. He'd almost reached his home, tapping his way with his white stick, when a large dog had barged past him, nearly causing him to fall. He was becoming quite frantic, feeling around in the dirt, when the stranger came to his aid.

"May I help you Brother?" John asked. "What have you lost?"

Peter was immediately on his guard. Throughout his life people were more inclined to ignore him, or worse, be cruel to him, than to offer him help, but if he couldn't find his keys, he would be outside all night and it was beginning to rain. He'd have nobody to turn to because the Council offices would be shut now and he'd have to wait until morning to get any assistance. So he took a chance.

"I've dropped my keys and I'm blind. I can't see where they fell."

"Ah, your keys. They are very important. I will locate them for you," John said and he began to scour the pavement and roadside. After a few moments he said, "I have them, here they are, Brother. They had fallen into the gutter."

Peter felt the man grip him by the wrist and place the keys in his hand.

"Thank you, thank you very much," he replied, relief sweeping over him. "I'm indebted to you, Pal."

John had never been called 'Pal' before. He had no friends.

"May I walk with you, Brother? I'm new to this area and I'm not sure where to go. I need to find somewhere to eat. Perhaps you can direct me?"

"The blind leading the blind," Peter replied and he began to laugh.

"It's wonderful that you can make fun of your affliction," John said smiling. "God has made you strong."

"If only that were true, Pal," Peter replied. "I'm blind, I've got a bad heart and I have no family. You're the first person I've spoken to in three days. Sometimes I think I'm invisible."

"Like you, Brother, I have no family. They are all dead. Do not despair, Brother, God sees you, and I see you. We are both his children. My name is John," he added, reaching out, and taking Peter's hand in his, he shook it vigorously.

"Hello, John, I'm Peter, Peter James. Pleased to meet you."

"You've been named after two apostles. Peter was a favourite of Jesus, you know? He and John were friends. I am a minister of the Lord," he added.

The two men fell into step as they walked along the pavement.

"Maybe we'll become friends," Peter replied. "If you're planning on moving into the area I could show you around, if you'd like?"

"Yes, Peter, I would like that very much, but first, will you break bread with me? May I buy you dinner?"

Peter lived on a tight budget funded only by the various benefits he received, so the offer of a meal was most welcome.

"It's getting quite late and I'd like to get home. Why don't we go to the supermarket and you can buy some food then we can eat it at my flat. The shop is only a few minutes away and I live just around the corner from here. We could buy a bottle of wine to have with the food and it would still cost less than eating in a restaurant."

"That sound like a good idea," John replied. "I would like to visit your home."

"Do you have somewhere to stay tonight, Pal? Is your church putting you up? Or have you checked into a hotel?"

"No, Peter, I have not. Can you recommend somewhere?"

"Tomorrow, yes, but tonight you can stay at mine if you want. I have a sofa bed. It'll be nice to have company."

Being blind, Peter had no idea what his new friend looked like and, since shaving off his hair and beard, no one else would easily identify John either. Peter didn't realise that he'd invited a monster to join him. Even if he could see, the photograph of the escapee from the secure hospital, which was now being shown on the news, depicted a much younger, thinner, man. John was soft spoken and very polite, he didn't give out any signs of the madness within, so, for the time being, at least, he could blend into the background, and now he had a friend and a place to stay.

As the men walked towards the supermarket they chatted amicably to one another.

"So, Pal, what's all this about you being a minister?" Peter asked. "What are you doing in this neck of the woods?"

"I go where God takes me, Brother. I travel around spreading the Lord's word. He led me to this place. I think he meant for us to be friends."

"I've never had a friend before, Pal. My life has been quite lonely, but I've just got to keep on going. No point feeling sorry for myself and spending my life moaning. I'm luckier than most. I've got a nice flat, paid for by housing benefit. I can heat my house and feed myself. So it's not so bad."

"I am never lonely," John stated. "The world is full of my brothers and sisters. If I ever feel despair, the Lord supports me and when I enter a church, I am safely home, in my father's house."

"Maybe I should join a church. Do you think they'd want a broken down, old soul like me?"

"They would welcome you with open arms, Brother. Jesus would cherish you. He would keep your soul safe. He would guard it from the devil."

"Sounds very dramatic, Pal. Jesus sounds like some kind of modern-day superhero."

"I suppose Jesus is the original superhero," John replied laughing. "He is the saviour of us all."

When the two men entered the brightly lit supermarket they were an incongruous sight. John with his bald pate and round, flat face, was dressed in a top-of-the range track suit and trainers. And Peter, with his emaciated frame, thin straggly hair and near toothless mouth, was dressed in a three-piece-suit which had seen better days. It was shiny from wear. People seeing them would naturally assume that Peter was a poor, disabled soul and John was his carer.

As neither of the men could cook and both had poor taste, they chose sausage rolls, microwave chips and onion rings for their main course with sticky toffee pudding and tinned custard for dessert. Then they bought a bottle of cheap red wine to wash it down and a box of after dinner mints.

"This is a feast, Pal," Peter said, as they made their way to the check-out. "Good food and good company. It's lucky I dropped my keys."

"Yes, Brother," John agreed. "The Lord works in mysterious ways."

As they walked the short distance to Peter's house, the rain became heavier and the men were pleased to get indoors. When they entered the narrow hallway it was very dark. John reached for the light switch and to his relief the ceiling bulb lit up. Peter heard it click on.

"Sorry, Pal, I don't bother with the lights very often. It makes little difference to me. I only use them so people think someone's home, so they don't break in. Not that I've got much to steal."

There were doors on either side of the hall and it opened to a T-shape at the top.

"Bedroom left, lounge right, kitchen top left, bathroom top right," Peter explained. Do you have a bag or a case? You can put your stuff in the lounge then we can go and eat in the kitchen."

"I have a holdall," John replied. "Let me heat our food and serve you, Brother. You sit and relax."

"Thanks, Pal, that'll be a first. Nobody's cooked for me before, not since I was a wee boy in care, that is."

John was surprised at how sparse the house looked. It held a few sticks of furniture, no knick-knacks or pictures, and the surfaces, such as they were, were devoid of clutter. But then, he reasoned, what use would a blind man have for such things. He couldn't see pictures or read books and, being a single man, he was unlikely to want fussy ornaments or soft furnishings. The furniture was solid but very old, the carpets completely flat with age and the wallpaper was decades old. John was sure that the woodwork had been painted white at some time, but it was so yellowed now, it was hard to tell.

"If you need a mirror, there's one on the medicine cabinet in the bathroom. I shave by touch so I don't use it," Peter explained. "There's clean bedding for the sofa bed in the hall cupboard. I'll let you sort that out if you don't mind."

Within twenty minutes the men were seated at the table eating, drinking and talking. John felt very comfortable in Peter's company. For the time being, at least, these circumstances would suit him very well. He would remain a guest here for a while, he thought, and if Peter had any objections, or caused him any trouble, John would deal with it. After all, he reasoned, there would be nobody to miss Peter if he simply disappeared.

Chapter 6

When Angela arrived at the office the next morning she knew she looked tired. Her charcoal-grey coloured, tailored suit fit like a glove over her long, lean frame and her crisply-ironed, white shirt looked sharp, but the normal healthy glow from her skin was missing and the colours drained her. Her thick, long, black hair was brushed and tidy but looked flat and dull and her normally sparkling, blue eyes were veined with red.

Frank was at the coffee machine in the main office when she entered. He stared at her for a minute making her feel self-conscious.

"What?" she asked. "Why are you staring at me?"

"I'm trying to decide if you look like shit because you've been awake all night partying or if you've not slept 'cause your fretting over Harvey Stone."

Angela scowled. "Of course I'm not fretting over Harvey Stone and before you ask, I wasn't partying either. If you must know, I didn't sleep well. I admit I was disturbed by the scene yesterday. It was too close to where I live."

"Yeah, it was pretty gruesome," Frank admitted. "We should find out pretty soon if the perp is known to us. Then we can see what we're dealing with."

"Have you any thoughts on who it might be, boss?"

"I can't be sure. But at the moment my money's on the escaped loony. He's called John Baptiste and he's a religious nut. He thinks he's John the Baptiste. He's a dangerous fucker, a complete nut job. He battered one nurse, locked him in a cupboard, killed another, stole her keys and her swipe card, then he strolled out of the hospital unchallenged."

"That would explain the crosses on the wall."

"Yeah, that's my feeling. I'm having his profile sent through to us. It shouldn't be too long before we catch up with him. He's quite distinctive looking although the photo we have of him is quite old. He wouldn't allow a photo to be taken in hospital, said it was against his human rights, and some do-good, social worker agreed with him."

Frank handed Angela a coffee just as Paul entered the room.

"Christ, you look even rougher than her," Frank exclaimed staring at him. "What happened to you? Who gave you that shiner?"

Paul held his hand to his forehead. "When I got home last night the place was bedlam. Our neighbour was trying to cope with my kids, but she was having a hard time. By the time my wife came home with Michaela from the doctor's it was late and everyone was hungry and tired. The kids were all acting up. I felt like running away and I wish I had," he added wistfully. "The older ones were carrying on, banging their spoons off the table and singing 'why are we waiting', and when I leaned over to place a bowl of soup in front of Grace, her spoon caught me on the eye."

Showing no sympathy, Frank began to laugh. "Serves you right for being such a randy bugger," he said. "I told you to have a vasectomy after kid number four, but no, you wouldn't listen. Are you trying to fill that chapel all by yourself? You must be the number one Catholic in the diocese. I bet the priest loves you."

For a moment Paul looked pained then he began to laugh. My wife is popular with Father Quinn. She lords it over the other mothers like a queen bee. You're just jealous of my nocturnal gymnastics, you sad old sod."

"I'm not jealous of the consequences though," Frank replied. "And I'm not sporting a black eye. Anyway, let's get down to business."

Just then the phone on Angela's desk rang. She reached over and picked up the receiver.

"And he's been taken to the Vicky," she said. "Is he still unconscious? Mrs Graham spelled 'ham' not 'eme'. And she's the church cleaner. Yes, give me her address, please."

When she hung up the phone Angela had Frank's and Paul's full attention.

"There's been an incident at the Church of Scotland in Clarkston," she said. "The cleaner arrived this morning to discover the church door open, and when she went round to the warden's house, it had been ransacked and the warden was unconscious on the floor. He's been taken to the Victoria Infirmary."

"This has to be connected to the murder. The church connection is too much of a coincidence," Paul said.

"Did I hear right? Is the warden still unconscious?" Frank asked.

"Drifting in and out, they said. He's been lying on a stone floor all night so it might be hypothermia rather than a broken head," Angela replied.

"I'd like you two to nip over to the hospital and assess the situation. By the time you get back here I should have an update on the fingerprints. In the meantime, I'll read up on John Baptiste. Even if he's not our man, he's still out there and he has to be caught. Oh, and pick up some sandwiches on your way back and something sweet. It's going to be a long day," he added.

Paul offered to drive. Angela was grateful because she felt lethargic and her eyes were tired. The journey, which should have taken only ten minutes or so, was arduous and frustrating. As well as hitting the tail end of the rush hour they seemed to be stopped by every red light along the way, and, to cap it all, at a particularly narrow part of the road, a lorry driver making a delivery, halted the flow of traffic for several minutes.

"This is absolute Hell," Paul said. "I feel as if I've done a morning's work already."

"I'm so glad you're driving," Angela replied. "I'd have been crying by now."

"Well, you see that's the difference between boys and girls," Paul retorted. "Boys get on with the job while girls are just big cry babies."

For once, Angela didn't rise to the bait. They eventually did arrive at the hospital which had buildings on both sides of the main road. To their left, was a modern clean-looking building of concrete and glass, and to their right, was a towering Victorian stone structure.

"He's in the old Vicky, but park wherever you can," Angela advised. A task which proved to be impossible. After driving round the car parks several times, Paul managed to find a space on the street towards the back of the old building.

"What on earth would you do if you were an outpatient coming here for an appointment?" Paul asked.

"Parking's always been a problem," Angela agreed, "But it seems to be even worse now".

They made their way through the building. "It's so old fashioned. No wonder they want to close it down," Angela observed.

"Yes, but if you're having a heart attack and you live in the south side of the city, you could make it to this hospital and they'd have a chance of saving your life. If you had to get all the way to the Southern General, the journey might take forty minutes or more and the chances are you'd be D.O.A. It would take even longer if there was a match at Ibrox, you'd have less chance of surviving than Rangers."

"I'd better not have a heart attack at home then," Angela replied.

When they arrived at the ward they were surprised to see Kenneth Scott, a freelance reporter who mostly worked for a local rag, sitting outside, writing up some notes.

"What are you doing here, Kenny?" Angela asked. "Is one of your relatives sick?"

She'd known Kenny for years. They'd both attended the same swimming club when they were children.

"In a manner of speaking," Kenny replied.

"What's that supposed to mean?" Paul cut in. He was in no mood for games.

Kenny's chin was practically resting on his chest. He looked up smiling sheepishly. "I've been to visit my brother, Freddy," he said.

"But you don't have a brother," Angela replied.

"They don't know that," Kenny answered, pursing his lips and pointing his thumb at the ward door.

Paul held his bottom lip between his thumb and forefinger for a moment then it dawned on him. "Freddy, is Mr Gordon, the church warden. You've wormed your way into seeing the victim of a crime by lying to the staff."

"A man's gotta do what a man's gotta do. Everyone has to make a living," he replied. "Anyway, it was pretty much a waste of my time. He's mostly talking gibberish. The only thing he could tell me was that he opened the door and a big, black, bugger punched him in the face. After that, nothing."

Kenny replaced his notebook in his pocket and stood up to leave. "Nice to see you again, Angie," he said before nodding at Paul and scuttling off.

"Cheeky sod," Paul said scowling. "I hope you didn't date him. I hope you've got better taste."

"Well I managed to repel your advances, so I must have," she fired back.

Their thoughts returning to work, they realised that what they'd been told by Kenny was enough for them to consider he'd probably had a run in with John Baptiste.

Chapter 7

Kenny Scott was smart. He knew that although he hadn't gleaned much information from Mr Gordon, what he did have was dynamite. He was more than capable of thinking outside of the box. After running to his car, he took his laptop from the boot, and began to write his editorial, under the heading, 'Madman on the doorstep'.

When Kenny first became a journalist he dreamed of stories like this, but although he'd always worked, plodding along with tales of local events and achievements, he'd never had a scoop of this magnitude.

It had been a massive decision on his part to leave a safe career, working in Social Services, and instead enter the precarious field of journalism. His parents thought he was crazy and maybe he was. They were of a generation who believed that when you got a job, you should keep it for life, especially if that job was a good one with steady pay. But Kenny had hated his work. It was tiresome and the people he had to deal with had problems he couldn't identify with or understand. After two years, he needed to get out. Fortunately, his wife Caitlin agreed with him.

She was already working for the council when they met and subsequently married. While he struggled to earn recognition, she supported them. And when she had their son, Ben, he became a stay-at-home dad while her career continued to take off. Now Ben was nine and Caitlin was a high flying executive. Even though earning a steady living was difficult for Kenny, he loved his work, and besides, his family were comfortably off and, more importantly, happy.

He, like many other journos, had spent much of the previous evening camped outside of the house where Rachel Stone had been murdered. Like them, he'd wondered whether her death might be the work of John Baptiste. The religious aspect was his style. But after hanging around for hours, that was all they had, speculation.

The police evidence wouldn't reveal any proof, in the form of DNA or fingerprints for some time yet and, whilst none of the others could positively place John the Baptist in the area, thanks to the statement from the church warden, he could. When Mr Gordon said he'd been battered unconscious by a big, black man, Kenny was ecstatic. It didn't really matter if it was John or another big, black man who'd landed the punch. For the time being at least, there was enough evidence to justify the speculation. Kenny had his story. He had a scoop. All he had to do was type it up then decide which of the big papers to sell it to. He couldn't waste any time. He had to be quick to beat the pack and make the deadline for the next publication. His heart thumped in his chest and he was wired with adrenalin as his fingers flew across the keyboard.

* * *

Angela and Paul got nothing from the church warden. By the time they arrived on the ward the consultant was doing his rounds and they had to wait. Then, when they were finally admitted, Mr Gordon was deeply asleep and, as he'd suffered a head injury, they weren't allowed to disturb him.

"Shit," Paul said. "What do we do now? What do we tell the boss?"

"We tell him Mr Gordon was punched by a big, black man," Angela replied.

"But we didn't get that information from the victim."

"The boss doesn't know that, and I, for one, don't want to enlighten him. Do you?"

"I don't suppose old Freddy in there will remember who he spoke to or what he said," Paul replied. "I'm with you, Angela, the information isn't definitive anyway. It just makes us look as if we've done our jobs."

"Let's get a coffee, Paul. I need a hit of caffeine to wake me up. There's a cafe in the new building. I'm paying and I'll even stretch to a piece of carrot cake, if you'd like."

"You're on, Murphy. My eye is really aching and I could do with some TLC. Half an hour out of the day probably won't make a difference to the case at this stage, but it'll give us strength for what lies ahead."

They walked across the main road and entered the modern building. It was a stark contrast to what they'd just left. The brightly lit corridors were modern and clean, although every area looked the same and the signage was confusing. A person could easily get lost in the building. The cafe had the feel of a commercial coffee house rather than a hospital canteen and within a few minutes they had selected a table and were tucking into their coffees and slices of cake.

"This is great, Angela," Paul said beaming. "I feel better already. Sometimes a bit of what you fancy does you good," he added, licking his lips and leering at her suggestively.

"You've recovered quickly," she replied laughing. "Is food and sex all you need to live on? Are you that base and shallow?"

"Yes and yes," he answered. "I am that base and shallow. A piece of carrot cake and a pretty smile and I'm anybody's."

After a few moments, Angela was surprised to see Kenneth Scott enter the cafe.

"A wonder what he's still doing here?" she said.

He bought a coffee then walked towards them.

"Aw, shit, that's all we need," Paul replied, "Just when I was beginning to unwind."

"Mind if I join you?" Kenny asked, sitting down before they could refuse. "I've just sold my story to one of the majors," he said smiling happily. "When do you think you'll know who killed Mrs Stone? The word is that you got plenty of forensic evidence and lots of fingerprints."

"You know I can't discuss the case, Kenny," Angela replied, "Especially not with a journalist. You wouldn't want me to get a reprimand, would you?"

"Aw, come on Angie, we go back a long way. I'm not asking you to do anything illegal. Just give me the head's up whenever you can. You'll need the press if the murderer turns out to be John Baptiste and if he also attacked Freddy Gordon. You'll need us if you want to track him down."

Kenny reached into the top pocket of his jacket and extracted a business card.

"Please, take my card. You never know when you'll need a friend in the media."

Reluctantly, Angela accepted it. She didn't want to disappoint him, but was fairly certain she wouldn't use it.

"Can you give me your number Angie? In case I need to get in touch. I might get information you'll want to use."

"Don't push your luck, Mate," Paul cut in. He didn't like the way this guy was putting Angela on the spot. He had little patience with journalists at the best of times.

Kenny held up his hands defensively. "Sorry, I'm sorry. I didn't think asking for a phone number was overstepping the mark."

"It's okay, Paul. I don't mind giving out the work mobile number." Then to Kenny she said, "Only use this if you've got something for me. Don't call if you're simply fishing for information, because I can tell you now, you'll be sadly disappointed."

"I understand. Thanks, Angie," he replied, taking her card and standing to leave. "Good luck with your case. I hope everything goes well for you." Then he turned to Paul, "Nice to meet you," he added, grinning.

"Cheeky bastard," Paul retorted. "I can't stand these smart arse types. Who the hell does he think he is?"

"Calm down, Paul. He's just trying to do his job. Besides if he hadn't told us about what the church warden said to him, we'd have absolutely nothing to take back to the boss."

"I suppose you're right, Angela, but I still can't stand the creep. Journalists are such parasites."

They finished their coffees, left the building and had just climbed into the car when Angela's phone rang. She could tell from the caller display it was Frank.

"Come straight back to the office," he said. "Our murderer is John the Baptist. His fingerprints match. We're in trouble. He's a complete psycho. We need to find him before the bodies start piling up."

Angela felt a chill run down her spine. The colour drained from her face. He's a complete psycho and he's on my patch, she thought.

"When will the media get hold of this information, boss?" she asked. "Is there likely to be panic?"

"There's going to be an announcement in the lunchtime news. So we can warn the public not to approach him, but still get everyone looking for him. It might cause panic, but we've no choice. He could turn up anywhere. Where are you now? Are you on your way back here?"

"Yes, we're on our way, boss. We'll be with you soon."

The phone went dead. Frank had hung up.

Angela reached into her wallet and took out Kenny's card. She would let him have this piece of information as it was going to be public knowledge anyway.

It would mean that he'd owe her one, and it would give her a favour she could call in at a later date. She dialled his number.

"Hello, Kenny, Angela here. Today is your lucky day," she said.

Chapter 8

When Paul and Angela arrived at the office the whole team had been assembled. People were standing around or sitting on or at desks, chatting and drinking coffee. The door to Frank's room was open and Angela could see him talking to a stranger inside. Paul stopped to say hello to a colleague.

"I'd better let the boss know we've arrived," Angela said and she headed for Frank's room.

"Nice of you to join us, Murphy," Frank said when she knocked on the door. "I take it your side-kick's with you."

Angela was alarmed to see that Frank's face was the colour of a lobster and shiny with perspiration. She knew he used to look like this quite often when he was drinking. She glanced at the whisky bottle beside his desk and was relieved to see it was still full.

"Paul's waiting in the main office," she stated.

"Good, that's good," Frank replied. "Let me introduce you to Doctor McLaren, from the secure unit. He'd been treating Mr Baptiste for several years before his escape. He's here to tell us a bit about the man and what to expect."

Doctor McLaren was short and slim. He looked about fourteen. The skin on his face was as smooth as a baby's bottom, as if he'd never had to shave. His hands were long and elegant, like a woman's, and he wrung his fingers constantly. When Angela reached out to shake his hand his fingers were clammy and his grip weak. It felt like a limp, wet fish slipping through her grasp. His shirt collar seemed too big for him, like a child wearing his father's clothes. From Frank's tone and his demeanour, Angela could see that he was no more impressed with the man than she was.

"Well, now, Doctor, if you'd care to join me, we'll get this show on the road. Find the doctor a seat, please, Murphy."

When they emerged from Frank's room, everybody sat down and the chatter ceased. After a quick introduction, Frank began.

"Following the murder of Rachel Stone and the assault on Frederick Gordon, we know who we're looking for. I'm now going to give you a brief rundown of John Baptiste.

Mr Baptiste first came into the system when his parents died. He was fifteen. We don't know how his parents died, but we do know that something tipped him over the edge and he was held under a compulsion order until he was eighteen."

A hand shot up from the crowd interrupting Frank.

"Yes, Baillie, what is it?"

"Why don't we know what happened to his folks or why he was locked up?"

There were murmurs from the gathering.

"He was a minor at the time and his records haven't been released to us. We have requested them though. Anyway, people, if you would please settle down and save your questions for the end. It won't take me long to run through this."

Silence ensued and Frank continued.

"After his release from hospital, Baptiste was in and out of trouble, everything from petty theft to aggravated assault. He spent brief spells in jail and psychiatric hospitals, sometimes volunteering for care. When he was thirty, he murdered his next door neighbour, a known drug pusher. He was found to be unfit to plead and acquitted on the grounds of insanity. That's when he came under the care of Doctor McLaren."

The doctor smiled awkwardly and held up his hand in acknowledgment.

"He'd been in the hospital for just over five years, when he escaped. He'd been a model patient. He was usually calm and quiet and was trusted to move fairly freely about the hospital. He had access to the day room and to other patients. He was regularly given medication to control his condition, but the doctor believes he went off the rails because he stopped taking his drugs."

A ripple of voices went round the room.

"I'm going to hand you over to Doctor McLaren now and he's going to tell us what happened on the day Baptiste escaped, the day the nurse was murdered. If you would, Doctor, please," Frank said, holding out his open palms, offering McLaren the floor.

The doctor stood and cleared his throat, "Good afternoon," he said. "Firstly, I must tell you, I won't pull any punches," he began. "Although he was trusted, we were probably too complacent where John was concerned. There is no doubt in my mind that he's a psychopath and a sociopath and, while off his medication, he's about as dangerous as they come. Make no mistake, he won't follow any rules, and he's a danger to anyone he comes in contact with."

All of a sudden McLaren seemed to grow in front of their eyes. What he lacked in stature, he now made up for in presence. His speech was forthright and direct. Every man and woman in the room was shocked into silence and his words chilled them to the bone. You could have heard a pin drop. After a brief pause, he continued.

"The day of John's escape began like any other. He seemed exactly the same as before. He followed the same routine, took his drugs from the nurse, as usual, and he was calm. We didn't know that instead of swallowing his medication, he'd been concealing it. We had no reason to doubt him."

The doctor paused, drew his open palms down his face then rubbed his eyes and cleared his throat.

"I'm sorry, but what happened next is very disturbing for me," he said.

"Take your time, doctor. We know what it's like to deal with violence and death," Frank said kindly. "And we know you've lost a colleague."

Another murmur went round the room. Then McLaren began again.

"John presented himself at the nurse's room complaining of stomach pains. In hindsight that should have alerted us, as stomach pain could have been a sign that he was off his meds. There were two nurses on duty Barry Andrews and Mary Gregory. It seems that Mary went into the next room to get medication for John. She would have used her swipe card to open the door and would have then closed the door behind her, before opening the drug cabinet. Once in that room she wouldn't have been able to hear what was going on next door because of sound-proofing."

Doctor McLaren paused. His hands had been clenched into fists, but he now relaxed them and began to wring them again. His face developed a nervous tic at the side of one eye.

"Excuse me, please," he said and he turned his back on the room, took a handkerchief from his pocket and blew his nose loudly.

Everyone held their breaths, unsure whether he would be able continue. Frank held up his hands in a placatory fashion, indicating for silence. After a moment, and to the great relief of his audience, McLaren turned back to face them and spoke once again.

"The attack on Barry happened so fast he had no indication of it coming. One minute he was standing in the room, the next he was coming round, with his hands, feet and mouth bound by 'Tensoplast' heavyweight tape. He'd been pushed into a metal locker usually used to hold coats. Barry is a big chap. He couldn't move an inch while he was in the locker. He realised very quickly that he'd been briefly knocked out, but there was no way he could alert Mary to the danger."

He paused again and held his hand against his forehead. "I'm sorry, but may I have a glass of water, please?" he asked, then he sighed deeply.

Once again, a ripple of voices went through the room. Paul was next to the water cooler and he quickly filled a plastic cup and gave it to the doctor, who gulped it down before beginning again.

"Mary re-entered the room," he said, his voice breaking slightly. "All we know is what Barry heard. It seems she asked John where her colleague had gone and John said, 'he's with God'. John obviously thought he'd killed him. Then Barry heard scuffling and Mary cried out. He heard John referring to her as a whore and making some reference to Mary Magdalene. Then he heard… then he heard…"

Doctor McLaren began to sway slightly as if he might faint. Frank reached for a chair, grabbed the doctor by the elbow and sat him down.

"I know this is very distressing. Take a moment," he said.

"No, no, I'm okay," the doctor replied, but he didn't stand up. Instead he continued from his seat.

"Barry heard the sound of fabric being ripped. He assumed that like him, Mary had been gagged, but he could still hear her screaming through the tape. John raped her. She'd been married less than a year to her childhood sweetheart and she was three months pregnant."

The doctor swiped his eyes with his handkerchief as tears ran down his cheeks. He breathed deeply then began again.

"Using Mary's keys, John took a scalpel from the cabinet and he cut off her head. He cut off her head," he repeated as if he could hardly believe what he'd just said. He stared around the room, swallowed hard then continued, "Barry heard John ranting. He heard him praying, asking God to take Mary's soul. Then he heard the door close and there was no further sound. He knew John had left. He was frantic, desperate to help Mary, but he couldn't move. About half an hour later, a security guard did a random check via the CCTV and saw that something was seriously wrong. When we entered the room, Mary's body was on the floor. There was blood everywhere. We found John's blood-stained clothes in the adjacent shower room. He'd washed himself, then he calmly went back to his room wrapped in a towelling robe. Afterwards, he dressed in outdoor clothes and, using Mary's swipe card to open the doors, he walked out of the facility. He hasn't been seen since."

There was an uncomfortable shifting of feet and clearing of throats when the doctor finished his brief. No one knew what to say. The gallows humour that usually kicked off at these meetings didn't materialise. Everyone could identify with the victims in some way or other and they all felt sympathy for Doctor McLaren. He seemed so broken. Not only for the loss of his colleague, but also for his clear misjudgement of John Baptiste. This underestimation was the reason for the complacency which doubtlessly led to Mary's death. When Frank finally showed the doctor out of the door, there was an audible sigh of relief.

After he left, the brief continued for a further half hour. They were each advised of the work they would be responsible for and what they should expect over the coming days. They were also advised, that the only available photograph of John Baptiste was taken by the police, when he was twenty-one years old and was, therefore, very out of date.

"So how are we meant to identify the bugger?" one of the officers asked. "We can hardly ask every big, black man to give us a DNA test, can we? For all we know, Joshua here could be the killer," he added, playfully boxing his colleague on the arm. "He's a big, black bugger, and he's got a foul temper," he added laughing.

"Watch your step, white boy," the officer replied, "Or you could be my next victim. I'll make an ornament out of your peaky, fat head."

Everybody laughed. To their collective relief, humour had returned.

"To get back to the job in hand," Frank cut in. "It's going to be a real problem, because until he shows his hand, we could have difficulty recognising him."

"So we've got to catch him red-handed, committing a crime or rely on a member of the public getting to know him and turning him in," Angela stated.

"Yes, I'm afraid that's about where we're at," Frank replied. "As you all know, the most difficult person to catch is the fucker who murders a stranger."

The subdued mood returned and Frank drew the meeting to a close. The atmosphere was very low as everyone dispersed and went about their business. Soon, Paul and Angela were the only ones left in the main office.

"Are you okay, Paul?" Angela asked with concern. "You've gone awfully pale."

"Well thank God for that," he replied, as quick as a flash. "At least I won't be mistaken for John the Baptist."

Chapter 9

Angela was shattered when she got home from work and she was experiencing a number of emotions, none of them good. She felt heavy with sadness, imagining Mary Gregory's terror, her pain and her anxiety for her unborn child. She was unnerved and edgy, fearing that John Baptiste could be just around the next corner, waiting to strike again.

When she entered her house all was quiet. Bobby should have been home, she thought, a jag of fear hitting her in the chest. She called out, "Bobby, are you in? Are you okay?" She was met with silence. Leaving the front door open, 'don't bar your escape route', a voice in her head warned, her police training kicking in. She made her way through the house towards the kitchen, checking the front rooms on her way. No longer calling out as she didn't want to alert a possible intruder to her whereabouts. There was a roasted chicken resting on the hob and a bowl of savoury rice on the work top, so he had been home. She glanced at the peg board and there was a note. 'Back in 10, love Bobby', it read. Relief flooded over her. Quickly, she ran back to the front door and shut it, then, feeling like an idiot, she began to weep.

Angela didn't want Bobby to return and find her in this state, so she went upstairs, gathered casual clothes from the bedroom, and went to have a shower. However it was a short lived affair as, while standing under the jets of water, all she could think about was the scene from the film 'Psycho'. She'd returned to the kitchen and was sitting at the table, half way through a glass of red wine, when, a few minutes later, she heard Bobby's key in the door.

"I'm in the kitchen," she called, not moving from her chair.

"Sorry I wasn't in when you got home," he called back. "I went to 'La Brava' to buy some of that Scottish tablet ice-cream you like, so we can have it for dessert."

When Bobby entered the kitchen he was accompanied by a very wet, large dog. It was tall and lean, had a beige and black short coat and kind eyes.

"I can explain," he said, before Angela could respond. "He was tied to a lamp post outside the bistro and when I went in to buy the ice-cream, Aristide, the chef, came over to speak to me. He knows you're with the police and he wanted advice about the dog. He said a young couple with a baby tethered the dog. One of the customers saw them. He kept expecting them to return, but they didn't."

Neither he nor the dog moved. They stood side by side as Bobby spoke, with the dog occasionally glancing from him to Angela and back again, as if he could understand every word.

"Anyway, when I went over to the dog, he was very friendly and he licked my hands. I found this baggage label tied to his collar."

Bobby held out a crumpled piece of cardboard. When he realised that Angela wasn't going to take it from him he read, "Please take me home. I'm kind and gentle. I'm three years old and my name is Rex."

He paused, waiting for a response and when one wasn't forthcoming, he continued.

"I couldn't just leave him in the street, standing in the rain. Look at him. He's soaked through."

As if on cue, the dog shook himself, covering every surface with spots of water.

Bobby stared at Angela's horrified face. "Don't worry. I'll soon have this cleaned up, and I'll get a towel for Rex," he said.

They were already on first name terms, it seemed.

"What are we going to do with him?" Angela asked. "It's far too late to take him to the Dog and Cat Home. And what will you feed him on? We don't have any dog food."

"I'm sure he'll enjoy some of the chicken and rice. I've made loads. There are a couple of old bowls under the sink that I can use for his food and water and a car rug in the garage that'll do for his bed. He can sleep in the kitchen in case he has an accident through the night. I'm sure he'll be fine, but no point taking any chances."

"And what about after tonight? What then?"

Bobby's expression was full of hope and longing. "I thought I might keep him," he said. "I work from home, so he wouldn't be alone. He would be company for me. It would force me to go out and get fresh air and exercise instead of poring over a computer all day."

The dog sniffed the air and licked his lips then stared hard at Angela and wagged his tail.

"I think you'd better feed him soon, before he slavers all over the floor," Angela replied. "And I'm pretty hungry too. I haven't had time to eat much today," she added pointedly. "He can stay for a few days. Just a trial run, then we'll decide."

Bobby grinned. He bent down and ruffled the dog's ears. "Mummy said, yes, Rex. She said, yes. You're staying boy. You're my lovely boy, now. Let's carve up that chicken, Rex, you must be starving."

Great, Angela thought, now I'm second best to a mutt.

The food was delicious. While working from home, Bobby had become an excellent cook. After eating, they took the remaining wine and adjourned to the lounge. Rex joined them. Stretching himself out on the rug in front of the fire, he promptly fell asleep, occasionally twitching and snoring through doggy dreams. He was utterly relaxed, as if he'd always lived with them.

Angela was almost asleep in her chair when her work mobile rang. She stirred and reached for her handbag.

"Drat, I'd better answer it," she muttered. There was no caller ID visible.

"Yes," she said.

"Hi, Angie, it's me, Kenny Scott. Thanks for the info earlier. I really appreciated it. I'm returning the favour now. I've got something for you, not much, but it might help."

Angela was suddenly wide awake. She sat up in her chair.

"Hi, Kenny," she replied. "No problem. Glad to help. What have you got for me?"

"It's about John Baptiste. The photos on the news show him to be thin, young and with a black beard and afro-style hair, but he doesn't look like that now. His face is wider and he's shaved off his beard and all of his hair. He looks like a black, Uncle Fester from the Addams Family film."

"How do you know this, Kenny? Was it from a reliable source?"

"Straight from the proverbial horse's mouth, Angie. My brother Freddy told me when I visited him this evening."

She was about to say again that he didn't have a brother when she stopped. "You went back to see Mr Gordon? But the nurses knew you weren't a relative. How did you get in?"

"Ah, well, you see, the day shift knew I wasn't really his brother, but the evening shift had no idea. Anyhow, by tomorrow he'll be on a general ward and everyone will be able to visit."

"You're a real chancer, Kenny. You know that, don't you?"

"Maybe so," he replied chuckling, "But I got the info and we'll both benefit from it. While I'm on the phone, I'd like to ask, do you and your husband ever go to the Stamperland Club for a drink? My wife and I are going on Friday. Just for a beer and a game of snooker, nothing heavy or formal. I thought it might be nice to meet and catch up."

Angela thought about it. It might be pleasant to socialise with them. He was always good company when they were youngsters. They didn't go out with Jake and Miranda much now, since he was caught out to be a serial womaniser, so befriending another local couple, to have the occasional drink with, might be rather good.

"Thanks for the info, Kenny. Let me get back to you about the Club. I'll have to check with Bobby first. I'll call you tomorrow."

"Who was that?" Bobby asked when she ended the call.

"An old friend. He's a reporter. He'd like us to meet him and his wife for a drink."

"And would you like to go out with them?"

"Yes, I think I would."

"Make the arrangement then and we'll do it."

Bobby was usually rather shy around new people, but at the moment he'd agree to anything that would draw attention away from Rex. Although the dog was meant to be with them for a few days trial only, Bobby was determined to hang on to him.

Angela phoned the office with the information she'd been given from Kenny. They now had the new description of John in plenty of time for a statement to be made on the ten o'clock news. At least now, everyone would know what he looked like.

After following up with a call to Frank, she settled back in her chair and stared at the big dog lying by the fireside. She was actually rather pleased to have him in the house. He would be a good deterrent for criminals. Not many people would take on a big dog, she thought, possibly not even John Baptiste.

* * *

When John had woken at Peter's house that morning it had taken him a few moments to remember where he was. He shivered under the threadbare blankets, the room was cold and it felt damp, not at all what he was used to. He remembered that before he'd lived in a modern building which was clean, bright and draught free. He knew it was a sort of hospital, but he couldn't remember why he'd been there. He didn't feel ill, so he must have got better.

John rubbed his face with his open hands and tried to clear his head. Gradually a memory of helping Peter to find his keys came back to him. God had brought him to this place. He didn't always understand why God made suggestions to him, but he knew He had a plan for him. He had a plan for all of his creatures.

John rose and quickly dressed. The floor felt cold beneath his feet so he pulled on his trainers. He'd better buy some clothes today, he thought. He had a holdall with some bits and pieces, but he'd need more. Perhaps Peter would like to join him and show him around? He knew there were a number of charity shops in Victoria Road because he'd seen them yesterday when they'd walked to the supermarket. John had plenty of money in his wallet, so he could afford to buy a few things.

As he made his way to the bathroom, he heard Peter moving about in the kitchen. A smell of slightly singed toast reached his nostrils and his stomach rumbled. John was used to a full English breakfast, but he was pretty sure that wouldn't be on offer today. Peter had little money, but he was generous of spirit and he was a good man.

John washed and shaved using Peter's razor. Luckily there was a packet of new blades in the medicine cabinet. Then he went to the kitchen to get some food.

"Good morning, Pal, did you sleep all right?" Peter asked cheerily.

"Yes, Brother, thank you. Although the day feels cold."

"I don't put the heating on through the night," Peter explained. "It costs a fortune to heat this old tenement flat with electric. There is a working fireplace in the lounge where you slept, but coal costs a fortune too."

"Your flat is very spacious and well placed. With a bit more money you could be very comfortable."

"I just wish someone would tell that to the council," Peter said. "Anyway, Pal, I've made you breakfast. It's not much. Just some toast and jam and a pot of tea, but it'll keep you going until we get some shopping in."

"You're very kind, Peter."

"I've been thinking, John and I've had an idea about where you can stay while you're in the area. You'll probably think it's a stupid idea, but I'll run it past you just in case. Instead of booking into a hotel, you could live here with me. I wouldn't charge you any rent, but you could share the bills. We'd be company for each other. What do you think?"

John smiled to himself. He'd always planned to remain here, with or without Peter's blessing.

"I would be honoured to share your home and your companionship, Brother," John replied. "Honoured."

Chapter 10

When Angela came downstairs to the kitchen she'd forgotten that Rex was there and was startled to see him. He lay on the car rug on the kitchen floor, relaxed, as if he didn't have a care in the world. The dog didn't get up when she entered the room, but merely lifted his head and wagged his tail, making a thumping noise against the laminate floor. When she said, "Hello Rex," he stood and stretched, made a 'humph' sound then came over to her and nuzzled her hand. As she prepared breakfast he sniffed the air, licking his lips expectantly.

Angela opened the back door to let the dog out and he immediately went to the back gate and relieved himself against the gate post. Then, after a quick surveillance of the garden, he left a large, steaming deposit on the patio before returning to the kitchen. I'm not cleaning up after him, she thought, clearing poo would be Bobby's new job. He'll soon learn that having a dog is a big responsibility.

When Bobby entered the room she said, "I've got to go or I'll be late. I don't know what to give the dog to eat, but I think he's hungry. You'll need to sort it. Oh, and he's done a big poo on the patio, so you'll need to clean that up too. I might be home late again today. It all depends on what happens with the John Baptiste case. I'll phone Kenny Scott and arrange to meet them in the club tomorrow, if you're still good with that."

She stopped to draw breath.

"I'll take care of everything. Don't get stressed and please be careful. Don't take any chances where this nutter is concerned. It'll be good to get out for the evening tomorrow, so go ahead and arrange it if you can. I love you Pet, and thanks, I'm really pleased we're keeping Rex."

Bobby opened his arms and Angela went over to him for a hug and a kiss before leaving.

"I love you too," she replied. "And don't worry about me, I'm always careful." Even as she said the words, she knew that was a lie, but it kept him happy.

Arriving at the office fifteen minutes late for her shift due to a problem on the road, she was surprised to see that neither Frank nor Paul was there yet. More surprisingly, Jack Dobson was still poring over his computer typing something up. His shift should have been over and he was usually quick off the mark.

"No home to go to, Jack?" she asked. "Wife finally seen sense and locked you out?"

"For your information, my wife and I split up two weeks ago. I don't think you're very funny."

Angela was shocked. She knew they'd gone through a difficult patch over a year ago, but she thought they were rock solid now.

"I'm really sorry, Jack. I honestly had no idea or I wouldn't have made the joke," she replied, feeling sick.

"My God you're a gullible wench, Murphy. Got yah," he replied laughing.

Angela walked over and punched him on the shoulder. "Bastard," she said.

"Ow, that hurt, police brutality, I could charge you, you know?"

"Serves you right, I hope you get a bruise. Why are you still here? Where's your partner? I thought you had a rookie shadowing you this week."

Jack Dobson sighed, he was no longer young, and he'd been passed over for promotion several times. Although he'd been a cop for years, he was generally lazy and lacked any ambition to progress his career. He stank of stale cigarette smoke, was always shabbily dressed, and looked as if he needed a good wash. He looked particularly grubby against the stark newness of the recently refurbished office.

"Don't talk to me about him," Jack retorted. "The boy is straight out of university, sharp as a tack and he thinks I'm an old codger. We were called to a suspicious death at Knightswood. Some guy found at the bottom of a stairwell having fallen from a great height. Everything points to it being murder. He's known to us, and he's a bad one, goes by the name of Howard Hughes. Have you heard of him?"

"Can't say I have," Angela replied. "Famous name though, maybe he thought he could fly," she joked.

"More likely he was launched," Jack replied.

"Anyway," Angela continued. "That doesn't explain why you're still here and your rookie isn't."

"We didn't get back here until five minutes before the end of our shift. I said to Tony, why don't you get off, Son, and I'll write it up. I expected him to say, no Jack, you get off and I'll do it. After all, I'm the senior and Detective Khan is the kid. But no, the cheeky sod said, okay ta, and he was off like a rocket. He moved so fast you'd think his arse was on fire. So I'm stuck here and the wee shite will be half way home by now."

"Tony Khan? That name's a mixture of cultures if ever there was one."

"Aye, his mother's Italian and his father's Pakistani. They're academics, scientists I think."

"Well their boy certainly knew the formula for getting out of here early," Angela laughed. "You'll not be so quick to offer your services next time."

"Damn right. Anyway, I don't know why you're so cheerful. Have you not seen the list on your desk? Every crackpot under the sun has been calling in, thinking they've seen your murderer. I didn't know there were so many black men living in Glasgow."

"Aw Hell, no wonder Paul is late in. He's probably hoping I'll be landed with making the calls."

"I guess you've been stiffed with a crap job, too, Murphy. At least I'm out of here now. Good luck. You're going to need it."

"Before you go, Jack. Is there any chance your flier could have been hefted over the banister by my man?"

"Doubt it. But when there's a maniac on the loose, who knows. You can look at the case if you want, but you've probably got enough on your plate. I'm outta here now, before the boss arrives and finds a reason for me to work a double shift. I'm going home to have breakfast with my estranged wife," he added with a wink.

Angela intercepted Frank as soon as he came into the office, before he had the opportunity to disappear into his room.

"Where's Paul?" he asked her. "Isn't he in yet?"

"I haven't seen him, but it doesn't mean he's not in the building," Angela replied, trying to protect her partner.

"He'd better have a good excuse for not being here," Frank grumbled. "What do you want, Murphy?"

"Jack Dobson has been dealing with a suspicious death in Knightswood. I'd like to spend an hour and go through his notes. I want to make sure there's no connection to our case. It means Paul will have to start our follow up calls himself."

"Knock yourself out, Murphy. I heard all about it from George at the front desk. I don't think there's a snowball's chance in Hell they're connected, but it's better to be sure. I'm guessing most of the calls about Baptiste will be fucking useless anyway. I've spoken to the people who sifted out the real dross and they're not very hopeful. Let Paul call the do-gooders and the cranks. That'll teach him to come in late for his shift."

Paul arrived just as Angela was leaving Frank's room. He looked awful, pale and tired looking with red-rimmed eyes.

"What happened to you this morning?" she asked.

"Nothing good," he replied.

He didn't even challenge the issue of the follow up calls. He just flopped down at his desk and picked up the phone. Angela went to the machine and poured three coffees, handed one into Frank then returned to her desk.

"Here," she said handing one to Paul. "I shouldn't be long going through Jack's case notes then I'll give you a hand."

Paul nodded his acceptance then returned his attention to the list.

It didn't take Angela very long to establish that Howard Hughes had a fight with another known criminal, only a few hours before ending up dead at the bottom of the high rise building. The fight was witnessed by a pub full of people, and several overheard threats being made, so she was pretty sure his death was unconnected to Baptiste. Paul was on his ninth phone call, and was slouched in his seat, when suddenly he sat up and reached for a pen, patting the desk to get Angela's attention.

"And you're sure he said he was visiting churches?" Paul asked. "And your name is Elizabeth Andrews. Sorry Libby, but I need to take your official name for the paperwork. Can you come into the office and make a statement and perhaps look at some photos? Good, yes, ask for Detective Sergeant Costello, Paul Costello, when you arrive at the reception desk. I'll see you in an hour then."

"Yes!" Paul said when he ended the call. "I've got a charity shop worker who saw our man. She can place him in Clarkston and she actually spoke to him. I'm going to get an artist to sit with her and produce a more accurate picture of him. At least we'll have a fighting chance of the public identifying him then."

"How did she make the connection?"

"She said he was a bit odd. When the newsreader read out the description you got from the reporter, and mentioned that he was always spouting religion, she put two and two together. She described the track suit and trainers he was wearing and they sound like the ones stolen from Rachel Stone's house."

"Let me see the list of calls," Angela said. "Are there any from bus drivers or car drivers who could have given him a lift?"

She and Paul both scoured the list.

"Here," Paul said excitedly. "Good call Angela. Charlie McBride, driver of a number six bus, thought he picked him up at the bus stop at Clarkston Toll. I'll phone him next."

"Just keep your fingers crossed that Charlie boy remembers where he got off. That would tell us where he went. With any luck he might still be in that area," Angela said.

"Yes, and hopefully it's nowhere near where either of us live," Paul replied.

* * *

John knew, from hearing the news report on the radio, people might be looking for him. His description, including the clothes he'd been wearing, was accurate. It troubled him. He didn't wish to be apprehended at this stage of his journey, because he had so much work yet to do. Why couldn't these people realise that God guided him? The very souls he was here to save would deny him. The Lord knew all about denial. One of his best friends denied him not once, but three times, and he was betrayed by those he trusted. John had to change his appearance. He had to remain free to complete his task.

He searched through Peter's meagre belongings when his friend went to the corner shop for milk. He found a flat, tweed cap to cover his bald head, and a pair of dark glasses. John stared at his image in the bathroom mirror. It changed him considerably. Next, he dressed in the dark suit he'd bought at the charity shop. He was comfortable in his track suit, but it would have to go. A wool 'Gap' coat, another charity shop find, added the finishing touch. No one would recognise him now. With the dark glasses, and accompanied by his blind friend, he would appear to be just another man with poor eyesight.

Peter entered the flat. "Hi John," he said sensing his friend's presence. "I got the milk and some of those French rolls, the crescent shaped flaky ones, to have with our tea. Now we're sharing the bills, I can afford a bit of luxury. I bought some cheese and ham too. We'll soon be cutting the crust off our cucumber sandwiches, just like Prince Charles," he joked. "Oh, and I bought you a newspaper as well. They were really surprised when I bought that, I can tell you," he laughed. "They didn't know what to think, a blind man buying a newspaper, indeed."

John was mildly annoyed. Even though he knew Peter meant well, he didn't want him drawing attention to their situation. If he persisted, he'd have to be stopped.

Chapter 11

Elizabeth Andrews liked to talk and she had opinions on every subject. Whether it was the price of bread, the weather, President Obama or Dancing on Ice, Libby had something to say about it. Paul had been with her in the interview room for over an hour and had yet to get all the answers he required. He really didn't have the energy for Libby Andrews this morning. He was finding it difficult to get a word in edgeways, let alone steer the conversation in the direction required.

"So Miss Andrews, you're absolutely sure he said he was going to visit the Evangelical Church? That's the one at Busby?"

"Yes, that's what he said, but I don't think he knew the area, and he didn't actually say he was going to Busby. It's a lovely, friendly church, the Evangelical, he might have gone there and then gone on to the Church of Scotland. He was very polite. I can't believe he would commit such a terrible crime. Are you a member of a church, Officer? If you are, you'll know how shocking this is for me. If a man of God can do something so heinous, what hope is there for the rest of the community?"

Paul was sick of this stupid woman. He was desperate to escape the confines of the interview room. He fancied a coffee, needed the caffeine, but he didn't want to offer Libby one in case it added to the time he had to spend with her and prolong the torture. There was a loud knock on the door. Paul jumped to his feet to answer it, thankful for any distraction. When he opened the door he saw it was the artist.

"Hi, Glen, I'm so pleased to see you," he said, practically pulling the poor man into the room. "Miss Andrews, this is Glen Wilkes, the artist. He's going to sit with you at the computer and see if he can construct a photo image of the man you saw. I'm nearly finished. I've just got a couple of sentences to write then, if you're satisfied the statement is correct, I'll get you to sign it, please."

Glen hadn't even managed to get his backside onto a chair, before Libby was off on another tangent. Paul's final sentence was written so quickly, it was little more than a scrawl, but he could smell freedom, so he didn't care. It was a further fifteen minutes before he could extricate himself from the room, abandoning Glen to the agony of Libby's inane chatter.

When he returned to the main office, Paul was informed that Charlie McBride, the bus driver, had arrived to make his statement. After his experience with Elizabeth Andrews, he begged Angela to accompany him to write up his statement. Seeing how exhausted Paul looked, she agreed without comment. She didn't know what his problem was, but was sure he'd tell her in his own sweet time.

Angela phoned through to the front desk and asked that Mr McBride be shown into an interview room. Then she grabbed Paul by the arm and practically dragged him along the corridor.

"After this, we're going out for lunch, my treat," she said. "You look as if you could do with some sustenance."

Paul smiled wryly. "Thanks, Angela, my stomach's rumbling at the very thought of lunch and, with the current state of my finances, I'd be delighted to let someone else pay."

It must be money that's his problem, Angela thought. Paul earned considerably more than she did, but he had five kids to support on one wage, whereas she and Bobby had two salaries coming in and no dependants. It couldn't be easy for Paul with so many mouths to feed.

When they entered the interview room, Charlie McBride rose from his chair.

"I'm DS Costello and this is DC Murphy," Paul began. "And, you're eh... you're eh..."

"A bus driver," Angela cut in. "Please do sit down."

Charlie McBride began to laugh. "You're surprised I'm black, aren't you?" he said to Paul. "Charlie McBride is such a Scottish name for a black guy, isn't it? Don't worry. I get that all the time."

Paul's face reddened, he didn't know how to respond.

"The good news is, that based on the description given on the telly, I'm ninety-nine per cent sure your man got on my bus. You see, not all black men look the same to me," he added with a chuckle.

Mr McBride was offered tea, which he declined, then the interview began with Angela asking the questions and taking notes while Paul listened in.

"If we could please establish which bus stop the man got on at," Angela asked.

"Outside the Cancer Research shop, only a couple of folk got on and he was the only one who paid cash."

"And where did he ask to go to?"

"He didn't. He just put two pounds into the box for his fare. The fare all the way into town is one pound ninety pence, and we don't give change, so he could travel anywhere for that."

"Where did he actually get off?"

"Victoria Road. He thanked me as he got off. He had nice manners."

A well-mannered psycho, what next, Paul thought, but he said nothing.

"Did you notice anything unusual about him or his behaviour, anything that would draw your attention to him?"

"Only that he paid in cash instead of flashing a travel pass and he looked sort of out of place. I couldn't quite put my finger on what it was. Something just didn't seem right about him, as if he was unfamiliar with his surroundings. He stood out, if you know what I mean."

"Would you recognise him again? Do you think you could sit down with our artist while he puts together a photo likeness of the man?"

"Aye, no problem. When I told my boss I wanted time off to come here, he said I could take as long as I needed. You could have a raging toothache or be getting married and you'd have to beg for time off, but helping the police to catch a murderer, no problem. My boss can dine out on that, you see," he joked.

Angela liked Mr McBride, he had an easy manner and he was relaxed and funny.

"Are you always on the same route?" she asked, as an afterthought.

"Usually, why do you want to know that?"

"If Baptiste got on your bus again, we'd like you to alert us right away, please?"

"Damn right, I would. I can make a call for assistance if I'm ever in any trouble. And don't you worry, I'm not daft and I don't have a death wish. If he got on my bus, I'd drive straight to Toryglen police station and let your lot sort him out. I've never understood these movies where a person goes to investigate when they know a maniac is on the loose. They always end up getting hacked to death. Trust me. I'll be the snivelling coward who runs away and lives to fight another day."

After they finished their interview with Charlie McBride, Angela and Paul thought they'd better go back to the hospital and have a talk with Freddy Gordon. It was just a formality as they already had all the information they needed. Nevertheless, they knew they must take a statement directly from him and not simply rely on hearsay.

"As we're heading back to the Queen's Park area, is there anywhere on the south side you'd particularly like to eat?" Angela asked Paul.

"I'm really famished, Angela. If we're going to the south side anyway, why don't we go to the Ruby Palace restaurant on Clarkston Road and fill up with Chinese food? It's a top quality place. The food is really tasty and very good value for money, so I'll be a cheap date."

"You're always a cheap date, Paul. There's not a classy bone in your body. Personally, I couldn't eat a lot at the moment, but I fancy vegetables and noodles, so I could order that while you pig out on the three course lunch."

Paul's reply was to grunt and squeal like a pig. Angela threw him a look usually reserved for precocious children.

They took Angela's car and were soon seated in the restaurant which was situated only a short walk from Angela's home. She could have popped back to the house to see Bobby for a few minutes, but knowing Paul was finding money tight, she didn't want to flaunt her high standard of living in his face. As it was, he commented on the affluence of the area.

"I'd love to move my family to one of these big, sandstone houses. We're really cramped where we are now," he said.

"You're living in Kings Park, aren't you, Paul? It's a nice area."

"Yes, it is, and we've got great neighbours, but the house is far too small and it costs so much to move these days."

Angela felt the time was right to broach the subject of Paul's troubles.

"You've seemed a bit stressed recently, and you're always tired. Is there a problem? Anything I can help you with?"

"Only if you've got a spare fifty grand lying around, that's the shortfall I'd need to make a move to a bigger house in an area with good schools. Don't get me wrong, being a cop, I can easily get the mortgage for the full amount, but it's the monthly repayments that would be the problem. If you must know, I'm tired because I've been moonlighting. I'm doing odd jobs for extra money. I know we're not meant to, but I really need the cash. Only last week, three of the girls had to get new shoes. Over a hundred quid they cost me. Just like that, and they weren't even the designer ones they wanted, just ordinary black, school shoes. It's outrageous."

"Who did the mortgage calculations for you? Did you go to a financial advisor?"

"No, I thought it would be a waste of time. I just did the sums myself based on what I'm paying at the moment."

"Did you take into account the term of the loan? You must have paid off at least ten years by now, and you're still young, so you could take the new mortgage over a twenty-five year term. That would reduce the monthly repayments. It could make a huge difference."

Paul stopped shovelling food, his loaded fork held midway to his mouth. "Who should I go and see? Do you know someone?"

"Go to your own bank. They'll have a person who deals with things like that."

"Thanks, Angela, you've renewed my hope. I've been feeling really low recently. I've got someone who might be interested in buying my house, but I thought we had no chance of moving to where we'd prefer. I'll phone the bank this afternoon and see if I can get an appointment."

"Just don't move next door to me," she said wagging her finger at him. "I'm sure your children are delightful, but the thought of living next door to five kids, terrifies me."

"You should try living in the same house as them," he replied smiling.

When they returned to the office, Frank was pacing the floor.

"Where the hell have you two been?" he stormed. "How long does it take to write down a sentence or two?"

Angela and Paul glanced at each other, but said nothing.

"I've had Rachel Stone's family on the phone, twice," he added grimly. "They keep going on about their religious beliefs. They want to bury her, but her body's not been released yet. The brother-in-law, the rabbi, said he's coming in to speak to me. What the fuck am I meant to tell him? I'm not good around very religious people. They make me nervous. I don't want to fuck up and be accused of prejudice."

"It's not your fault, boss. If the body's not been released there's nothing you can do. It's not something you have any control over," Angela replied, trying to calm him down. His fat face was alarmingly high coloured, his eyes protruding. He looked as if his head might explode.

"He's due to arrive at any moment," Frank said, glancing at his watch. "One of you two will have to see him. Tell him I've been called into a meeting. I've got enough to stress me out. God is looking for a quick result on this case. I don't need this. Besides, I haven't had the benefit of a long break. I've been working flat out while you two have been swanning around being ladies who lunch."

There was no point in Angela or Paul protesting. They both knew the boss wasn't good at dealing with these sorts of situations. The DCI, God, as he was known by those beneath him, could be a real pain in the ass. Often being downright unreasonable. So they understood the pressure Frank felt.

"I'm going out for a sandwich. I might be some time," Frank said and he strode briskly out of the door.

"Do you think he's had a drink?" Paul asked. "His face was very red."

"I'm not sure, but I'd be willing to bet he's on his way to a pub and he won't be back anytime soon," Angela replied, "So which one of us is going to deal with the rabbi?"

"Rock, paper, scissors, okay," Paul suggested.

Angela won.

"Best of three?" he ventured.

"Not a chance," she replied.

Chapter 12

John and Peter very quickly fell into a living arrangement that suited them both. Peter provided John with the perfect cover. Who would suspect that the mild mannered, near blind, black man could ever commit a violent crime? When they went out to the local shops or got on the bus to travel into the city centre, they looked like a couple of poor souls indeed. One tap tapping his way with a white stick, while the other grasped his arm and held his stick in front of him. Both wore dark glasses. John would have preferred to wear the stylish Raybans he'd stolen from Rachel Stone's house rather than the plain, ugly pair that were Peter's spares, but why draw attention to himself?

John was careful, mimicking Peter's mannerisms until he could play the role with ease. Although his vision was near perfect, nobody would ever know it. He learned to accept assistance when shopping. He didn't directly face people when he stopped to speak to them. Instead, he would let his head loll back and slowly roll it from side to side, as if he had no point of focus. He could have won an 'Oscar' for his performance.

For his part of their arrangement, John brought money to the household. He proved to be an excellent beggar easily relieving people of their hard earned cash and, in particular, unsuspecting elderly ladies of their pensions. He gently cajoled them into parting with their money, a pound here a tenner there. Of course he didn't tell them the whole truth, but implied the money would go to a charity for the blind. He knew it was wrong to lie, but he repented for his transgressions, praying for forgiveness every time he strayed from the straight and narrow path. God loved sinners and John knew he'd be forgiven.

The Govanhill area of Glasgow suited John very well. It was a melting pot of races and cultures. He didn't stand out from the crowd. Historically, it had become a first home for migrants from diversified backgrounds. Jews escaping from Eastern Europe, Italians, Pakistanis, Irish, they all arrived with little, but with hard work and initiative they succeeded and built communities. It had always been considered to be a relatively safe area. People knew their neighbours. They shared what they had and they helped one another. Many of these incomers became successful businessmen and businesswomen and some became the backbone of society. But times could change. A recent influx of economic migrants, coming from poorer Eastern European countries, had brought high levels of crime to the area. They clashed with the well-established, mostly Asian community. No one felt safe anymore and the escalating level of violence was alarming. Someone like Peter, or John in his current disguise, was seen as an easy target.

John hadn't noticed the shadowy figure standing in the doorway as he walked along the dimly lit, Torrisdale Street, until he was grabbed by the arm and pulled off the street. It was seven o'clock in the evening and he was meant to be meeting Peter at the pub for a beer. The attacker held a long-bladed knife in front of his face.

"I have a knife," the heavily accented voice of a pockmark-faced young man said. "Give me your fucking money and your fucking watch," he demanded.

He was tall and wiry. John could smell a clean, freshly laundered scent emanating from his clothes. He wore a hoodie and denim jeans, the standard uniform favoured by thugs and junkies, but John was pretty sure he wasn't a junkie. His pallor was too healthy.

"Brother," John replied, "What use would I have for a watch? I am blind."

The man smirked, momentarily dropping his guard. It was the seconds John needed. He threw his head forward, in a motion known as a Glasgow kiss, catching the man square on the nose. There was a satisfying crack followed by a gush of blood. The robber didn't have time to realise what had happened before John brought his knee up, hitting him in the groin and doubling him over. The robber gasped, fighting for breath. He fell to the ground, landing with a thud, on the cold, damp concrete of the close. As he lay there, writhing in pain, John assessed him. Here was a sinner who obviously didn't need money to pay for an addiction. He simply had seen his victim as a vulnerable man, easy pickings for the opportunist thief. John was instantly outraged, how dare he, he thought.

"You must learn from the error of your ways, Brother," he said. "Your sin cannot go unpunished."

With all the strength he could muster, John stamped on the man's right hand, crushing and breaking bones. The man screamed, in agony. He raised his left hand to try to protect himself, unsure where the next blow would land. John stamped down again, reducing the hand to blood and pulp. The man passed out.

"In the holy land, your hand would have been cut from your body. You cannot steal. You have broken God's commandment. I pray you will now repent," John preached.

He looked out of the close entrance to make sure nobody was about then turned and walked quickly down the dark street towards Victoria Road, without looking back. John had to get home. He had to get back to Peter's flat to clean up before going on to the pub. He couldn't risk being seen in this state, not with the man's blood on his clothes.

* * *

Angela and Bobby arrived at the club just as Kenny and his wife came walking down the hill towards it. They waited for them to reach the door before all four entered together. Kenny was a few years older than Angela so she assumed Caitlin was aged about the same, but she looked much younger. She was stunningly beautiful and it was hard to believe she had a nine year old son. Caitlin was slim, blonde and petite. Her hourglass figure was clothed in a plain, cornflower blue, shift dress the colour perfectly matching her large, bright eyes. Her face was heart shaped with her red lips forming a cupid's bow. Bobby couldn't take his eyes of her and neither could Angela.

"Where do you work?" Angela asked when they were seated, secretly hoping she was a cleaner or a factory worker or employed in some other unsexy job.

Caitlin smiled shyly, "I work for East Renfrewshire Council," she replied, "In the offices."

"She's being modest," Kenny said. He and Bobby had returned with their drinks in time to hear the tail end of the conversation. "Caitlin's a senior accountant in the finance department. She's the main breadwinner in our household. I'm a stay at home dad."

"So you just work part-time as a journalist?" Bobby enquired.

"Yes, I'm freelance. The pay is sporadic. Luckily, I'm a kept man," he added laughing.

"I work from home too," Bobby said. "Angela and I earn about the same, but her job is much tougher than mine," he stressed.

"So how do you and Kenny know each other?" Caitlin asked. "He didn't say."

"We attended the same swimming club when we were children. Being a few years older than me and my friends, Kenny was allowed to help the instructor by teaching us the strokes. All the girls fancied him. I thought he was a God."

Kenny blushed scarlet.

"Well I assume you've got over that now," Caitlin replied shortly.

Kenny's face fell. He looked at Angela, clearly dismayed by his wife's response.

Oh, my goodness, Angela thought, surprised by the rebuke. She's jealous. She looks like a goddess, yet she's jealous. She's not perfect after all. Angela couldn't help feeling smug then she was ashamed. Caitlin seemed nice enough, but the poor woman was obviously insecure. Angela wondered why she had such low self-esteem.

The conversation covered every subject from sport to holidays, but inevitably, after about half an hour's worth of small talk, the main focus was on the murder of Rachel Stone. A couple, who were sitting at the adjacent table and who were known to Caitlin and Kenny, leaned over to join in the chat. They were introduced as Mags and Derek.

"It sounds as if we live very close to you," Derek said to Angela. "In fact, I think we're practically your back to back neighbours. We've been living in the Avenue for ten years, but I don't think we've met before."

"Actually, I think I've seen you in Sainsbury's, Bobby," Mags said. "Am I right in assuming you work from home?"

"Yes, that's right. I have my own company, so I can make my own hours."

"Your work must be fascinating, Angela," Derek said. "I bet you know where all the bodies are buried," he joked.

Angela felt uncomfortable. Her current case was no laughing matter and she quickly tried to change the subject.

"I heard that the Jewish lady had her head cut off. Is that true?" Derek asked, determined to keep the line of conversation open.

"I'm sorry, but I can't talk about my work," Angela replied, clearly irritated by his persistence.

"Aw, come on Angela, just a juicy morsel or two. Just enough for us to dine out on," he persisted.

"She said no, Pal," Bobby replied, standing up to lean over Derek. "Which part of no, did you not understand? We're here for a night out with our friends. It's nice to meet you, but if you don't mind, we'd rather be alone."

Mags grabbed her husband by the arm, "Come on, Babe," she said. "We can take a hint. We know when we're not wanted." As they moved to another table Mags said in a loud voice, "Stuck up cow, probably works as a clerk. And I'd be willing to bet he's, unemployed."

Kenny was horrified. "I'm really, really sorry," he said. "They were very rude and we hardly know them. I think they've had a lot to drink, but it's no excuse. I promise, we won't talk about work anymore. This is meant to be a social evening."

"Don't be upset," Angela replied. "It happens all the time. As soon as people discover I'm a detective it's open season I'm afraid."

For the next hour, every time Angela glanced up, Mags was looking at her and glowering. Silly woman, Angela thought, no wonder they're on their own.

The evening progressed very well. The two couples were enjoying each other's company. Kenny was very witty. Bobby and Angela found themselves laughing out loud at some of his anecdotes. Even Caitlin managed to relax. By eleven o'clock they'd had a couple of rounds of drinks and the boys had played two games of snooker, winning one each They were planning to have another night out the following Friday when the conversation was interrupted by Angela's work phone ringing.

"I'm sorry," she said. "I'll have to take this call. It must be important if they're calling me out of hours."

Kenny glanced at her, expectantly.

"I see, boss," she began. "I'm sorry but I can't drive. I've had a couple of drinks. Well, it is Friday, and it's my evening off. No, I'm not complaining about coming in. Of course not, but you'll have to send a car to pick me up. No, Bobby can't drive me. He's been drinking too." Angela's voice was rising. She was obviously annoyed. "Why don't you pick me up then, if it's not a problem? I see. No, I didn't think you'd have your car. How did you get in then?" she snapped, her irritation changing to anger. "Twenty minutes at my house. No, I can't be ready before that." She ended the call. "Well fuck you too, you old bastard," she said.

"I'm afraid I've got to go into work. They've got a young man at the Victoria Hospital with a broken nose and a mangled hand. He's claiming he was assaulted in Torrisdale Street by a black man matching the description of John

Baptiste. It's probably a waste of time, but I'll have to go. I'm really sorry. The three of you should stay on though. I've just to pop home and change then a car is picking me up."

"I'll walk you home," Bobby said. "I don't want you out there on your own with that nutter walking about. We're getting together next week anyway. It's been great meeting you both," he said to Kenny and Caitlin.

"I know we said we wouldn't talk about work, Angela," Kenny said. "But please remember me if this does turn out to be the work of John Baptiste."

"Don't worry, Kenny. You'll be the first reporter I'll tell," she assured. "But between you and me, I hope this isn't his work. It's still too close to home."

Chapter 13

A young uniformed officer arrived to collect Angela and, when he rang the doorbell, Rex barked as if they were under siege.

"Good boy, that's right, you tell him," Bobby said, proudly. "He's a great guard dog, but don't worry, he won't hurt you," he assured the young policeman when he let him in.

"I'll take your word for it," the officer replied.

Meanwhile he didn't offer Rex his hand to sniff, even after Bobby suggested it, and he stood in the hall with his back to the wall never taking his eyes off the dog. Sensing the upper hand, Rex let out a low growl every time the young man moved. After a false start, because Angela couldn't locate her house keys, the policeman audibly sighed with relief when he and Angela eventually left the house and were on their way to the hospital.

The journey took less than fifteen minutes. When the car arrived, Frank was waiting for her at the main entrance, smoking, and pacing up and down impatiently.

"They've only had to cut his fucking hand off," he said by way of a greeting. "His face is smashed up. Broken nose, broken cheek bone, jury's still out on the eye socket. He's in a right mess."

"They've amputated his hand? Oh, my God," Angela replied. "Will he be able to speak to us?"

"Yes, I think so, just so long as he doesn't have to use sign language," Frank joked. "He's back on the ward now and I've already had a chat with his doctor. Not the surgeon who operated. He's away home. But the wee boy who's in charge of the ward. He told me what the patient said when he was first admitted."

"What have we got?"

"Well, the lad, Arek Bronsky's his name, said he was attacked in an entranceway in Torrisdale Street. The ambulance driver confirmed that's where he picked him up. A man found him lying in the close and called it in. That was at around eight-thirty."

"And he said he was attacked? Out of the blue? He did nothing to warrant it?"

"Ah, well, there's the thing. That's what we have to find out. The description of the assailant loosely fits John Baptiste, but Arek told the doctor the man was blind. Doesn't seem right, does it? A fit, young lad randomly attacked by a blind man. It sounds like the start of a bad joke, 'What do you get when you cross a Pole with a big, black, blind bugger, etcetera, etcetera'."

"What's the plan, boss? Shall we go and interview him now?"

"Aye, I've finished my fag. It's fucking freezing standing at this door. Are you not cold? Where's your coat."

"Hanging on a peg at home. I forgot it in the rush to get here. I told you I've had a couple of drinks. It might be better if you write down the notes."

"No, you're all right," Frank replied. "I'm sure you'll manage. Besides, you'll be typing it up when I'm on my way home to my bed," he laughed.

Angela gave him a wry look. "I don't think so, boss. I think tomorrow morning will be soon enough for that, don't you?"

They took the lift to the ward and were admitted by a staff nurse.

"If you could keep your voices down, please," she said, "Everyone's asleep. Arek's been dozing on and off. As you can imagine, he's very shocked by what's happened to him. He's still mildly sedated, but he's aware he's lost his hand."

"Poor bugger," Frank replied. "Terrible thing to happen to a young man."

"Just so you know," the nurse said, "He told me he tried to rob the man. He's full of remorse now, of course, but you might want to have your people look around in the close for a knife. Although, given the area where he was picked up, someone might have lifted it already for their own use."

They were led to a small side room where Arek lay. Even though Angela had been warned about his condition she was sickened by what she saw.

Frank muttered, "Bloody hell," then coughed to hide his shock.

Arek's eyes were swollen shut and his face was almost completely covered in purple-black bruises, highlighted by patches of blood red. His arm was heavily bandaged, but it was clear the hand was gone.

"Arek," the nurse said softly. "These people are here to talk to you, but only if you feel up to it. They're detectives."

He opened his eyes, but the lids parted to barely more than a slit.

"He was blind. A blind man did this to me. He could have killed me."

"Would you mind starting at the beginning, Mr Bronsky and my colleague will take notes? If it becomes too much for you we can stop. We know you've been through a terrible ordeal," Frank said, signalling for Angela to sit down.

"May I have some water, please?" Arek asked, and the nurse lifted a cup with a straw to his lips. Once he'd had a few sips she replaced the cup on the trolley which stood at the foot of the bed and left the room.

The interview began with Arek giving his full name, date of birth and address.

Then he said, "I tried to rob him. "I hold my hand's up to that." The implication of his words suddenly hit him and a sob escaped from his lips. After a few moments Arek managed to compose himself and continue. "He kept preaching. Stuff about God and sin. He was black and big, but I thought he couldn't see. I thought I'd be in and out. Two minutes to take his wallet and watch and I'd be home and dry. I just wanted the money to buy my girlfriend a piece of jewellery for her birthday," he added, as if that somehow justified his actions. "I didn't expect him to fight back or be able to identify me."

Angela and Frank exchanged glances.

"Did he say anything that would give you his name?" Angela asked. "Do you remember him mentioning a name from the bible?"

Arek considered the question. "No, nothing," he replied. "He just spoke about God and the holy land." Then Arek shut his eyes. "I'm sorry, but I'm exhausted. I can't talk anymore."

"You've done very well, Son," Frank said kindly. "We'll catch the man who did this to you. Mark my words."

"But I tried to rob him," Arek said. "I guess you think I deserve this."

"No one deserves this, Son," Frank replied. "No one deserves what he did to you."

Leaving Arek to sleep, Angela and Frank quietly left the ward and returned to the lobby.

"That was awful, boss," Angela said. "It'll take a long time for him to recover."

"Yes, it's truly shocking. But if the assailant was John Baptiste, then that young man is lucky to be alive. Look what happened to Rachel Stone."

* * *

John knew he had to change his appearance and he could no longer live at Peter's flat. It was a shame because he had a nice set-up. Leaving Peter's spare white stick folded on the table he laid the dark glasses he'd been wearing beside it. Then, discarding his suit, he changed into a pair of jeans and a bomber-style, denim jacket, both charity shop finds. Instantly he looked younger and trendier, no longer like a formally dressed, middle-aged, blind man. He was pleased with his appearance. Over the past few days he'd grown a moustache which he shaved into a modern shape, letting the ends join up with a goatee beard. His hair had grown into designer stubble and he shaped that too with the razor. Without actually punching a hole in his ear, he used a small, gold loop from a key ring as a single earring, to finish the effect. No one would recognise him now, he thought.

John assumed, if he didn't turn up at the pub, Peter would come home when he ran out of money. He could tell him he didn't join him because he'd felt unwell. Then later, when Peter was asleep, he would pack his bag and leave in the morning before his friend awoke. He wouldn't need to move very far away, which was good because he knew the south side of Glasgow very well now. Just to another district where people wouldn't recognise him. One way or another, he'd soon find a place to stay, he thought. The Lord would guide him.

Chapter 14

"Oh, God, oh God, oh God," Paul said over and over again.

"Please stop fantasising about me and jerking off, Paul. I'm in the room now," Angela said.

"Oh, God," Paul repeated. He looked up and stared at his colleague. His desk was piled high with files and his computer screen was switched on. He looked serious and his eyes were watery as if he might cry. "These are the reports on John Baptiste," he said. "He murdered both his parents. His father was a monster."

Angela wandered over to Paul's desk.

"When did this come in?" she asked staring at the screen.

"I'm not sure, but the files only landed on my desk about an hour ago. The boss phoned and called me in. He said there'd been an incident last night, probably when you were out drinking with your new best friend, that cocky reporter."

"I'll have you know that when you were sound asleep in your bed, I was attending that incident. Why do you think I'm in here on a Saturday morning when it should be my day off? I have to write up a report."

Frank entered the room moaning and groaning. He looked tired.

"I hope you two are working," he said. "Have you written that report yet, Murphy. I hope you're not keeping Costello from his job. He's a lazy sod as it is. Don't give him any excuses."

Paul kept his head down, trying to avoid any further interaction with him, but there was no escape.

"Well, have you discovered anything from these files yet, Paul? Anything that might lead us to our man? Do we know what makes him tick?" Frank persisted.

"Have you seen any of this, boss? It makes shocking reading. Did you know he killed his parents?"

Frank walked over to stand beside Angela and they both stared at the screen each leaning a hand on Paul's shoulders.

"According to this psychiatric report, he was forced to rape his mother while his father stood over him. His father regularly raped his mother making John watch. Christ, what a crazy fucker the father was. No wonder John became nuts," Frank commented.

Paul read aloud, "The father frequently battered both John and his mother. Hah, it says here that Baptiste senior had mental health issues. Mental health issues? He was a psychopath, for God's sake. Baptiste junior killed his old man when he was fifteen years old. Christ, he crucified him. Do you see that, boss? It says here he crucified his father. The coroner estimated it took days for him to die. Baptiste senior died from dehydration."

Angela shuddered, her face paled. "Why didn't anyone notice something was wrong? Where were the teachers? Where were the social workers? Surely someone saw something? He was a child."

"Aye, but he was a mighty big and powerful child according to this," Paul said. "He was five feet ten when he was arrested and he weighed twelve stone six. His father was a weedy little guy. He obviously controlled his wife and son by fear. Then John grew up and probably couldn't take it anymore so he fought back. Being forced to rape his mother was probably the last straw."

"He nailed the father to the wall with a nail gun. Bloody hell, can you imagine how sick he was to do that? He told the shrink he strangled his mother to save her soul for the Lord. He said she sold her body to men and gave the money to his father. When John tried to protect her, Batiste senior threatened to cut off her head if John didn't rape her too. The father told him all women were whores," Frank read.

"He raped the nurse he killed. Her colleague heard John calling her a whore, when he was shut in the locker. Then he cut off her head, just like his father threatened to do to his mother. His actions all seem to be connected," Angela said. "This reads like a horror story."

"It is a horror story," Paul replied.

"Oh, my goodness, look at this entry," Angela said, pointing to the screen. "His maternal grandmother was his next of kin although she had severed all ties with the family when he was still a child. Her last known address was

Clarkston. She once lived at the same address as Rachel Stone. He might have been going after the grandmother when he went to that house. If he'd been locked away with no contact he wouldn't have known that she'd moved out of the district. And he probably didn't know what she looked like, not after all those years, so he wouldn't have had a clue who he was attacking."

"We'd better try to find her. See where she is, if she's still alive that is. We don't want to be seen to be neglectful if he suddenly turns up on her doorstep and bumps her off," Frank added.

"Never mind that the poor soul could be at risk. As long as we're not neglectful," Paul muttered.

"Don't push your luck, Boy," Frank replied. "When I go home at night I don't give a monkey's fart about Baptiste's relatives, and neither should you. I have no connection to them other than this job. The mad fucker's hurting people all over the place, but as long as they've nothing to do with us, we should all just be thankful. We can't save the world, Paul."

Suitably chastised, Paul concentrated on the screen in front of him and said nothing more on the subject.

"If he attacked Rachel Stone because he thought she was his grandmother that doesn't explain his assault on the church warden," Angela said. "He had no connection to him."

"He didn't need a connection," Frank replied. "He's been off his meds for ages. He's completely off his trolley. Besides, from what I gather, the church warden upset him because he refused to unlock the church. The young man from last night tried to rob him. He's becoming crazier and more random. Nobody's safe."

By lunchtime, the latest description of John Baptiste hit the television news and by the afternoon the phone began to ring with sightings of him. One unfortunate man, who was both black and blind, was set upon by a mob, convinced they'd caught the murderer. People were frightened and when a crowd was scared they behaved unpredictably. Instead of just being at the office for a couple of hours, Angela and Paul saw the day looming large.

* * *

Peter was woken at nine when he thought he'd heard the front door close. It wasn't banged shut, on the contrary, it was very softly clicked on the Yale lock, but he heard it. Being blind, his other senses were sharp and he could literally hear a pin drop. He didn't know where John had gone, so he waited, hoping he'd soon return.

By five-thirty, Peter began to worry about him and he searched the flat for any clues to where he might have gone. Sometimes John would leave an empty milk carton on the kitchen table to let Peter know he'd gone to fetch milk. Another time he'd leave his newspaper from the previous day spread out on the sofa so Peter knew he'd gone to buy a paper. In the short time they'd lived together, they'd devised a number of ways to communicate when the time wasn't opportune to talk. By five forty-five he realised that John had left, taking his stuff with him. Fifteen minutes after that, he listened to an item on the radio and his blood ran cold.

Peter didn't have a television and he almost never listened to the radio preferring his music CDs. He'd had no idea the police were searching for someone called John Baptiste. Surely his friend, John, couldn't be that monster? He was such a mild mannered man, kind and generous, but it was an awful coincidence that the killer had been acting as if he was blind. He remembered all the times John had gripped his arm while they were walking. Was that part of his act? And besides, if he wasn't the criminal, why did he leave?

Peter was utterly bereft. His life had improved a hundredfold whilst he'd had John living with him. He could afford life's little luxuries with his friend's contribution to the household budget and he'd had someone to help with the shopping. No more mistaking soup for beans because he was in a rush and didn't notice the supermarket shelves had been changed. Most importantly, he'd had company. The sheer joy of having someone to talk to was a pleasure he couldn't even have imagined before John arrived.

Peter felt he should do something, perhaps tell the police about John, but he didn't really want to speak to anyone, especially not someone in a position of power. They made him nervous. He didn't want to look pathetic and stupid. How could he tell a cop he'd had a murderer living with him for days and he didn't even know it? But what if John came back? What if he wanted to shut Peter up? Maybe silence him for good.

Peter felt weak and helpless. His heart was throbbing in his chest. His ribcage was sore, constricting his breathing. He'd had heart trouble from birth and was meant to avoid stress. Large teardrops ran down his cheeks and he sobbed loudly. "You're a pathetic piece of shit," he said aloud, angry at his inadequacies.

"You'd be better off dead. What use are you to anybody? Even a murderous maniac couldn't stand living with you."

Chapter 15

Jack Dobson and Angela entered the building at the same time. She expected him to hold open the door for her, but instead, he raced through in front of her and let it swing shut behind him, then he turned and laughed.

"Not quick enough, Murphy," he said.

"A gentleman is meant to hold a door for a lady, you're not ten years old," she chided.

"Well there you are, Murphy, you've got your answer. I guess you're no lady."

Angela stuck her tongue out at him. "What are you doing here anyway?" she asked. "I don't usually see you from one week to the next and, I must say, I prefer it that way."

"Yeah, me too," he replied. "It's all your friend, Paul's fault, so you can take up your grouse with him. He's had to take a day's leave all of a sudden, compassionate grounds, the boss said. Some old aunty of his has popped her clogs."

"Did he say who? There are hundreds in the Costello clan."

"Bridget Quinn, the boss told me. Not that the name meant anything to me."

"Oh, I don't think she's his real aunt, but they were very close. She was a neighbour of his folks when he was a wee boy and she had no family of her own. Paul often spoke about her. They were closer than most of his real relatives. I think she made him her heir. He'll be very upset."

"Yeah, but he might get over his grief quite quickly if she's left him something in her will. Mind you, some of these old birds leave all their worldly goods to the Cat and Dog Home. He could end up with nothing and have to pay for a funeral as well," Jack replied.

"Is money all you can think about? Poor Paul's just lost someone who's been part of his life since he was a child."

"Don't be such a simpering softie, Murphy. Everyone has to go sometime. Meanwhile the lucky bugger's got a day off and I'm stuck with you. You'll have to bring me up to speed on the sinister minister," he laughed. "The rapist papist, the..."

"Enough," Angela shouted, holding up her hands. "I give in. Stop it with the rhyming jokes. You're not clever or funny or even accurate. If you have to work with me behave yourself or else, I swear, I'll tell the boss you've been telling lies about him behind his back."

"But I haven't," Dobson protested looking hurt. "That's not true. The boss and I go back years. I like the man."

"That might be the case, but who do you think he'll believe," she said with a mock smile.

"You really are a first class bitch, Murphy," he replied. "No wonder Costello's taken the day off. He probably bumped off the old aunty himself, just to get away from you."

"Are you kids fighting already? I hope not. You've got a lot of phone calls to get through this morning." Frank's voice boomed across.

"Hello, boss. Coffee?" Angela called back.

"Crawler," Jack muttered.

They were no sooner sitting at the desks in the main office, sipping coffees, and discussing the strategy for the day, when a call came through for Jack.

"David Hughes, you said? Any relation to Howard Hughes, my flyer found in the stairwell? His brother. Christ! Yeah, give me the address. Say I'm on my way."

Jack scribbled down an address then ended the call. He turned to Frank and Angela.

"A Mr David Hughes, brother of Howard. Thrown through the window of a top floor flat in Hathaway Lane at Maryhill, or rather North Kelvinside if you're posh, about a couple of hours ago, in plain sight of the neighbours. We've got another murder and it's connected to the first flyer. It seems the brothers were pimps, each running two or three girls from their respective rented flats. I'll have to attend, boss. Tony won't get in here for another hour at least. What do you want me to do?"

Frank sighed, "We need more people. You'll have to take Angela with you. I've got a meeting in ten minutes. When Tony gets here I'll get him to start on your calls, Murphy. There's nothing else we can do. Between days off and with this vomiting virus that's going around, we're awfully thin on the ground."

Angela's face fell. She hated working with Jack. She thought he was lazy and sloppy.

"Don't give me that face, Murphy," Frank said, noticing her scowl. "I know he's the last person you'd want to partner, and he reeks of cigarette smoke, but this is Jack's case and he needs assistance. So bury the hatchet you two, and not in each other. Get out of here and phone me with information as and when you get it."

"We can take your car, Murphy. I'll shut my eyes and have a wee nap while you drive," Jack said.

"Oh, no you don't. You're not making my car stink of stale smoke. I've just had it valeted. We'll take your car and I'll wear one of the forensics masks infused with menthol, so I can breathe."

"Suit yourself. You drive like a girl anyway."

"I am a girl, not that you'd notice, faggot."

"And you're a ball breaking lesbo," Jack replied.

"Are we finished now? Truce?"

"Aye, I suppose so. Save the malice for the punters. It's not a very salubrious area. They'll all have something to say and I'd be willing to bet, a lot of it won't be sensible or sober."

The journey was stop start all the way because of heavy traffic. By the time they arrived at Maryhill Road, the rain was becoming heavy and the sky was the colour of grey steel. Jack opened the boot of the car and took out two waterproofs, handing one to Angela.

"It's my wife's," he explained. "I think you'll need it. It's fucking freezing. I don't want you moaning you're cold," he added, embarrassed by his own kindness.

"Thanks," Angela replied. "At least this one doesn't smell of smoke."

Jack laughed, but said nothing more.

There were no entrances opening onto the front part of Maryhill Road as the whole ground level section was shops. They walked round and cut through a side street, entering Hathaway Lane, which formed the rear of the building. It was an unusual setting, but rather quaint and trendy and, being only a ten minute walk from the University of Glasgow, meant it was an area favoured by students.

When they approached the flat they saw that the entrance had been cordoned off. A small crowd of people were standing in the street to the side of the police tape. They looked frozen and they were moaning and complaining.

"Davy was flung out of his window, not mine, why can't I go back into my flat? I'm on the ground floor, nowhere near him," one man said.

Aye, we're all freezing our nuts off here, ma weans don't even have their jackets on," another added.

"I'm Mrs Perry and these are my daughters," another said, pointing to two short, fat, identical looking girls. They had flat, pug-like faces and reminded Angela of drawings she'd had in a book when she was a child, depicting Tweedledum and Tweedledee. "They have bad chests," the woman continued. "They shouldn't be out in the rain."

"I'm sorry folks, but this close is a crime scene. Until forensics is finished you can't go back into the building," Jack said, much to the relief of the young officer who was manning the entrance.

"Why don't we all adjourn to McDonald's, along the road? We can have a hot drink and get out of the rain. You can tell us what you saw and heard and, with a bit of luck, we'll be able to let you back into the building soon," Jack suggested.

"Aye, very good, mate, you turf us out of our houses then invite us to spend money we don't have at a fancy place like McDonald's," the first man said.

"Don't worry," Jack replied, "I'll be paying for the hot drinks and I might even stretch to a McMuffin."

All of a sudden, at the thought of something for nothing, the assembled group cheered up. Even Tweedledum and Tweedledee managed smiles on their previously sour faces.

Jack turned to Angela. "This place is crawling with uniforms and forensics is already here. We'll have a quick look at the layout, a gander at the corpse then we'll get ourselves out of the cold and eat breakfast at McDonald's, courtesy of Frank."

"Shouldn't we just take the names and addresses of this lot and hang about here for a while. There's a lot we can do and see," Angela replied.

"Look, Murphy, there's three separate households here. One of the bottom flats is boarded up so including the corpse, five out of six in the block is accounted for. Look at these people. They're the dregs of the earth. It might be days before we can track them down again. Once we let them back in they'll all be off down the pub to tell their tales. I say, we take what we can while we can. Besides, I'd rather be hearing what they have to tell us while seated in McDonalds, than standing out here in the rain."

Angela still wasn't entirely sure about Jack's motives, but what he said did make some sense. They had a uniformed officer lead the motley crew in the direction of the fast food outlet, with instructions to keep them there. Then the detectives donned protective suits and made their way inside the tent, which was used to hide the corpse from public view, to examine the landing place of David Hughes.

"I take it the fall killed him," Jack said, addressing one of the forensics people who was taking measurements close to the corpse.

"Actually, no," the man replied. "Landing killed him. Falling just scared the shit out of him, literally," he said chuckling at his own joke.

"Hello, Mack, I see you've not lost your sense of humour," Jack said. "Angela, this is Mighty Mack Bain, so called because he's a fat bugger. He has to get XXL coveralls or he bursts them. Mack, this is Angela Murphy. She's a real pain in the arse, but she's smart," he added, by way of a backhanded compliment.

Angela was touched by the praise, especially coming from Jack.

"I can't tell you much yet, Jack," Mack began, "Except that I think he was thrown through the window by two people. They must have swung him back then launched him, like you'd throw a heavy sack. That's why he landed a distance from the building. There's broken glass from the said window, all around, so they didn't open it first. We found footprints all around in the mud as well. From what I can see, it looks as if they came down here to check he was dead before they left."

"I guess it wasn't accidental death then," Jack said.

"Not unless they expected him to sprout wings and fly."

"Murphy and I are going to talk to some of the residents of the close. Is there anything we should know?"

"Only that this happened in broad daylight. The perpetrators had no fear of being identified. In fact, I'd say they wanted everyone to see what they were doing. They were in no a hurry to leave the scene. I suspect it's related to gang activity and this is some kind of warning. Two brothers, both being thrown to their deaths from a great height, is not a coincidence. They've stepped on someone's toes."

"If he was thrown from the top, back window, could the neighbours have actually seen anything?" Angela asked. "Other than the criminals leaving, that is."

"You'll have to ask the residents of the close, of course, but from what I've heard, there were four men. They removed two young women from the flat under duress, forcing them to go with them. One neighbour said the girls were hookers who worked out of the premises. Oh, and another thing, it seems there's a third girl who's not arrived back here yet. As I said, you'll have to confirm that. Anyone passing by at the time would have seen everything. Through the day, this place is crawling with students and the unemployed, but I don't suppose they'd have hung about. And who could blame them?"

"Thanks Mack, we heard that Hughes was a pimp, so your information's probably correct. I suppose we'd better look for those girls. Although I think they'll be safe enough. They'll just have a new boss now," Angela replied.

"A live prostitute definitely has more earning potential than a dead one," Mack agreed.

"Aye, but sometimes it's hard to tell if they are actually alive," Jack added, "When these lassies are full of heroin."

On that sombre note, Jack and Angela said their goodbyes to Mack. After a brief chat with members of the scene of crime team, and with heads bowed against the wind and the now driving rain, they made their way towards McDonald's.

Chapter 16

The neighbours of the unfortunate Davy Hughes were assembled in an area normally reserved for children's parties. There was an excited chatter. Suddenly their mundane lives had stepped up a notch.

"Jesus, what a circus," Jack observed. "They look like a freak show or a day trip from the funny farm."

"How do you want to handle this?" Angela asked, not looking forward to the task ahead.

Jack sighed, blowing air out through his puffed cheeks. "You take the wee man with bad teeth, Mr ground floor flat. I'll take the man with skelly eyes and the scabby looking brats. He seems to have acquired a wife, the woman with horse teeth and frizzy, bleached hair. We'll tackle Mrs Perry and the teenage twins from Hell, together."

On seeing them enter, the uniformed constable in charge of the group came swiftly over to Angela and Jack. "They're all moaning, saying I've to buy them teas and muffins. The woman with the fat teenagers said they haven't had breakfast. They want quarter pounders and fries. I've got no money on me. I didn't know what to do. Are we meant to buy them food?"

"You're a new boy, aren't you?" Jack said.

"I've been in this job for three months, Sir," he replied.

"Watch and learn, Son. Watch and learn."

Jack strode into the middle of the rabble. "You, Sir," he said, pointing to the wee man with few teeth. Everyone stopped talking.

"Who, me?" the man replied.

"Yes, Sir. What's your name?"

"I'm Mr Harkness."

"Right, Mr Harkness, you're at that table with Detective Murphy. Please move over there now. And you, Sir? Yes, you with the two youngsters. Is that good lady your wife?" Jack pointed to the horse teeth woman with frizzy hair.

"I'm Mr Collins," the man replied. "Joe Collins and this is my wife, Mercedes."

It would be Mercedes, Jack thought, even though she looked more like an old banger. "Okay, I'd like you and your family to sit at that table by the window. Mrs Perry, please stay seated with your daughters and we'll get to you as soon as we can."

Jack signalled for the shop manager to come over.

"This is official police business," he said. "Each person can order a drink and a McMuffin. The two teenagers over there can have quarter pounder meals. Give the bill to me. If anyone wants anything else, they pay for it themselves, okay?"

To the constable he said, "No one leaves until I clear them. Get yourself a drink and sit at that table over there. It's at the entrance to this seating area, so nobody will slip out past you. Right, Angela, let's see what, if anything, this lot knows. Good luck."

He walked over to the table with the Collins family and sat down then Angela joined Mr Harkness.

There was a distinct smell emanating from Mr Harkness. A sour alcoholic aroma was clinging to his skin and clothes. His teeth were rotten and, when he grinned at Angela, his breath was foul. Before she could ask him a question, he spoke.

"I can give you a description of the four men who did for Davy, and the lassies who worked for him. He was a pimp you know," he said matter-of-factly. "I knew he was a bad boy, but he was good to me. He gave me a bottle of Buckfast on ma birthday and he let me visit his girls from time to time, no charge."

Angela felt sick at the thought. How could anyone let this ghastly man touch them, let alone have sex with them?

"I always chose to go with the lassie who wisnae in when the men came round. They men probably never even knew she lived there. Her name is Ann-Marie and she wisnae a junkie like the other two. I never went with either of the others because I was a bit nervous going with a junkie, in case they had that HIV disease. Anyhow, I was at ma window when Ann-Marie came walking towards the close, so I waved at her to go away. I think she'd been out for fags at the Asian shop. I don't know where she is now, but at least she had the good sense to stay away. The men took the other two lassies with them when they left."

The manager brought two teas and a muffin for Mr Harkness.

"Thanks, Pal," he said, before turning his attention back to Angela.

"Can you give me your personal details, please?" she asked. "Then, if you don't mind, I'll get a description of the girls who worked at the flat, the four men you saw, and a brief account of what took place. I'll write down everything you tell me then I'll give it to you to read. If you're satisfied it's a correct account, I'll ask you to sign it, and it will be your statement. Do you understand what I've said, Mr Harkness? Is that okay?"

"Aye, lass, that's fine. I'm just sorry you've to do all that writing. It would take me hours. My writing's not very good, but I can read all right," he assured.

It took Angela over forty minutes to complete the task, but by the time Mr Harkness was ready to sign his statement, she had plenty of useful information. She discovered that the Hughes brothers both worked in the construction industry, but their main income had come from living off immoral earnings. The three prostitutes lived at the flat full time, but Davy came and went. Mr Harkness speculated that he might have another house elsewhere. Two of the girls, Katya and Inga, were Eastern European, but the third girl, Ann-Marie was from Glasgow.

"Ann-Marie's mum lives in Harland Street at Scotstoun," Mr Harkness added. "You might find the lassie there. In times of trouble everyone wants their mum, don't they?"

"Do you know her mother's name?" Angela asked.

"Something Irish sounding, Fitzwilliam or Fitzpatrick, it was unusual," he replied.

"You've been extremely helpful, Mr Harkness, thanks."

"Is that me done? Can I go home now?"

"As far as the interview is concerned, we're finished, but whether you'll be able to get back into your home yet, I'm not sure."

Mr Harkness stood to leave. He offered Angela his hand to shake. "If you find Ann-Marie, please tell her Willie Harkness was asking after her. Tell her to ring my doorbell if she's in the area."

"I'll be sure to do that," Angela lied, briefly shaking his hand.

After he'd left, Jack came over to speak to her.

"Collins recognised the crims, Jackie McGeachy and his gang of thugs. They're known to me. They work for the Chinese."

"So they're responsible for killing Howard and Davy Hughes, but does it end with them, or do we have to go after the Chinese gang?"

"As far as I'm concerned, McGeachy sent the brothers flying, so he's the one I aim to track down. I don't want to get involved with the Chinese. I'd prefer to live a lot longer, thanks very much."

At that moment, Mrs Perry came walking over to them.

"Everyone else has gone home. Are you ready to speak to me and my girls yet? We've been here over an hour and I've only had a cup of tea and a muffin. See, it's way past my lunch time," she said, holding her fat wrist in front of them, displaying a rhinestone encrusted watch. "And my girls are getting hungry again," she added.

"Now then, Mrs Perry," Jack answered. "Please go back to the table. We're coming to speak to you right now and I'll order something more to eat and drink. We can't have your girls wasting away, can we?"

Satisfied, she returned to her seat.

Angela stifled a laugh. "If they ate nothing for three months, they wouldn't come close to wasting away," she said to Jack. "These two girls must each weigh at least fifteen stone and they're still teenagers."

"Aye, but look at the size of their mother, she's like a hippo in drag," he replied.

Before they sat down, Jack spoke to the uniformed officer and asked him to return to the crime scene. Then he ordered more food for the Perry family. Disappointingly, the interview revealed nothing. They couldn't even confirm anything Mr Harkness or Mr and Mrs Collins had told them, so after only fifteen minutes, Jack said they could go.

"They cost us a fortune, ate their way through half a cow, and knew nothing," he grumbled. "What a complete waste of space and time that lot were. All Mrs Perry did, was complain about having prostitutes living in the same close as her daughters, and moaning that the police did nothing to stop them. It's not our fault unsavoury characters visited them at all times of the day and night."

"They did establish one thing," Angela said. "We now know that there is nobody else in the building. As well as the boarded-up flat, and the four we can account for, the only other one is empty, because the tenant was recently evicted with an ASBO."

"Aye, but what if the evicted person had a grudge against Hughes? What if he told tales and led McGeachy to his door? We'll still have to find the bloke and interview him."

"I don't think it's very likely, but I guess you're right. You'll be able to get the details either from the local community officer or the ASBO people."

"I think we're done here for the time being," Jack said. "We'd better get back to the office and see how Tony's getting on with the phone calls about Baptiste. At least with my case, we know all the facts. We even know who we're looking for because they didn't care who saw them. They probably think everyone will be too scared to give evidence against them in court, and they might well be right."

"Yes," Angela agreed, "That's often the way of it. We do all the work. Spend a great deal of time and money pursuing a case. Then the whole thing falls apart when the witnesses change their statements because they've been frightened off."

"In this instance, I can't say I blame them. I wouldn't want to speak out against something the Chinese gangsters were involved in. I wouldn't want to risk losing my balls, or having my eyes, ears and tongue cut out. Remember the three wise monkeys? Well, this wise monkey knows when to turn a blind eye."

Chapter 17

Tony Khan was speaking on the phone when Angela and Jack returned to the office. When he saw them enter, he held up his hand in a wave and grinned, then slapped his forehead in mock despair. He had a well-scrubbed, healthy glow, as if he'd just stepped out of the shower. His tailored suit and white cotton shirt were immaculate and expensive looking. Angela wondered how he could stand working with a slob like Jack.

"I'm just going to talk to the boss," Jack said. "You'd better see how Tony's getting on with your calls. Thanks for your help today, Murphy. I owe you one."

"Yes, and don't think for one moment, I'll forget it," she replied, their previous banter returning.

She walked over to her desk where Tony was seated and was mildly annoyed to see that he'd reorganised her belongings. The previous chaos of pens, files, notes and other assorted accoutrements had been tidied. The surface of the desk had been wiped clean where before it had been splashed with spots of coffee. He'd even washed her mug, removing brown tea stains from the inside. She was impatiently waiting for him to get off the phone so she could pull him up for it, when he pointed to the notes in front of him and indicated that she should read them. On seeing the progress he'd made, she swiftly changed her mind about complaining. Tony had almost completed the phone calls. Managing to contact and speak to all but two of the people on the list. Clearly, he didn't just look tidy and efficient, he was tidy and efficient.

"I've got some really good results, Angela," he said when he ended the call. "Four of the people who contacted us, gave the same location for Baptiste. They've all given me the name of a blind man who they say is a friend of Baptiste's. They think our killer has been staying at the man's flat in Govanhill."

"Great work, Tony. Did you get an address?"

"Yes, one of the guys I spoke to, works in a charity shop, he knows the man well. He gave me an address in Alison Street. He said the man we want to contact is called Peter James. Everyone told me that the black man often made religious comments. They all thought he was a gentle soul, softly spoken and polite. Of course, they also thought he was blind."

"You've done a great job, Tony, and you've got through a shed load of work. I'm really impressed. If the boss says that it's okay, would you come with me to interview some of these people? I'd like to get their statements as soon as possible and, as you know, the department's a bit stretched for detectives at the moment."

"Well now, let me see," Tony replied. "My options for consideration are one, being stuck with Jack and putting up with the stink of smoke and his slovenly behaviour, or two, travelling to the mean streets of Govanhill with a smart and fragrant, young woman. No contest, you win hands down Angela, if you'll have me."

"I see that you're particular about being clean and tidy," Angela observed, staring pointedly at her desk top. "I've just spent a few hours with Jack and I'm desperate to have a shower. How do you stand it?"

"Oh," he replied blushing. "I'm sorry about your desk. I have to have everything tidy when I'm working. I didn't mean to offend you. It's just my way. I've always been organised in everything I do. I'm probably a bit OCD and Jack brings out the worst in me."

Jack and Frank came out of Frank's room and approached Angela and Tony.

"How're you getting on, Khan?" Frank asked. "Have you got anywhere with that list for Angela?"

"Actually, yes, Sir. I've done rather well."

Jack rolled his eyes at Tony's cultured accent. "Christ, you sound like you've a plum stuck in your mouth. Can't you talk normally, like the rest of us? You public schoolboys make me laugh," he said.

"Leave the lad alone, Jack," Frank cut in. "Just because you've no fucking class, you think the rest of us were born in the slums. Murphy, here is a very posh bird and I can speak cultured when I have to."

"Aye, the phrase posh bird is very cultured, boss," Jack replied. "As is the use of the word, 'fucking'. I can tell right away you're no peasant."

They all began to laugh. It lightened the mood and the enormity of the tasks they faced.

After a brief discussion it was decided that uniformed officers would try to locate the killers of Davy Hughes. They would also search for the girls who'd been taken from the flat. Jack would attempt to find Ann-Marie, whose second name turned out to be Fitzherbert. He intended to call round to her mother's home in Harland Street before finishing up for the day. He particularly wanted to contact Ann-Marie and get her statement before Davy's killers tracked her down. This left Angela and Tony to follow up on the Baptiste case.

They decided to drive to Alison Street to see if they could interview Peter James and they took Angela's car. When they arrived, it was rather late in the day. The sky was darkening and the rain was an icy drizzle.

"I'll be glad to finish up and get home tonight," Tony said. "I'm going to order a curry then put my feet up and watch telly."

"My husband is cooking our meal," Angela replied. "I can't wait to get home. It's been such a miserable day."

She turned into Alison Street and tried to find somewhere to park. Not an easy task. Cars seemed to be abandoned along the whole length of the street, parked haphazardly, with wheels on pavements and noses or tails partially blocking the lanes which led to the rear of the tenement buildings. The kerb sides were strewn with empty fruit boxes and litter. Much of the street contained fruit shops and all of these seemed to be owned by Asians. Eventually Angela managed to squeeze into a space vacated by a woman with a car load of rowdy children.

"That was absolute hell. Do you think my car will be okay here?" she asked.

"I think you should be all right. Look around. It's not the only BMW in the street," Tony replied.

They climbed out of the car with difficulty. Tony could hardly open the door wide enough because of the debris on the pavement and Angela had to wait for several minutes until there was a brief break in the traffic. As they began to make their way towards Peter James' address, the street suddenly filled with a large number of Pakistani men. They seemed to be everywhere, congregating on street corners or in doorways, chatting.

"What's going on here?" Angela said. "Where did they all come from? Do you think there's going to be trouble?" Her voice quivered, nervously. "Should we get back in the car?"

"Relax, Angela," Tony replied reassuringly. "Prayers are over and the mosque has emptied, that's all."

People stared at them as they walked along the street. Angela felt most uncomfortable.

"Are they staring because of me?" she asked. "I seem to be the only white face in the street at the moment. Is it a racial thing?"

"Angela," Tony replied soothingly. "You arrived in a BMW. You're wearing a smart business suit as am I. Look around you. Everyone here is dressed for working in the shops or they're unemployed. Any professionals who live in the district will still be at work. Their staring isn't anything to do with colour or race. This is a close knit community and we seem out of place. Strangers dressed like us, in the middle of the day, are likely to be debt collectors, tax inspectors or benefit investigators, and none of them are welcome here. Just keep walking, you're not in any danger, we're nearly at the flat."

"I have worked in Govanhill before, you know?" Angela replied, anxious not to seem weak in front of her colleague. "I felt a bit intimidated by the large number of men suddenly appearing, that's all," she added.

"You don't need to explain, Angela. They made me feel a bit nervous too, until I realised what time of day it was," Tony replied. "But rest assured, we're perfectly safe, these are religious men, not troublemakers."

When they reached the ground floor flat belonging to Peter James, the curtains of the front room windows were shut, so Angela couldn't see inside. They entered the close and banged on the door of the flat, but it wasn't answered and they heard no movement coming from inside.

"There are no lights on," Tony said as he peered through the letter box. "He must be out. Why don't you scribble a note on your card, asking him to call, and post it through the letter box?"

Angela sighed, "For a smart guy, you can be so dumb sometimes," she said. "The man is blind. How will he read a note? I'm afraid I'll just have to keep coming back here until I get him in."

Tony slapped his forehead with his open palm. "Sorry, Angela, I didn't think. Well, on a positive note, at least the people living here will get used to seeing you around. Who knows, they might even speak to you."

"I'd rather not be here at all," she replied. "The chances are, Baptiste is long gone and I'm just wasting my time."

* * *

Peter heard the bang, bang, bang, on his front door and immediately felt scared. He's back, he thought. John's come back. He didn't know what to do. He sat on the sofa in the lounge, drew up his knees and hugged them. What if John broke in? What if he'd come back to kill him? His heart was pounding painfully with unbridled terror, and tears spilled down his cheeks. His skin was damp with perspiration and his whole body shook uncontrollably, making his teeth chatter. Peter was usually lonely and hemmed in by the darkness. He often felt unhappy and helpless. But one thing he knew for sure, miserable as his life was, he wasn't yet ready to die.

Chapter 18

Angela woke and glanced at the clock on her bedside cabinet. The luminous yellow, digital display read six-nineteen. The alarm was set for six-thirty, but she always seemed to wake before it rang out. Angela reached for the button to switch it off, so it didn't disturb Bobby. Then she remembered it was Sunday. With relief, she rested her head back down on her pillow and pulled the duvet up to her chin. Sunday, glorious Sunday, and she had the day off. Frank had said there was nothing she personally had to work on that wouldn't keep until Monday.

At six thirty-five she heard the creaking sounds of the radiators heating up as hot water flowed through the pipes, causing them to expand. Normally, by this time, she would be under the shower, but not today. Angela shut her eyes and tried to go back to sleep, but it evaded her. After a few minutes of tossing and turning, she heard the bedroom door swing open, soft padding feet walked towards the bed, warm fur brushed her face and a wet, sniffing nose was thrust in her ear.

"Rex," she hissed, "You're not meant to be in here." A wagging tail beat a tattoo against the side of the bed and a heavy paw reached up, settling on the side of her arm. "Get down, Boy," she said, gently returning the paw to the floor. He licked her face. "Okay, okay, I'm getting up. Move and let me out of bed." The dog backed off. With tail still wagging, he licked his lips then gave a snort of approval as Angela slid out of bed.

"What time is it?" Bobby asked drowsily.

"It's early, go back to sleep," she replied.

"Why are you getting up? It's Sunday."

"Your dog wants company and he prefers me to you."

"Rex? Is Rex in here?" Bobby asked, half sitting up and resting on his elbow.

The dog made his presence felt by giving a woof. Then he leapt up onto the end of the bed and crawled towards Bobby. When he reached the top of the bed, Rex laid his head on Bobby's chest and sighed contentedly.

"Hah, and you thought he preferred you," Bobby said triumphantly.

"Well why on earth did he wake me then?" Angela replied indignantly.

"He woke you so you could fetch the breakfast, Woman," Bobby laughed and, as if on cue, Rex woofed again.

"In your dreams," Angela retorted. "I'm going for a shower. You boys can make the breakfast. I think I'll have a full English today. It's not often I get the chance."

"Anything your heart desires, My Sweet."

"Whatever you're after, forget it. And don't you, 'My Sweet' me. You can take Rex to fetch the Sunday papers. It's pouring with rain and I'm staying indoors. Oh, and I'll have scrambled eggs not fried with my breakfast."

"You're a hard woman, Angela. She's a hard woman, Rex," Bobby said to the dog. Rex licked his lips and barked. "I suppose you want breakfast too. Would Sir like scrambled eggs or fried?" he quipped. The dog barked again.

"Scrambled it is then," Bobby said.

As he rose from the bed, he reached out and grabbed Angela by the arm, pulling her towards him. He was about to draw her close for a kiss, when Rex pushed his way between them.

"Aw, Rex, back off," Bobby protested.

"Kids, who'd have em," Angela said laughing. She pulled from his embrace and ran towards the bathroom for her shower.

"Killjoy," Bobby said accusingly to the dog. Whose reply was once again, to bark and to wag his tail.

Angela decided to have a long, luxurious soak in a bubble bath instead of her usual shower, while Bobby and Rex went for a walk to the newsagent to pick up the Sunday papers. As they returned and entered the house, Angela emerged from the steam-filled room wearing her favourite towelling robe. She was relaxed and glowing. By contrast, Bobby and Rex were soaked to the skin and chilled to the bone.

"I think, perhaps, I should cook breakfast while you two dry off," she offered.

"Thanks, Angie. It's absolutely chucking it down out there and, just as we were about to cross the road at Muirend, the number six bus raced past us, straight through a huge puddle. We were nearly drowned. He must have seen us. I'm sure the bastard did it on purpose."

Angela tried to look sympathetic, but seeing the pair standing there bedraggled and dripping water made her smile. They looked so comical yet so appealing.

"I'm glad you think it's funny," Bobby said, but he too was smiling.

"I'm not laughing, honest. I'm sorry for you, really I am," she replied.

"Are you sorry? Are you? Give us a kiss then," he said holding out his arms and walking towards her.

"No, no, don't touch me," she squealed backing away. "Please, no," she begged. "I'm warm and clean and you're so wet and dirty."

"I thought you liked me dirty," he leered, reaching out for her laughing.

"I swear, if you touch me, I won't be happy. Do you want us to fall out? Do you?" she threatened.

Bobby leaned towards Angela and planted a kiss on her forehead. His wet hair flopped forward and dripped water onto her face. She squealed again and squirmed away from him.

"I'm going to dry Rex then I'll have a quick shower," Bobby said. "I'll be ready for that breakfast you promised in about twenty minutes. A full English, remember. Oh, and Rex wants his eggs scrambled," he added before disappearing to find a towel for the dog.

By mid-morning they were relaxed in front of the coal fire after pigging out on too much food, Rex was asleep and snoring loudly, when Angela's mobile rang.

"I wonder who that could be," she said.

"Ignore it, let's take a day off from everything," Bobby suggested.

Angela glanced at the caller ID. "That's odd," she said. "It's Kenny. Why would he be phoning me at this time on a Sunday morning, on my work number? I'd better answer it."

"Hi Kenny."

"Angela, I dialled 999. I'm not sure if the call was real. I'm in the office of the Gazette. I've been sharing a news desk. My stories on the Baptiste case gave me the chance. I'm only here because I forgot my house keys. I'm not meant to be working today. I just came in for five minutes and I answered the phone."

Kenny was rambling. Angela sat up in her armchair. "What's happened Kenny? Try to calm down and tell me what's going on."

"A man phoned. He said he was going to fly two birds off the roof of a building. He said they were the girlfriends of Davy Hughes. I told him I didn't understand, then he said I'd get it when the birds landed. He laughed and told me to watch the skies over the Kingsway. Do you think he's going to kill two women? I dialled 999. I didn't know what else to do."

Angela felt sick to her stomach. Acid bile rose up in her throat. She swallowed hard.

"You did exactly the right thing, Kenny. I take it you told the police everything you've just told me?"

"Yes everything," he confirmed. "What will happen now? What should I do? Can I leave the office or should I stay here?"

"Did you give them all your details, name, home address etc.?"

"I told them everything. I want to use this story, Angela. It's the biggest thing that's ever happened to me. How do I find out what's going on? How will I know if the call was real or simply a crank? Can you help me?"

"I'm going to drive to the high flats at Knightswood, that's where the Kingsway is. I'll call my office on the way and try to find out what's happening. I'll phone your mobile if I hear anything. You should grab your camera and get along Dumbarton Road until you see the buildings. I'll meet you there. Whatever happens, you'll have your story because you took the call."

"Promise me, Angela, you'll tell me when hear something, anything."

"I promise, I promise, now please get off the phone. I can't do anything until you hang up."

"Okay, right, bye," he said and the phone went dead.

"That sounded very serious," Bobby said. His expression was one of deep concern.

"Someone called Kenny's paper and he answered the phone. They threatened to chuck two women off the top of a high rise building."

"Bloody Hell! Do you think they'll really do it or are they just nutters trying to cause a scare?"

"If it's the people who killed Howard and Davy Hughes then they are nutters. They're also capable of carrying out their threat. Jack Dobson and I attended the murder scene of Davy Hughes. We know for sure, that the killers took two girls with them when they left his flat. It's not technically my case, but I'm going out there anyway. I'll phone the office on the way, so much for us having a lazy Sunday."

"Maybe they won't need you. Maybe they'll have enough people to deal with it."

"Really, do you think so? And when exactly did you see those pigs flying by?"

Chapter 19

Angela threw on smart clothes, pulled her hair into a ponytail and applied a pink lipstick. She was in her car and on her way in less than five minutes. As it was Sunday and still relatively early in the day, the traffic was light. Her call to Frank's mobile was answered on the second ring.

"Hello, boss. It's me, Angela. Have you received a call about the Hughes case?"

"Yes, I'm on my way to Knightswood at the moment. My wife's driving me. Where are you?"

"I'm heading over there too. I got a call from Kenny Scott. He's a friend of mine."

"Good girl. Have you got your car? Are you driving?"

"Yes, and I'll be able to take you back home if no one else turns up. Who have you called?"

"Jack was out on the town last night. He's had too much booze to be able to respond. Tony is half way to Inverness. I was about to phone Paul, but if you're on your way anyhow, I'll not bother. Steve Murray is attending, but he's already worked for seven days solid, so I'd like to let him go home."

"No worries, boss. I'll be able to stay. I'm about ten to fifteen minutes away, traffic permitting. How about you?"

"Yeah, yeah, about the same. We're really under pressure with two big cases on the go at once. I just hope we can manage to cover everything. We could do with more people, yet the powers that be are talking about cutting our budget again. It's totally ridiculous."

Angela heard Frank say something indecipherable to his wife then the phone went dead. He had a habit of hanging up without saying goodbye, so she was pretty sure the call was over.

As she drove along Dumbarton Road the car behind her flashed its headlights and she realised that it was Frank's wife driving. She pulled in to park so he could join her and they could continue together. Within a couple of minutes he opened the door and climbed in.

"I just got a call from the uniform boys. They said the eagles have landed. But don't panic. They didn't throw the girls off. An eye witness from an adjacent block said he saw the girls on a top floor balcony. They were screaming their heads off. But what they actually threw off the building was shop mannequins dressed as tarts. This all happened a few minutes before the uniforms got there."

"So it was all an elaborate stunt. Why?"

"To scare off anyone trying to muscle in on their patch. They made an example of the Hughes brothers and now they're putting the fear of God into the tarts."

"That's shocking. Why haven't we arrested them yet? We know who they are."

"Knowing who they are, is one thing, finding them is a different story. Besides, you can be damn sure when we do pick them up, they'll all have solid alibis."

"But Jack and I have witness statements," Angela protested.

"Aye, and how long do you think it'll be before their statements are retracted? These people would rather be charged with wasting police time than be launched off a roof. And who could blame them?"

Angela drove up to the police tape which was blocking the road and flashed her ID to the officer in charge. He moved people back to allow her to park, then she and Frank got out of the car. While Frank spoke to the policeman on duty Angela stepped over to the tape where she saw Kenny. She drew him aside and quickly filled him in about what had taken place.

"Oh, thank God," he said. "Nobody in this crowd seems to know what actually happened and the police are saying nothing. Some people were saying that two women were thrown off the building. I'm so relieved it was just dummies. Is it okay for me to write this up now? Because I took the call, I'm the first journo on the scene and now I've got the right information. This is pure gold for me."

"Of course, Kenny. Make the most of it. Just stick to the facts and don't mention me, okay."

"My lips are sealed," he replied grinning and making a sign as if zipping closed his mouth. Then he quickly left, fighting his way through the growing crowd.

When Angela and Frank were back in her car driving towards his home, he ran through all the jobs that needed to be dealt with.

"Jack will have to find the third prossie who worked for Davy Hughes. She's at serious risk of being harmed. With regard to the Baptiste case, I can't understand why no one has seen him since he moved out of the blind man's flat. Have you managed to speak to Peter James yet?"

"No, boss. He too is lying low."

"Could Baptiste have moved town? Perhaps he's a master of disguise," Frank laughed. "Maybe instead of being a big, black bugger, he's now a small, white bastard. Either way, we have to find him before he goes nuts again."

* * *

John had booked into a small private hotel at Charing Cross. The room price was great value for money and it included a buffet breakfast. He wasn't short of cash, but he knew it wouldn't last forever. Charing Cross was only a five minute walk from the heart of the city and he liked the buzz. He missed having company. Peter had been far from ideal as friends went, but he was better than nothing. John needed a plan, something to let him move on. At least he was sure of one thing, nobody he'd come in contact with, had recognised him.

He was using the name Mark Lucas now, borrowed from a guy he'd met on the bus while travelling into town. Mark had given John his card. He worked as a financial consultant for a large insurance company and John pretended he might be interested in buying life assurance. The phone number he gave Mark in return was fictitious, of course. He had no intention of ever meeting with the man again. He used Mark's card as ID when he'd booked into the hotel. Normally they'd have wanted to swipe a credit card, but as he paid cash in advance for a three day stay, plus a fifty pounds deposit for extras, they gave him the room key. So for the time being, at least, he was safe.

On the suggestion of one of the receptionists, John attended a Sunday service at St Mungo's Church which was to the east of the city centre. A large number of the congregation were from Nigeria, so John's black skin didn't look out of place. The people were beautifully dressed, obviously, to them, Sunday best still meant something. At the end of the service people didn't rush to leave, but instead they stood around chatting. John noticed a plump, young woman smiling shyly at him. He smiled back.

"Are you new in town, Brother?" a voice said. John was startled. He turned to see three men standing at his shoulder."

"I'm living at Charing Cross, but I came across town for the service here. I was born in Glasgow, but I've been living away for many years. My father was African," he replied ambiguously.

"We are all from Nigeria," the man explained. "We're all studying for our Masters degrees in business studies at the University of Strathclyde. My name is Leonard and my friends are Jacob and Jonah."

The man offered John his hand.

"Hello, Brothers, I am Mark, Mark Lucas," John replied.

"What did you think of the service?" Leonard asked.

"I liked it. I liked it a lot. It was relevant to my circumstances. I am relying on the friendship of strangers at this precise moment. I have some money, but no job and I have no family or friends nearby."

"Have you somewhere to live, Brother?"

"I am staying in a hotel for another day then no, I have nothing else arranged."

"We are renting a flat beside the University. It has four bedrooms and we are just three. We could let you rent the extra bedroom. As we are studying all hours and we don't have much time, if my brothers agree, you could clean the flat, do our laundry and cook our food. In return we will cover the cost of your accommodation and pay for what you eat. Would you be willing to accept that, Brother? Would the arrangement suit you?"

"It would suit me very well, if your friends agree. I am a very good cook, by the way," John added smiling.

Everyone nodded enthusiastically and shook hands. John was delighted. The Lord had provided for him once again. The young woman he'd noticed earlier came over to the group.

"What are you boys plotting?" she asked. "Watch out for them, Sir. They are bad boys," she said smiling and wagging her finger at them.

"Miriam is always giving us a hard time," Jacob said.

"But she likes us, really," Jonah added.

"Let me introduce you, Mark. This is our good friend, Miriam. She is studying too. She flat shares with a girl called Adeline," Leonard said. "Where is Adeline today? Why is she not in church?" he asked.

"She is sick. She has a bad cold. I have to leave soon to make her lunch. I just came over to say hello to your new friend."

"I hope I can be your friend too, Sister," John said. "Miriam is a beautiful name. She was the sister of Moses who led the woman out of Egypt," he informed.

"You are very knowledgeable, Brother. Perhaps we'll see about the friendship," she replied, dropping her chin and smiling shyly. "I'll give you my phone number if you'd like."

"Thank you, Sister, I'd like that very much," he replied.

As she left the group the other boys slapped John on the back, congratulating him.

"You move fast," Leonard said.

"She never gives out her number," Jonah added.

"Miriam never goes on dates," Jacob said. "I've been trying to get her number for months. She is a very respectable girl," he added. "Her father is a preacher."

John couldn't believe his luck. In the space of a morning he'd found a community, new friends and board and lodgings. Now a pretty, chaste, young woman was showing interest in him.

"Thank you Lord. I won't let you down," he whispered and, at that precise moment in time, while his dangerous mind was lucid, he truly believed what he'd said.

Chapter 20

On Monday morning Paul arrived at the office looking bright and rested. Even though he'd had to deal with the death of his beloved aunt, having time off from the job had revived him. Angela, by contrast, looked like a wet weekend. She was really tired and very troubled about the cases she'd been working on. John Baptiste was one of a handful of people in the world who were deadly dangerous, yet most of the time, could seem completely normal. Psychotic sociopaths who became serial killers were fortunately extremely rare individuals, but they were unpredictable, were incapable of empathy and had no conscience. They could live in a community, interact with people then, without notice, strike out indiscriminately.

As for Jackie McGeachy and his gang of thugs, they were pure evil. Heartless and cruel they brutally crushed anyone who stood in their way. Just like the Kray brothers, they had no fear of being recognised, because they knew nobody would dare point the finger at them in court. Worse still, McGeachy answered to a known Chinese gang master and no one in their right mind took him on. Angela didn't know who frightened her more, the dangerous psycho or the brutal murderer.

"Morning Angela," Paul said. "You look awful. Partying again?"

"Shut up Paul. I'm not in the mood. I'm sorry about your aunt, by the way."

Paul placed a large, paper bag in front of her.

"What's this?"

"My daughter, Michaela, made it. Surprisingly, it's bloody good. Fudge tray bake, she calls it. I'll fetch the coffees then I want to ask you something."

When Paul returned he drew a sheaf of papers out of a brown A4 sized envelope.

"This is Aunty Brigit's stuff. She lived in a council house all of her days, but I had no idea she'd bought the house eight years ago. She's left it to me."

"I'm sorry about your aunt, Paul, but wow, even the cheapest house is worth thousands. You might be able to move your growing brood after all," Angela replied.

"Yes, it seems like it. I'm sad that Aunty Brigit's gone. I loved her very much, you know. When I spoke to her doctor at the hospital, I discovered she'd had terminal cancer. She hadn't said a word to me about it."

"Is that what killed her? I thought you took the kids to see her only last week. It must have been very quick."

"That's just it, Angela. She didn't die from the cancer. Aunty Brigit tripped on a kerbstone on the way home from bingo. She hit her head on the pavement and died instantly. It was a complete accident."

"Oh, my goodness. You know, Paul," Angela said, "If I had a terminal illness, something that was going to take my life little by little, robbing me of my dignity. I think, given the choice, I would prefer a swift end. Although it was shocking for you and your family, Brigit didn't suffer."

"You're right, Angela. I keep telling myself that."

They sat in silence for a few moments, sipping their coffees and eating Michaela's tray bake. Then Paul said, "Brigit had life insurance. She'd been paying it for years. It's a guaranteed lump sum of fifty thousand pounds. It would have been worthless had she died from cancer because it was an accidental death policy, but of course Brigit's death was an accident. She's named me as the beneficiary. I feel bit guilty now, wishing for fifty thousand pounds to help me move house, then she dies and I find the policy. I have it here. Would you look over it for me, please? Tell me if you think I'm reading it correctly."

Angela reached out for the paperwork. "You've no need to feel guilty. You loved her and she loved you," she said. Then she scanned the document. "It's with a reputable company. You are the beneficiary and it does cover accidental death." She read further. "Yes, Paul, it all seems to be in order. Have you spoken to the solicitor yet?"

"I didn't want to look like a money grabbing idiot. That's why I needed someone to look over it first. I wanted to get all my facts right before I went to see him. He's very old and a bit of a fuddy-duddy, but the firm's been around for ages and Brigit trusted him."

"I guess you'll have to arrange to sell her house as well. Where did she live?"

"She lived in Castlemilk, in a cottage flat. It's in a very nice, quiet street, with good neighbours. I think these houses fetch around sixty thousand pounds, possibly a bit more."

"Even after costs and the funeral expenses, with the money from the house sale and the policy, you'll be around a hundred thousand pounds better off. You'll easily be able to afford to move now. Would you like me to start looking for a house in my area? In case something comes on the market."

"There's no harm in looking I suppose," Paul replied. "I don't want to seem like a ghoul, but I must admit, I'm excited about the money. I've been worried sick about moonlighting, but we've been finding it really tough recently."

"Muirend or Netherlee would suit you ideally. The red sandstone houses have very big rooms and there are quite a few which have four bedrooms. If you choose Netherlee, you'll be in the East Renfrewshire district and in the catchment area for all the best schools. St Ninians, the Catholic secondary school, is one of the best schools in Scotland."

"I've heard of it. I'd love to give my kids that standard of education. I'm sure Brigit would have approved too. She was always telling me how important a good education was."

Angela hit some buttons on her computer. "Here we are Paul, Clarkston Road, just up from the shops. That's quite close to me, but not so near that your kids would drive me mad," she laughed. "Four bed, two public, stunning kitchen, offers around £285,000. It will probably go for a bit more. It looks fab. The garden's a good size too. Why don't we make an appointment and have a look. Then you can see the sort of thing that's available."

Paul leaned over and stared at the screen. "It's amazing. You could fit my current house into the downstairs. You won't tell anyone about Brigit's money, will you? I don't want anyone else knowing my business."

"No problem, Paul, just so long as you don't move next door to me. In fact let's leave a distance of say twenty houses in every direction, okay?"

"Yes, okay, but what makes you think I'd want my children to live near to a grouch like you?" he replied. "One day you'll have a family and, when you do, you'll be delighted to live next door to an experienced babysitter like me. You mark my words. Your time will come."

Angela knew Bobby was desperate to have a family, but at this point in time, the very thought of it horrified her.

"Murphy, get your arse in here," Frank's voice boomed across the room.

"Oh, shit, I wonder what he wants now," Angela said. "Yesterday, when I was the only idiot who offered to come into work, he acted like I was his new best friend."

"He's got the memory of a gnat and the temper of a Tasmanian devil. Good luck," Paul replied.

"Thanks a bunch."

Angela walked into Frank's room. "Did you want coffee?" she asked.

"No," he growled. "And I don't want to be your personal secretary either. Your friend Liz Brown phoned and the call was put through to me. She said she's working with Mighty Mack in forensics this week and she wants you to get in touch. I thought she was in uniform. What's she doing in forensics?"

"She did a college course and loved it. Now she's working on her degree."

"Is she still seeing Bill Cruikshank? They were dating weren't they? He moved to a job in East Ayrshire, Kilmarnock, I think."

"Yes, they're living in Southcraigs. They're engaged to be married and they've bought a house there. We meet up about once a month."

"Yadda, yadda, enough of the small talk, back to work, Murphy. And yes, bring me coffee and whatever you and Costello are eating. And for God's sake call Liz Brown and remind her only to phone here if it's business related," he barked.

Angela was about to remind him that forensics was business related, but when she saw his thunderous look, she thought better of it. The boss was obviously under a lot of pressure and his high red colouring frightened her. He looked as if he was ready to have a stroke.

"Well, what did he want?" Paul asked when she left Frank's room and went to the coffee machine.

"Some of Michaela's tray bake and a coffee," she replied.

"He's not having any of the tray bake. There's just enough for us. Take him the squashed Twix that's in my desk drawer. He won't know any different," Paul replied. "Was that it? Coffee and food?"

"Yeah, nothing sinister."

Angela didn't know why Liz was trying to get in touch with her, but she decided to keep it to herself until she knew more. Liz had worked with her on her first major case. They'd become good friends, but It was unusual for her to call Angela at work.

Angela lifted her mobile from her handbag and went to the front door to make her call.

"Angie, hi, how are you? I see Frank Martin's the same grumpy old devil he always was. Did he moan at you because my call was put through to him by mistake?"

"He's under a lot of pressure at the moment," Angela replied. "He really likes you because your whole family are cops, but he did mutter something about personal calls."

"Yeah, he said something to me about not being your PA. Anyway, much as I love to chat, I was calling about business. It's about the Hughes case. I'm working with the forensics team this week as part of my course work."

"How are you enjoying it? I hear good things about Mighty Mack's team."

"The guy's a God. I've learned so much from him already. He likes me and he said when I get my degree, I've to come and see him about a job."

"So you'll be leaving uniform then? I thought you loved your work."

"I did, I do, but this work is so fascinating. It really stretches my mind. Anyway, the reason I phoned was to give you information about the Hughes murder. The report won't be ready for a while yet, but just in case you pull in any of the McGeachy gang for questioning, I can tell you we've lifted two good prints from Hughes' trouser belt. One is a clear, right-hand, thumb print from McGeachy. It was on the back, right hand side of the belt. And the other is a clear, right hand thumb print from a known bad boy called Alec Keys, it was on the back, left-hand side of the belt. They must have grabbed him by his belt to chuck him out of the window. Being a cop and being familiar with the way McGeachy operates, I know your witnesses might become unreliable, but the forensic evidence is absolutely solid. You can use it however you see fit."

"Will Mack not be annoyed at you telling me this before the report comes out? You won't get into trouble, will you?"

"Not at all. Mack suggested I call you. He's old school and he knows my Dad. He wanted you to have the info before you interview any of the gang."

"Thank, Liz, that's so helpful. They might be able to nobble the witnesses, but they can't deny the forensic evidence."

"We found a number of hairs and other debris on the victim's clothing. We're still trying to identify who it belongs to. Oh, and some skin under the fingernail of his right hand."

"This is technically Jack Dobson's case, but don't worry, I'll get the credit for it. Thanks a million, Liz."

"Don't mention it. You gave me a break with the Thomas Malone case. I'm simply returning the favour. What are you and Bobby up to these days? Bill and I would really like to have you over for a meal. And don't worry, he's an excellent cook," Liz said, laughing.

"That would be lovely, thanks," Angela replied. "We've both been working long hours. All good though. Bobby's business is doing really well. Just tell me a date and time and we'll be there. I haven't seen your new house yet. Have you settled in?"

"You know what it's like, Angie, there always seems to be something to do when you move house, always boxes you haven't unpacked."

"There you are, Murphy," Frank's voice boomed out behind her making Angela jump. "That better be a business call," he added.

"Gotta go, Liz," Angela said. "I'll phone you later. The bear has woken up and he's got a sore head."

She turned to Frank who was hovering at her shoulder. "It was a business call, boss, and it's going to bring a smile to your grumpy face," she said.

Chapter 21

No sooner had Angela returned to her desk, than her mobile rang again. She saw from the caller ID it was Kenny Scott.

"Yes, Kenny, what have you got for me?" She answered rather shortly, expecting to be deflecting another personal call.

"Someone phoned me, Angela. He said he liked my reporting about Davy Hughes. I wasn't in the office when he first called, but they gave him my mobile number. I'm not sure what to do. The man said his name was McGeachy. He spelled it out so I'd get it right when I wrote about him. He sounded like a complete head case."

"McGeachy, you say? What did he tell you?"

"He said, and I quote, because he made me write it down. I'm going to roast some sitting ducks then they won't be quacking any more. He said if I wanted to get a scoop, I should head over to Maryhill."

"Oh, shit. Where are you now?"

"I'm in my car on my way to the building where Davy Hughes was murdered."

"Hold on a moment, Kenny. I've got to speak to my colleague. Stay on the line," she said.

"Paul," she said, tapping the desk in front of him to get his attention. "Put in an emergency call, all services, Davy Hughes's address, Maryhill. The reporter, Kenny Scott, has just received a threat against the tenants and the building. I've got Kenny holding on the line. The call went initially to the Gazette and they gave out his mobile number. Once you've called it in, tell the boss, please."

Paul picked up his phone acknowledging Angela with a nod of his head.

She returned to Kenny and, at the same time, she began to put on her jacket.

"How far are you from the flat?" she asked.

"Ten minutes at most."

"Don't arrive until you hear the emergency vehicles. It might be a set up. McGeachy might want to draw you out for some reason. I'm on my way. I'll meet you there."

"Bloody Hell, Angela, what would he want with me. You're scaring me now."

"I have no idea. It's probably nothing to do with you. He's probably trying to silence the witnesses, but don't take any chances. As you said yourself, the man's a head case."

By the time Angela ended the call Frank was by her side and, within a couple of minutes, they were in her car heading towards Maryhill. As they neared the address, emergency vehicles came racing past with sirens blasting. Smoke was seeping out of the entrance of the building when they arrived and Mrs Perry was screaming for help from her open window.

Frank looked grim. "Good call, Murphy," was all he said.

Within a short time of the fire brigade arriving, the front door of the close had been kicked in and the fire extinguished. It had been started by newspapers doused in petrol being pushed through a broken window in the door, then set alight. The fire damage was minimal, but the smoke was intense. Angela phoned Kenny Scott to see where he was and two minutes later he arrived at her side.

"I've been speaking to a fireman," he explained. "I'm just going to take statements from the tenants of the building. It won't take me long then I'll come back and talk to you. I won't mention your name in the article, but I am going to say that it was me who gave the story to the police. I'd particularly like a word with that fat woman who's sitting in the ambulance and a photograph of her with her soot-blackened face." Kenny couldn't suppress a grin. "This is magic," he said, "Pure magic."

As he left her side, Angela felt a tug at her elbow. It was Willie Harkness.

"I want to change my statement," he began. "I think I got it wrong. I didn't really get a good look at the men who killed Davy Hughes. I was just caught up in the excitement of what had happened. I'm not a reliable witness. I like a wee drink, you know."

Angela sighed. "I hear what you're saying Mr Harkness and I understand you're frightened, but are you sure you want to do this? You could be charged with wasting police time, you know."

"Charge me if you like, better a day in court than being burned alive," he replied.

Mercedes Collins stepped forward towards her. "Joe and I will be changing our statements too. I don't need to tell you why."

"But Mrs Collins," Angela protested. "That's exactly why these criminals get away with murder. They frighten witnesses. If decent people like you don't stand up to them, then they'll win and we'll all be living in fear."

"For God's sake, lass," she replied. "We've nearly been burned alive. You can't protect us. You don't live here. What do you expect us to do? What would you do in our circumstances?"

Angela didn't know what to say. Mrs Collins noted her silence.

"Aye, right, I thought so," she said. There's nothing you could do. We're on our own here."

With that said, she stormed off to speak to Mrs Perry, who was still sitting in the back of the ambulance.

Frank had been speaking to the uniformed officer who was in charge, before walking over to Angela.

"This is a fucking mess. We have to get these bastards off the streets. It's all getting out of control, and that reporter friend of yours isn't helping. His stories are giving these two-bit criminals notoriety. God knows what they'll get up to next."

"None of this is Kenny's fault," Angela protested. "If he wasn't writing the story, someone else would be. And, if he hadn't called me today, the residents of this building might all be dead by now."

"Believe what you like, Murphy," Frank replied. "But I still think he's adding fuel to the fire and, before you say anything, that wasn't meant to be some kind of sick joke."

* * *

John loved living with the students. The flat was lively and friendly, with people coming and going, sharing coffees and ideas. The Townhead area, in the city centre, was handy for everything and he enjoyed keeping the house clean. In return for his efforts, the young men were appreciative of his work and didn't abuse the situation. John bought a couple of cookery books in the Bargain Books store which were designed for students, so each recipe had few ingredients and was easy to prepare. He'd told the students he was a good cook to make them feel encouraged about offering him a home. But John then discovered that he was really talented in the kitchen and he was thrilled by the results he achieved.

"This food is delicious," Leonard stated, as they sat eating at the dining table in the lounge.

"My compliments to the chef," Jonah said.

"Absolutely," Jacob added, speaking through a mouthful of pasta.

"I don't know how you're doing it, Mark," Leonard said. "But you're managing to fill our bellies with first class fare and save us money into the bargain. We used to spend a fortune on ready meals."

John beamed with pride. He'd never been praised before. His father had always told him he was stupid.

"I like cooking," John replied. "And this is an easy house to keep clean as it is very modern. Just as long as you boys continue to keep the place tidy," he added pointedly.

"Miriam's coming round tonight with her friend Adeline," Jacob said, changing the subject. "They're going to bleach my hair for me. I've always wondered what I'd look like with blonde hair. Would you mind going out to the Tesco Metro after we eat, to pick up some chocolate biscuits, Mark? If you go, it will give us time to freshen up and tidy away our study books."

"Of course, no problem, when are they due to arrive?"

Leonard glanced at his watch. "Not for an hour and a half," he said.

"Do you think they would bleach my hair too?" John asked. "I think it would be very stylish. I've seen a black footballer with his hair bleached blonde, on the television. It completely changed his appearance."

"I'm sure they'd love to have another victim," Jonah said. "Rather you than me," he added. "Call me old fashioned, but I think blonde hair looks odd on black men. It draws attention to them and makes them stand out."

"You're old fashioned," Leonard and Jacob said in unison laughing.

Standing out from the crowd with a changed appearance might be a very good idea, John thought. Hiding in plain sight could work very well for him.

Chapter 22

With most of the i's dotted and the t's crossed in respect of the current major cases, the office returned to the mundane. The police still hadn't managed to locate Peter James, but that was hardly surprising. He obviously didn't want to be found and was in hiding. It was the same with the prostitutes connected to the Hughes case, although their disappearance was possibly more sinister. With no breaks for over two weeks, the team were walking on eggshells when around Frank. He'd gone through every emotion from shouting and stamping to morose and depressed. Now, he was simply quiet, locked in his office and encouraging no contact. Both of the major cases he was leading, were going cold and every day he worriedly awaited the wrath of God. Each time the office door opened there was a sigh of relief when it wasn't the Chief Inspector coming to call.

Angela felt stressed. She had worked hard and for long hours, made a good contact in Kenny Scott, but still seemed to be taking one step forward and two steps back. She was tired of it all and she needed a break from the intensity of the job. When her mobile rang, she pounced on it.

"Yes, Angela Murphy, who's calling please?"

"Angela, it's me," Bobby's friendly voice said.

"Are you up to company on Saturday evening? Are you off work this Sunday?"

"I should be off work. What did you have in mind?"

"A dinner party. I'll cook. I was planning to invite Kenny Scott and his wife and also Liz and Bill. What do you think?"

"That would be great. I'd like to catch up with Liz and Kenny's good company. Thanks, Bobby, I could do with some light relief."

"No worries, leave everything to me. I'll call the prospective guests and I'll organise everything. I'll see you later. Bye Darling."

Angela replaced the receiver and turned to Paul. "Anything new?" she asked.

"Not a dickie bird. Lunch?" he inquired.

"It's eleven o'clock," she replied.

"Morning tea, then? Out of the office."

"What about the boss? Won't he be miffed if we disappear?"

"He won't even notice," Paul said. "Besides, we could have another go at seeing Peter James. Then we've got a reason to leave. I'll pay for food," he added. "I can afford to now. Thanks for coming to Brigit's funeral, by the way. I really appreciated it."

"Don't mention it, Paul. We're mates."

"I've checked with the lawyer and we were right, the money from the insurance is being paid into my account next week and the house deeds are being transferred to me. I'm sorry Brigit's gone, but she certainly looked after me. Her bequest will change my life and the lives of my children."

"I'm pleased for you Paul. Oh, sod it, let's forget about Peter James. Why don't we go to the south side and trawl the estate agents to find you a new home? We deserve the time off with all the unpaid overtime we've been doing. Then we can grab a light lunch at the Laurels."

"Do they serve all day breakfasts? I'm famished," Paul said.

"Yes, and theirs is the best I've ever tasted, big portions of good quality food, so you won't starve," Angela assured.

When they stepped out of the stuffiness of the building, both inhaled deeply.

"I felt as if I was suffocating in there," Paul said.

"Yes," Angela agreed. "What with the artificial heat and Frank's mood swings, it was very oppressive."

They took Paul's car and, as they drove south past local authority housing then tenement buildings and onwards to the stylish red sandstone terraces of the suburbs, their moods lifted. They parked at Clarkston, close to the library then they crossed the railway bridge to the shops. Angela led Paul round several estate agents where they gathered brochures. They also picked up a newspaper featuring property which had been produced by Glasgow solicitors.

"We can peruse these as we eat lunch," Angela said.

"Peruse? My, don't you speak posh when you're in a wealthy area? Do the Laurels serve cakes?" Paul asked changing the subject.

"Lots," Angela replied smiling. "Nothing like getting your priorities right," she added.

He chuckled, "Of course," he replied.

They returned to the car and a few minutes later were heading back along the main road towards the coffee shop.

As they approached, Angela said, "Pull in over there. Can you see it, Paul? Look, there's one table and a couple of chairs outside for the smokers."

"Yes, okay, I see it. It's just a wee place, isn't it?"

"Yes, but trust me, the atmosphere is wonderful, the owners are lovely and, as I said before, the food is great."

Paul parked and soon they were inside being greeted by Cathy, one of the owners.

"Hello, Angela, you're in luck, you've made it just before the teachers are due to come in for lunch. Sit down. I'll just give Mr Hoey his meal then I'll take your order."

"Thanks Cathy," Angela said. "This is my colleague, Paul," she added pointing her thumb in his direction.

Cathy nodded a greeting then turned to a gentleman sitting at the adjacent table. "Black coffee and a wrap, coming right up, Archie," she called over.

"What's the problem with the teachers?" Paul asked as Cathy beetled off.

"Nothing, except there's a crowd of them and it takes a while to fill their orders. So it's better to arrive before they do," Angela explained.

They enjoyed a delicious lunch finished off by moist, carrot cake, while they short listed houses to view, finally narrowing the options to just two.

"Both of these look suitable," Angela said. "They're the right size, right price and they're well located. I think you should make an appointment to see them. Why don't you phone your wife and tell her about them. I'm sure she'll be excited."

Paul looked embarrassed. "I haven't told Gemma about Brigit's house yet," he said.

"What? Why ever not?"

"I wanted to wait until the deeds were transferred to me. Just so I was sure."

"But even without the house, there's still the fifty thousand."

"Ah, that. I haven't actually told her about the money either. I wanted to wait until it was in my bank account."

Angela raised her eyebrows.

"You have to understand, Angela. I'm not like you. I've had to struggle for every break. I was scared, that's all. Scared I'd wake up and it would all have disappeared."

Angela always thought Paul was full of confidence and a bit of a smartass. She was surprised to discover that he was just as vulnerable as everybody else.

"I still can't believe I'll be able to live in this upmarket suburb," Paul continued. "I can't get my head around it. I imagine my children going to a top notch school, enjoying all the amenities, the clubs, the parks. They'll probably grow up talking posh like you," he joked. "I know it's ridiculous, but the very thought of it, makes me feel so emotional, I could cry."

"It's not ridiculous Paul and, just so as you know, I never stop appreciating what I have."

Just then, Norman, Cathy's husband, approached to say hello.

"Well now, Angela," he said. "Have you caught the killer yet? Are we safe in our beds? It's a shocking case, isn't it? You don't expect anything like that to happen here."

"I'm sorry to say, but crime happens anywhere and everywhere," she replied. "Fortunately, serious crimes don't occur very often. I'd be more frightened because this degenerate wants to move into the district," she said punching Paul lightly on the arm.

Norman smiled at Paul. "He looks okay to me."

"He supports Celtic," Angela replied laughing.

"I guess looks can be deceptive," Norman said, rolling his eyes. "Never mind, I can forgive one mistake," he added laughing before going to serve another customer. Football often gave rise to friendly banter.

"He's a nice chap. Everybody we've spoken to has been so friendly," Paul observed.

After they finished their lunch and were back in Paul's car, he said, "I suppose John Baptiste is on everyone's minds. I hope we catch up with him soon. It's a real worry not knowing where he is."

"That's true, Paul, but while he's on the loose, less people will be looking for houses in this district. So you might get a real bargain."

"God, Angela, you're one tough cookie. I suppose you booked flights to the US during the Gulf War or to New York immediately after 9/11, when no one wanted to fly and the airlines slashed their prices."

Angela smiled wryly, "Actually, Paul, I did," she replied.

Chapter 23

Miriam found herself grinning whenever she thought about the time she'd spent dyeing the boys' hair. It had been such a good evening. Well, at least until it had been time for her and Adeline to leave. She couldn't understand why those local men always hung about outside, drinking. Didn't they have homes to go to? They weren't teenagers, they were all in their late twenties or thirties at least, and one man looked older still. What pleasure could they possibly derive from harassing decent, young women while they walked home? Neither she nor Adeline dressed provocatively. They didn't wear make-up or flashy jewellery. They were simply heading back to their flat, minding their own business. If it hadn't been for Mark looking out of the window and seeing them being hassled, who knows what might have happened? As soon as he and the rest of the boys came out of the flat to protect them, the drunks moved away. They were quite happy to start with two young women who were alone and vulnerable, but less willing to engage with four men. However, it didn't stop them from calling out racially abusive threats as they left, or lobbing their empty beer cans at them.

John had been incensed. How dare these devils frighten good, pious women? The Lord would punish them. They were an abomination.

"Are you okay, Mark?" Miriam's had asked, her sweet voice interrupting his thoughts. John had stared at her for a few moments then he'd gradually calmed down. "You were frowning," she'd continued. "You looked so angry."

"I'm sorry, Miriam," he'd said, "But I was outraged by these ignorant men. They blight the landscape. They are unclean spirits."

"My father is a preacher, Mark," she'd told him. "He is a very religious man. He warns about unclean spirits in his sermons, but I didn't realise they'd come after me, disguised as ordinary men."

John had smiled benignly. "Jesus gave his apostles power," he said. "In Matthew 10:1 it is written, 'and when He had called unto Him His twelve disciples, He gave them power against unclean spirits, to cast them out, and to heal all manner of sickness and all manner of disease.' These men are sick. Their brains are diseased from alcohol. Their unclean spirits must be cast out."

The group then stopped walking. They'd stood staring at John, listening to his words.

"Wow, Mark, you really know your bible," Leonard had said. "Did you study to be a priest?"

"My father was a very religious man," John had replied, fearful in case he'd drawn unnecessary attention to himself. "I'm sorry for preaching to you, but these men made me so angry."

"I know exactly how you feel," Jonah had said, "Someone should sort them out. Their behaviour is unacceptable, but the police don't want to know. They'll only be interested when there's an incident and a person is hurt. We have to put up with their abuse nearly every day and, if they're not annoying us, they're having words with someone else. They don't work, they take, take, take, and they're jealous of anyone who is trying to better himself."

"You're right, Jonah," John had replied. "They have to be stopped, but rest assured, the Lord works in mysterious ways. They will be judged and found guilty."

The group of friends had continued on their way and, as they walked, Miriam had shyly slipped her hand into John's.

As she sat in her bedroom now, recalling the incident, she felt a thrill whenever she thought about Mark. He was calm and strong and he made her feel safe. He was the sort of man she could proudly take home to meet her parents. Her mother would like his gentle manner and her father would approve of his knowledge of the bible. Finally, she'd met a man she could really befriend, future husband material perhaps. She'd prayed for someone like Mark to come into her life and God had answered her prayers.

* * *

John had been living with the boys for some time now, but he was finding it increasingly difficult to control his anger. It bubbled inside him like lava and he knew the slightest nudge would make it spew out in a fiery explosion. It was the men, the local gang of useless, drunken wastrels who roamed the estate looking for victims to terrorise. They were the cause of his rage. How dare they? Not a day passed when they didn't accost him or his friends. He began waiting to walk Miriam to or from university each day, too terrified to let her out of his sight. His friends teased him about it, but he didn't care, just so long as she was safe.

But this day he was ten minutes late in leaving the flat. It would be today, when she was working late. Jonah had forgotten his keys and the other two boys were out of town, so John had no option, but to wait and let him in. When Jonah did eventually arrive it was already dark. John ran from the flat towards the university only to discover that Miriam had already left. He began to walk in the direction of her home, knowing he wouldn't sleep until he'd made sure she was safely indoors. He took the short cut across the middle of the estate, hoping to meet her on route. As he walked past one of the high rise buildings which housed a bin store at ground level, he thought he heard a muffled cry.

"Hello, who is there?" he called through the slight opening of the bin store door.

There was a muffled scream.

"Shut the fuck up, bitch. You know you want it," a man's rough voice warned. "All you black bitches like sex."

John's blood ran cold. "Miriam, Miriam, is that you?" he called, as he hauled open the door.

Another muffled scream.

"Get her knickers off, Tam. It's okay, I'm holding her. You can fuck her first. Don't worry about Sambo. There're two of us and I've got a knife. I'll soon sort him out."

There was a sound of fabric being ripped and more muffled cries.

"Oh, would you look at that black pussy. Soft and sweet, just waiting for a poke," Tam said and he began to unzip his trousers.

John was screaming, bellowing like a bull, he was completely out of control. He flew at the group grabbing Tam, and hurling him against a wall, winding him. The other man loosened his grip on Miriam who scrambled across the litter-strewn, damp concrete to get away.

"Oh, shit," the second man said. "You are a big bugger, aren't you?"

He drew a weapon from his jacket pocket. There was a 'click' and a long thin blade sprang open. Tam had managed to get his breath back and was now standing again.

"Run, Miriam. Get out of here," John said, his heart breaking at the sight of the terrified, shivering girl. "Run," he shouted again.

Finally, holding her torn dress together as she went, she took off across the estate.

"I'll hold him Spike, and you stick him," Tam said. "Say your prayers, Sambo. You're not going home tonight."

"I'm gonna cut his fuckin' balls off," Spike replied.

With no sense of danger, Tam ran at John. He was as high as a kite, out of his mind with drugs and booze. As he came close, John reached out, grabbing the smaller man by the head and neck. He grasped Tam's chin with one meaty hand and the back of his head with the other, digging his fingers into the man's skin. Then with a powerful, quick twist, there was a sickening crunch as he broke Tam's neck.

"Jesus Christ," was all Spike could mutter before John fell upon him.

He wrenched the knife from Spike's hand, throwing it onto the ground. Then he repeatedly punched him on the head and face until the bones were shattered and crunched like cornflakes under the blows. Eventually, John released his grip of the man, letting his body drop to the ground. Then he sank to his knees and sobbed.

"Miriam. Miriam," he muttered over and over again.

It took him a few moments to regain his composure. Then John realised, with awful clarity and deep sadness that Miriam would have run to fetch help. He had to get out of there. Once again he'd have to move on. Mark Lucas must now disappear forever, and he would never see Miriam again.

Chapter 24

Shocked, and terrified for Mark's safety, Miriam ran towards the boys' flat. She had to get help. Mark was alone. The man had a knife. Her dress flapped open exposing bare skin and bra to the cold night air, but she didn't notice. She was too frantic. She pressed on the security door buzzer, but nobody answered. She pressed it again and again.

"Oh, go away, children. I'm tired," Jonah said aloud, assuming someone was pushing the bell to annoy him.

He walked over to the open window and looked out and that's when he saw Miriam banging on the security door and heard her cries for help.

Jonah ran out of the flat to the door and wrenched it open. Miriam practically collapsed into his arms. He pulled her dress closed and held her tight as he helped her into the flat. She was hysterical.

"It's Mark. It's Mark. I need help," she managed to say.

"Did Mark do this to you?" Jonah asked, unable to comprehend what she was saying.

"Two men. One has a knife. They'll kill him, they'll kill him," she cried, staring into his eyes and pulling at his sleeve. "Police," she screamed. "Phone the police. They're at the bin room of the high rise."

Finally, Jonah realised what she was saying and he immediately picked up the phone. Once he'd imparted the information, he left Miriam and ran towards the high rise building. Even though the police had told him to stay where he was, he ignored their advice. He had to help his friend. Jonah wished the other boys were with him. He wasn't a coward, but he was slightly built and the shortest of the group. However, as he ran across the estate, he was relieved to hear the sound of an emergency vehicle drawing near. He was pretty sure the police would arrive at the same time as him, and he was hopeful that Miriam's attackers wouldn't hang around when they heard the sirens approaching.

As he arrived outside the building, a police car pulled up, and he ran over to it.

"I'm Jonah," he said to one of the officers. "I called you. My friend has been attacked by two men. She is at my flat. My flat mate saved her. One of the attackers has a knife. I think they're inside the bin room." He knew he was rambling and he was shaking with emotion.

The policeman had no idea what he would find, but he didn't want this shocked young man getting in his way. He opened the back door of the police car.

"Why don't you sit in here," he offered. "It's a cold, damp night and you've no jacket. We'll deal with this now."

"I don't want to sit in the car, thank you. My friend's in there. He's being attacked. Hurry up, we have to help him." Jonah didn't want to be stuck in the vehicle. He wanted to be able to see that Mark was safe.

"Suit yourself, Sir," the officer replied, "But stay back. We'll handle this." He left no room for argument as he and his partner walked purposefully towards the doorway.

At first, when they entered the dark area, it was difficult to see much.

"Phew, it stinks in here," the first cop said. "Why do we get all the shitty jobs?"

"There, look, between the big metal bins. There are people on the ground. Call for back up and an ambulance, Jimmy," the second cop instructed.

Jimmy immediately did as suggested. Then the two officers walked forward cautiously, in case anyone was still hiding in the shadows, remembering that Jonah had told them someone had a knife. Once satisfied there was no risk to themselves, they inspected the men on the ground.

"Oh, my dear God. Oh, sweet Jesus," Jimmy said and he began to gag.

"Don't be sick in here," his partner warned. "It's a crime scene." They heard sirens from a number of emergency vehicles drawing near. "That's the back-up arriving. Go outside and meet them," he instructed.

Officer Seb Caine was a seasoned policeman, but even he was shocked by what he saw. Spike's face looked as if it had been minced. There wasn't one solid, identifiable piece left. No wonder his partner felt sick.

Jonah was relieved when he discovered the bodies were of Miriam's attackers and not Mark. However, when he heard about the injuries that had been inflicted upon them, he was unnerved, to say the least. And where was Mark?

Was he on his way back to the flat? Had he flipped? No normal man would do such a thing. Was Miriam safe? Perhaps he shouldn't have left her alone. The questions he asked himself were being mirrored by the police.

Although he would have been quicker on foot, he agreed to get into one of the back-up police cars and be driven to his flat with two officers, one of them a policewoman. When they arrived, the front door to the flat was lying open, Leonard and Jacob having come home only seconds before.

It took the rest of the evening and most of the night, before all statements had been taken and Miriam had been examined at the hospital and given medication for shock. During that time, John didn't return to the flat. His holdall of belongings was still in his room. His possessions were meagre and he always kept his money about his person.

Although the killing of Tam and Spike was brutal, the policemen knew it had been one man against two and, besides, the dead men were known troublemakers with a string of convictions. The world wouldn't miss them, they thought.

When John still hadn't returned by mid-day the next day, his friends were concerned for his safety and the police stepped up their search for him. When he didn't show up for a second night, alarm bells began to ring. He had, after all, been responsible for the killing of two men, and he would have to be charged for causing their deaths, however justified his actions might have been. The police returned to the boys' flat and removed John's holdall containing all that he owned, to see if it would give them any clues to his whereabouts.

* * *

As soon as John left Townhead, he jumped on a bus and travelled south, making his way to the ASDA store. He knew the shop in Toryglen was open 24 hours per day. He'd already discarded his jacket, which had blood on it, and he needed to buy new clothes and a razor to shave off his bleached blonde hair. He had to change his appearance quickly. When he entered the shop, it was surprisingly busy for the time of night. John helped himself to some shaving foam and a razor off the shelf then went to the toilets to shave his head, discarding the used products in the bin after use. Then he took the escalator to the clothes department on the upper floor and chose a hooded jerkin, a black knitted hat, plain black denims and a black, waterproof jacket. After paying for his purchases he returned to the toilet to change. As he looked at himself in the mirror a new man stared back. He looked like a security guard or a manual worker. Nobody would recognise him now. He hardly recognised himself.

He would go by the name of John George. John because it was his name and he was used to it. George, he took from the label on his clothes.

* * *

It was quickly realised that the latest deaths in Glasgow weren't gang related, but nevertheless they were the centre of much conversation and speculation. It was Officer Seb Caine who made the shocking revelation about the identity of the killer and he was now speaking on the phone to Angela Murphy. After the usual introductions, and small talk about colleagues they both knew, he began.

"It shocked the Hell out of me, I can tell you. We thought we were dealing with a straightforward case, nasty, but straightforward. It was only when the perpetrator failed to return to his home that we began to get the jitters."

"The violence sounds about right for John Baptiste, and the moral stance," Angela said.

"Yeah, he was defending a young woman and himself against two known villains. But, crikey, you should have seen the mess. No one would have been able to identify one of the victims if he hadn't been carrying ID. His face was smashed to a pulp. The second victim had his neck broken like a twig. Your man must be a big bloke."

"He is big and powerful and completely off his head. Bodies are beginning to pile up and there's not one specific thing that drives him. Anyone could be his next victim. This is one mean killer who we have to stop. I don't mind telling you, he scares the shit out of me. I think he'd be very hard to physically pin down and cuff," Angela replied with honesty. "Anyway, Seb, what have you got for me? What makes you think your man is Baptiste?"

"When he didn't return to his digs or come into the station, we searched his room. All I found was a holdall and some clothes. The clothes gave nothing away, but as a matter of course, I stripped the vinyl covered cardboard base out of the bag, and bingo, there it was. Stuck to the vinyl, trapped between the layers, was a broken key fob. There was most of a name on the fob. It read, 'RVEY STONE'. I remembered your murdered woman was called Rachel Stone and I put two and two together. Then when I checked, I discovered Baptiste had stolen a holdall from the Stone residence. I have CCTV evidence of the man walking to and from the bin room, but it's not very clear. I also have descriptions from his friends."

"Good work, Seb. I'll come and see what you've got. It looks like once again, we've missed our man, and once again, he's left a trail of destruction in his wake."

"God knows where he'll turn up next," Seb said.

"God seems to be the only one who does know," Angela replied wryly.

Chapter 25

The dinner party hosted by Angela and Bobby had been going swimmingly. All three couples were getting along really well and the quick-witted interaction between Kenny and Liz was very funny. When Kenny began describing a recent fishing trip he'd taken with his son, Ben, the others found themselves laughing out loud.

"I was with my friend Terence and we decided to take Ben along because Caitlin was working late," Kenny began. "The boat leaves from Largs at around six o'clock and we fish for three hours. So even though it was a school night, we weren't going to be home too late."

"That's a matter of opinion," Caitlin cut in. "Ben was so hyper afterwards, he didn't sleep for ages then he was tired the next day."

"Anyway," Kenny continued. "When we arrived at the jetty there was a drizzle of rain, and what does Terry do? He opens the biggest golf umbrella I've ever seen. Everyone is in old clothes, waterproof jackets and beanie hats except for Terry. He's wearing his best Armani jeans, a Pringle sweater and a shirt. You'd think he was going on a yacht, not a grubby, stinky, fishing boat. Ben muttered, 'What a tosser,' and for once, I didn't tell him off. He was right."

"You shouldn't have let him away with that," Caitlin cut in again. "It was very rude coming from a nine year old."

Ignoring her comment, Kenny continued. "So we were all climbing aboard by walking along a plank, but not Terry. He's so busy fiddling with the damned brolly, he starts to take a step into oblivion, between the boat and the jetty, missing the plank completely. If the captain hadn't grabbed him he could have fallen into the water or worse, been crushed between the boat and the wall. All Terry could do was wail and complain because in the struggle to get him on board, he dropped his brolly and a gust of wind carried it out to sea. The rest of us were roaring with laughter."

"Did you catch anything," Bobby asked. "I shouldn't imagine there's much left after all the factory ships have done their worst."

"It wasn't too bad, actually, we caught some rock cod, more mackerel than we could use, a few haddock, and we came across the biggest creature I've ever seen. That encounter caused even more hilarity."

He paused to gulp his wine then said, "We were all having a great time, the rain had stopped and we were munching sandwiches while we fished. Ben was grinning from ear to ear because he'd hooked the biggest fish of the day, when suddenly Terry began shrieking like a girl. 'It's Moby Dick,' he yelled, 'it's fucking Moby Dick. We're all going to die. It'll eat us alive.' "

"What on earth had he seen?" Liz asked. They were all agog.

"Well, Terry was right, it was huge and it could have toppled our boat, but as for eating us alive, not a chance. It was a basking shark."

"You never told me about this," Caitlin said, shocked. "You could have all been drowned."

"I promise you, Pet. We were never in any danger, apart from perhaps laughing ourselves to death. There we all were hanging over the side to catch a glimpse of the magnificent creature before it swam away. All of us except Terry, that is. He's on his knees, in six inches of foul, fishy-smelling water, praying and begging God to spare him. It was hilarious, absolutely hilarious, Ben nearly wet himself laughing."

"That poor man, no wonder he drew me a dirty look when I asked if you'd be going again," Caitlin said. "I was really pleased with the fish they caught though," she added, "It tasted so fresh."

"I wouldn't mind going fishing, if you'd like to do it again," Bobby offered.

"Count me in too," Bill said.

The girls all raised their eyebrows.

"Hunters and gatherers," Liz said.

"I'm so proud," Angela added sarcastically.

"Overgrown children," Caitlin hissed. "Well you're not taking Ben."

"Good," Kenny said. "We'll take some beer then, and we can get a train home. It won't matter if we're late."

With the tentative arrangements made, the conversation continued in the same light hearted vein until it inevitably turned to work matters.

"It sounds as if John Baptiste is like a chameleon," Caitlin said. "He seems to be able to change his appearance to match his surroundings. I can't understand why nobody recognises him. His picture has been in every newspaper and on the telly."

"Well the first man he stayed with was blind and John copied everything he did and disguised himself so he seemed to be blind too. All anyone saw, when they looked at him, was a vulnerable middle-aged man. Then he stayed in a student flat. Once again he changed his appearance. He dyed his hair and dressed and acted like a student. He even took someone else's name. So once again, he was invisible," Angela explained.

"My God, so the students were living with a crazed killer and they had no idea the danger they were in," Bill said.

"That's the thing, he didn't hurt them, in fact, he killed two men protecting a young female student who was about to be raped. He has these strong moral beliefs mixed up with his madness."

"And you're embroiled with another big case, Kenny," Liz said. "The McGeachy murders."

"Yes, that's right. For some reason McGeachy thinks I'm sympathetic towards him. At the time of the last incident, he telephoned me to give me the heads up on the story."

"I don't want Kenny to have any involvement with these terrible people," Caitlin said, her voice rising with alarm. "These men are murderous maniacs. They're frightening. I don't want them to be led to our door."

There was an awkward silence. No one could look her in the eye. Eventually, Liz answered, "Angela, Bill and I deal with incidents every day of the week. John Baptiste came to Rachel Stone's door even though she had no connection to him. Unfortunately, there are some dangerous people in our society, but thankfully they are few and far between. That's why they make headline news. Most people live their entire lives completely oblivious to them. There's no reason for you to feel scared."

"With respect, Liz," Caitlin replied. "Most people don't go looking for trouble. Kenny invites it in. I have every reason to be afraid."

While Liz had been trying to reassure Caitlin, Kenny had been deep in thought.

"The Chameleon Killer," he said, suddenly looking up and grinning. "What a great headline name. I'll use that for my next article.

"And McGeachy could be the 'Launching Liquidator'," Bill added trying to lighten the mood and raising laughter from Liz, Kenny and Angela.

"Sounds like a baddie from a superhero comic," Angela commented.

Caitlin shuddered involuntarily. She and Bobby stared into each other's eyes. Each had a serious expression on their face. They would never understand the graveyard humour the others shared and, from the cases that had just been discussed, they were understandably concerned for the safety of their loved ones.

After the evening wound down and the others had gone home, Bobby and Angela sat in the lounge drinking a nightcap.

"You were rather quiet towards the end of the evening, Bobby," Angela said. "Is everything okay?"

"Everything's fine, Pet. It's just that I didn't really consider the danger of your job until Caitlin voiced her fears. You'd never take any chances, would you? You wouldn't put yourself at risk? I couldn't bear it if you were hurt."

His voice had a tremor in it, as if he was near to tears. He'd had a lot to drink and the alcohol was making him emotional.

"Of course I don't take chances, Bobby. I'm far too much of a coward. If ever there's a dodgy situation, rest assured, I'll push my partner forward and I'll run away," she joked, but even as she uttered the words, she knew she'd told him the same lies before.

Angela would say whatever she had to say and do whatever she had to do, however risky, in order to stop John Baptiste, before he killed again.

Chapter 26

Angela looked bright eyed and bushy tailed when she arrived at work on Monday. It was a sunny morning and the sky was a clear blue. She'd had a great weekend. The dinner party had been a success, everyone had got on with each other really well. Their conversations had been full of banter and jokes. On Sunday morning, she and Bobby had driven down to Prestwick beach to give Rex a long walk and, once again, the weather had been fair. Then, in the afternoon, they'd visited the Barras market in the east end of the city, where Angela had managed to purchase a beautiful silver-topped claret jug at a bargain price from one of the antique stalls. She was delighted.

Paul too, had had a great weekend. He'd finally felt secure enough to tell his wife, Gemma about the extent of their legacy and they'd spent their time registering with estate agents then checking out all the local amenities, imagining themselves and their children making use of them.

"We could hardly believe it when we discovered the local secondary school is situated in a park and that it's right next door to a sports facility and a theatre," Paul said. "No wonder people are clamouring to move into the area. Even the private schools couldn't compete with these facilities and, the best part is, it's free."

Angela and Paul were deep in conversation, sharing their news and views, when Frank stormed over with his face like thunder.

"What the fuck is this all about?" he shouted, slamming the morning's newspaper onto Angela's desk.

Both she and Paul glanced at the headline. 'Chameleon Killer, police in the dark,' it read.

"Oh shit," Angela muttered. "Kenny Scott."

"Aye, fucking Kenny Scott. Your mate," Frank said glowering at Angela. "Who gave him permission to write this shite?"

"With respect, Sir," Paul cut in. "He doesn't need permission. He's a journalist. He can write whatever he likes as long as it's basically true."

"That man is meant to be your friend, Angela," Frank said accusingly, ignoring Paul. "He's made us look like idiots. As if we haven't a clue what we're doing. He's made that bastard, Baptiste, look like some kind of genius of disguise, some sort of murderous mastermind, who's running rings around us."

Angela bristled with anger.

"Firstly, boss, whether or not he's my friend is of little consequence. Secondly, we have no idea where John Baptiste is. We only know where he's been by the trail of bodies he's left behind. He might not be a mastermind, but for the time being, at least, he is running rings around us."

"That might well be true, Murphy," Frank spluttered, "But do we really want the world knowing about it? Could you not have stopped him writing this shite?"

Angela didn't reply and Paul kept his head down, so with that said, Frank stormed out of the office, kicking a wastepaper bin as he left. When he'd gone, Paul glanced at the newspaper article, then he began to chuckle.

"No wonder he's blazing," he said. "This article names Frank and points out that this is the second case he's dealing with that's going cold. It links his name to the Baptiste investigation and the McGeachy one. Your friend Kenny has really done a number on him, but it's a bloody good article, nevertheless."

The day didn't improve any, in fact, from that point in time, the morning got decidedly worse. Barely half an hour after he'd left, Frank came storming back into the office.

"Murphy, Costello, get your stuff and come with me, you're driving Murphy." And before they could stand up from their chairs, he added, "We've got two more corpses."

They travelled the familiar road towards Scotstoun, fortunately the traffic was light. As they drove, Frank spoke on the phone to Jack Dobson. Angela and Paul listened to the one sided conversation and tried to make sense of it.

"So you've just arrived with Tony? Two young lassies. Oh fuck, do you think they're Davy Hughes' girls? Are you sure? One's wearing a necklace with the name Inga. You're probably right then." Frank gave a low chuckle. "Tony's parting from his breakfast, is he? It must be bad." He glanced at his watch. "We'll be with you in ten. Get the kettle on Polly, it looks as if we're going to be stuck there for some time. Aye, three white coffees and I'll have a Kit-Kat." He looked at Angela and Paul and gave a thumbs-up sign. They both nodded. "Make that three Kit-Kats." Frank ended the call, then to Angela and Paul he said, "I think we've just found Inga and Katya."

When they arrived at the scene, which was a lock-up at the end of a narrow lane, Tony Khan was leaning against a wall, his face the colour of chalk.

"I thought it was hair that changed colour with shock. You could pass for a white man, Son," Frank quipped.

Tony shook his head and grimaced. "It's awful in there, boss. There's blood everywhere and it stinks. Here are your coffees," he added, proffering a brown paper carrier bag.

"I'd better have a look, then," Frank said. "Where's Jack?"

"He's inside with the uniformed officer in charge. Forensics has been called, but they won't be available for a while."

"Do you have your car here, Tony?"

"Yes, boss. I drove Jack."

"Good, that's good. You take Paul and go back to the office. Have another look at the file then go and speak to Davy Hughes' neighbours again. Ask around the neighbourhood and see if anyone can tell us anything that would help us to identify these girls. The names Inga and Katya, with no surnames, isn't much to go on."

Tony inhaled deeply filling his lungs, then exhaled, blowing the air out of his puffed cheeks. He was relieved to be able to leave the scene.

Even before Frank and Angela entered the lock-up, the sweet, cloying smell of death assaulted their nostrils. The profusion of blood gave Angela a metallic, coppery taste in her mouth. When they neared the bodies, the hideous sight made her gasp. Bile rose in her throat and she gulped hard to force it back down.

"You okay, Angela?" Frank asked. She could see that he too, was struggling to stay composed.

"I'm fine, boss," she replied, the words came out in little more than a whisper because her mouth was so dry.

"What about you, Jack?" Frank asked his colleague who was kneeling beside one of the corpses.

Jack stood. He had his scarf wrapped round his mouth to try to hold back the awful smell.

"Aye, boss, I'm okay. I've been here for a while, so I've got used to it. Although it'll take a strong detergent to get this stink off of me and my clothes. The young man who rents the lock-up, and who discovered the girls, is on his way to casualty, he's suffering from shock, and no wonder. The pile of sick over there," he said, indicating to a deposit near the wall of the building, "Is his breakfast. What a waste of a good fry up," he added, trying to lessen the horror of the situation, with humour.

"I hear forensics has been delayed," Frank said. "Are you okay to stay here until they arrive?"

"Aye, fine. The uniform boys are looking after me. Giving me cups of tea and the like."

"Have you noticed anything obvious from the crime scene or the bodies?"

"That hammer, lying close to Angela's feet," he replied. "Watch you don't stand on it, Murphy."

Angela stepped back. Her eyes had now adjusted to the dimly lit space.

"I believe that will prove to be the murder weapon. I think they were raped with the handle then bludgeoned with the head. There's a hell of a lot of blood pooled under their legs."

Angela felt tears spring into her eyes and, although she tried to blink them back, they spilled over her lids and streamed down her face. "They're so young," she managed to say, swallowing a sob. "They look like teenagers."

Her colleagues stared at their feet. They were uncomfortable discussing such brutality in front of a woman, even if she was trained to deal with such events. Nothing could really prepare any of them for a scene such as this. Jack cleared his throat.

"Each girl has a tattoo on her upper arm. It looks homemade, like a prison tattoo. They are both the same. They say 'property of McG'."

"Shit," Frank replied. "The bastard's put his mark on them. He wants us to know he did this."

"Why isn't he afraid?" Angela asked. "Does he want to be caught?"

"He thinks he's bomb proof," Frank replied. "He's absolutely positive that nobody will turn him in and, even if we do catch him, who in their right mind would give evidence against him. I'm pretty sure he'll have someone lined up to do the time for him and make sure he's never convicted."

"But what I can't understand, boss," Jack said, "Is why did he kill these lassies? Surely they were making money for him."

"It's a show of strength. To scare people into doing exactly what he wants. As I said before, it's the same sort of tactics the Krays used. And, by the way the witnesses to the Davy Hughes murder changed their statements, we know it works."

"I think there's a good chance he'll be contacting Kenny Scott about this," Angela said. "Should I be phoning him? Warning him?"

"I suppose so," Frank replied reluctantly. "Even though he's a pain in the arse, he's still a member of the public and, if he tangles with this slippery fish, he could be in real danger."

Angela stepped outside and inhaled deeply, trying to clear her lungs of the stench. She took her phone from her bag and dialled Kenny's home number, but the machine answered. She hung up then dialled his mobile, but it immediately went to voicemail. Angela felt the hairs on the back of her neck stand up. Common sense told her he was probably simply in a meeting or on the toilet, something innocuous like that. Although a nagging doubt in the back of her mind kept surfacing and filling her with worry. What if McGeachy had contacted him again? What if he was with him now?

Chapter 27

Angela's work was intense and exhausting, not to mention painfully depressing. She couldn't get her head around how one human being could so brutally hurt and destroy another. What on earth had occurred in McGeachy's life that turned him into such a monster, she wondered?

When she and Frank returned to the office late in the afternoon, Paul and Tony were already there. Their shift was actually over, but they sat at Paul's desk, drinking coffees and poring over his computer screen, discussing and uploading the small amount of new information they'd discovered. Angela flopped into her chair without saying a word. She looked as lifeless as a wet dish rag. Neither man spoke to her, but instead, they kept their heads down. They both knew how she felt and realised that one kind word might make her emotions spill over, neither wanted to be responsible for making her cry.

At six o'clock, Frank came out of his office and locked the door.

"Go home, all of you. We've done enough work," he said, and with the immortal words from the film 'Gone with the Wind', he added, "Tomorrow is another day."

He stood patiently while they logged off their computers and shut them down.

"Is anyone going near my house?" he asked. "Could one of you give me a lift home?"

"I'll take you, boss," Paul offered.

Angela was relieved. She usually volunteered, but today she felt spent. It would be a struggle for her to drive herself home, never mind adding on a further journey. They all left the office in a subdued mood with barely a word exchanged amongst them. As she sat in her car and put on her seat belt, Angela felt her eyes heavy. She opened the window fully and switched on the radio in an attempt to wake herself up and keep her lids from closing. She was desperate to get home. Even though she knew the statistics of accidents caused by drivers falling asleep at the wheel, she turned the key in the ignition and pulled her car out of the car park into the stream of rush hour traffic.

The journey felt long and tortuous. The dying sun was low in the sky making it difficult to focus and Angela managed to catch every red light. By the time she drew up outside her house, tears of relief rolled down her cheeks. She walked up the path and was about to put her key in the lock when Bobby opened the door.

"I saw you pull up," he explained. "God, you look awful. Are you okay? Let me help you out of your jacket. You're shivering. Come into the lounge and heat up. Dinner's ready. Shall I pour you some tea?"

"It's been a terrible day," Angela replied. "I'll tell you about it after dinner. I don't want to think about it at the moment. Oh, and I'd rather have a glass of wine, please. A large glass," she stressed.

While Angela walked into the lounge and sat in her favourite armchair Bobby went to the kitchen, quickly returning with a bottle of Merlot and two large glasses.

"Caitlin Scott has been trying to get in touch with you," he said. "She left one message on the machine at around five o'clock and she's just called again, about ten minutes ago."

"Caitlin? Do you know what she wants?"

"Yes, it seems Kenny's gone walk about and she's trying to find him. He was meant to be home at four o'clock for Ben coming in from school, but he wasn't there. By the tone of her message, at first she was annoyed because she'd had to leave work early, but by the recent phone call, she'd become rather worried. Seemingly, he'd left a message at her work to say he was meeting a contact about a story, but he'd definitely be back for Ben. So it's not as if he'd forgotten. She said that she'd tried to call his mobile several times, but it immediately went to voicemail, as if it had been switched off. For some reason, she thought you might know where he was."

Angela felt sick. "Don't serve dinner yet," she said. "I'll call Caitlin then I'll have to phone Frank. I've got an awful feeling, and I hope I'm wrong, but I think something might have happened to Kenny. I've been trying to contact him all day, both at his house and on his mobile, and I've not been able to reach him either. I attended the scene of a double murder today. I'm pretty sure it's the work of Jackie McGeachy. If you remember the conversation at our dinner party, Kenny is his new best friend. I warned him that the man is a dangerous, unpredictable monster, but he was having none of it. I think Kenny might be with McGeachy. I think McGeachy might have taken him."

After speaking briefly to Caitlin Angela then spoke to Frank, it was decided that she would go round to the Scott residence and see what she could find out. Frank thought it was a bit soon to start panicking. But, given the fact that Kenny's disappearance was out of character, together with him having close contact with McGeachy, he felt she should have a chat with his wife at the very least.

"Like you, I have a bad feeling about this, Angela," Frank said. "I could understand him getting engrossed in a story and losing track of time, but he didn't turn up for his son and that's very odd. He hasn't been contactable all day either. I'll have the office check the hospitals. You never know, he might simply have taken ill or been in an accident. Phone later, when you get back home. I'd like to hear your take on this."

"Sure thing, boss, but if you don't mind, I'm going to have something to eat first, so I might not call till after nine."

"Do whatever you have to do, Angela. This isn't urgent," he replied, "At least not yet," he added.

When she ended the call, Bobby said, "Well, what's it to be? To eat or not to eat?"

"That is the question," she added then she smiled. "Let's eat. Caitlin can wait a while. If we're lucky, Kenny will walk through the door before I have to leave here."

Bobby was pleased. After going to all the effort of cooking the food, he didn't want it to be wasted while Angela rushed around after Kenny Scott. He liked Kenny well enough, though he thought the man was a bit of an idiot. How he'd landed an intelligent, pretty girl like Caitlin was a mystery to Bobby. Bobby really liked the fragile-looking, young woman with the intense blue eyes. He'd found himself drawn to her at the dinner party. They'd even indulged in mutual flirting, making jokes which were full of innuendos. He loved Angela with a passion of course, but something about Caitlin's vulnerability turned him on. More than once, he'd felt a stirring in his loins when he'd thought about her and, now that she was alone and frightened, his natural instinct was to want to protect her. Although she had a high-powered job, she looked delicate, fragile almost.

"I'll drive you to Kenny's house, Pet," he offered. "You're already tired and you've had some wine."

"I've only had a couple of sips, but I'm really beat, so I'd be grateful if you would, she acknowledged. Perhaps you could keep Ben busy while I speak to Caitlin? There's no point making him upset, and I need to find out what she knows."

"Right, that's settled then. You sit down and I'll serve the food. We can finish the wine when we get home."

* * *

Kenny wasn't scared when he received the call from Jackie McGeachy, because he was excited by the prospect of another exclusive story. Neither was he scared when one of Jackie's men picked him up from outside the newspaper office and drove him to a house in Victoria Park Drive in a well-to-do area of Scotstoun. No, the fear came when he realised that the house had several dangerous looking men sitting in the lounge awaiting his arrival. And his fear grew to terror when the door was locked, trapping him inside and McGeachy began to describe what he'd done to the two, young prostitutes who'd formerly worked for Davy Hughes.

"Make yourself comfy, Clarky. You'll be here for some time," McGeachy said. The name 'Clarky' being a reference to Clark Kent, the journalist of Superman fame.

"I'm meant to get my son after school," Kenny tried to explain.

"Nay problem, Clarky. I'll have my man Alec, here, go and pick him up, if you'd like," McGeachy offered.

Kenny was frantic. Caitlin's fears about his work leading gangsters to her door came rushing back to him.

"No thanks," he said. "He wouldn't get in a car with someone he didn't know. I can text my wife to get him."

Kenny took his mobile from his pocket.

"I'll take that," McGeachy said, reaching out and removing the phone from Kenny's hand. "I'm sure your boy will be fine. I'll give you the phone back when we finish our business." There was no room for argument. "I want you to write my memoirs," he continued. "It'll be a best seller, Clarky. It'll make you a shed load of money. I've been diagnosed with terminal cancer, you see, and I don't have long left. It's in my lungs now. I want people to remember me when I've gone. I don't intend to wait until I'm a complete wreck to say me piece. Have you seen the way people with cancer end their days? It's not a pretty sight. One of my men is going to shoot me in the head before I get to that stage. It'll be quick and painless."

Kenny was completely shocked by what he'd heard, but relief flooded over him. He's not going to kill me, he thought. Thank God, I'm not going to die.

"Now then Clarky, get your notebook out, I'm going to tell you where all the bodies are buried," McGeachy said with a wry smile, and, not having a death wish, Kenny did exactly as he was told.

Chapter 28

John Baptiste felt completely alone. He'd spent the last two days moving from place to place, either on foot or by taking a bus, and he'd spent the last two nights in a hostel for the homeless. At least he hadn't had to sleep on the street, although the hostel was barely a step up. The man at the Salvation Army office in Clyde Street was kind and sympathetic. He didn't ask too many questions. He'd offered him a bed and food, when John was desperate, but he couldn't risk going back for a third night, someone might recognise him.

"Where are you, Lord?" he beseeched, as he stood outside Glasgow Cathedral.

People in the street stared at him. John held up his hand in a placatory fashion and quickly walked on. He was getting paranoid, believing demons were at his heels. He had very little money, no home and no friends.

"Have you forsaken me, my Lord? Please don't forsake me, Lord."

John jumped on another bus. This time he headed west. He kept his head down. Nobody sat beside him. At lunchtime he found himself outside a small burger bar in South Street, near the river Clyde. A couple of men were in the shop, eating burgers and drinking large mugs of tea. One of them nodded to him as he entered. John ordered a roll with Lorne sausage, the cheapest thing on the menu, carefully counting out coins on the counter.

"Do you want tea with that, Pal?" the server asked.

"Thank you, no. I have no more money," John replied.

One of the men who'd been eating came over to the counter.

"Give the man a tea, Chas," he said. "I'll pay. You cannae eat a roll and sausage without tea to wash it down," he explained to John.

"Thank you, my friend. You are very kind."

"My name's Alec," the man said offering his hand.

"John, I'm John George."

"I don't need your second name, Johnny. Isn't that right, Chas? Too much information is a dangerous thing."

A huge mug of steaming, stewed tea was placed on the counter in front of John together with the roll and sausage. Then a plastic bottle of ketchup, sticky round the top, was plonked down beside it.

"Short of cash, are you?" Alec asked.

"I have no money, no work and nowhere to live," John stated miserably. "The coins I paid over for my food were the last I had."

"So you're not worth robbing, then?" Alec said laughing.

"All I have left is my soul," John replied, "And the devil is knocking at my door for that."

"You're a big bloke. Isn't he a big bloke, Jackie?" the man said to his friend who was sitting at the only table. "Could we not use a big bloke like him?"

The other man stood up and came over to inspect John. "Do I know you, Pal?" he asked. "You're face looks a bit familiar."

John stood and stared into the eyes of Jackie McGeachy. "I don't think so, my friend. I'm new to this part of town."

McGeachy smiled, "You certainly look the part for a job I have in mind. It's a security job of sorts, looking after some flats I have. I have girls working in the flats and I need a big bloke to keep an eye on things, protect the lassies from overzealous visitors, buy them food, keep the close clean, that sort of thing. The pay is little more than pocket money, but you'd have a roof over your head, food in your belly and cash in hand. Alec and I have to leave just now, I'm writing my memoirs," he said, laughing loudly, until he coughed alarmingly. "Here's a tenner. Alec will give you an address. If you want the job, be there at six tomorrow. If not, you've won a cup of tea and some cash."

John took the money and the address. "Thank you, Sir. You are most kind. I'll be there at six," he assured.

When the two men left, Chas said to John, "Be careful, Pal, he's a bad one that Jackie McGeachy. He could be that devil knocking on your door."

"Maybe so," John replied. "But I have little choice. Besides, I have God on my side. He will protect me."

* * *

Jackie McGeachy hadn't been scared of anything his entire life. He wasn't even scared when his beloved father died in a prison knife attack when Jackie was just sixteen. He simply stepped into his old man's shoes, providing for the family. It was business as usual. He'd learned the skill of gathering damaged, dangerous people to him at an early age. He demanded total loyalty from his minions, and he achieved this, either by gaining their respect or by tapping into their fears. By making examples of the one or two who tried to leave his employment, he crushed the spirits of the others. There was only one way to get away from McGeachy once he had you, and it involved dying.

Now that he faced imminent death himself, things had changed. It wasn't the dying he feared, but what came after. He worried about what would happen to him when his soul left his body. Was there a Heaven and a Hell? Would he finally have to answer to a higher being? Would his mother be made to suffer for raising him to be the man he was? Jackie loved his old mum. She'd fought in his corner all of his life, but now she was frail and elderly. She'd have plenty of money, but who would look after her after he'd gone? More fear and uncertainty was creeping in under his skin and he didn't like the feeling.

With all this doubt coursing through his brain, Jackie had hatched a plan. He wasn't sure if recanting his misdeeds was the same as repenting for them, but he had to give it a shot, and besides, it was all he could think of to make amends and appease the wrath of God

Employing Kenny Scott was a good idea. The man clearly respected him. You only had to read his reporting to know that. Kenny Scott had made Jackie famous. Now everyone knew who he was and what he was capable of. Soon the journalist would have all the facts and he'd be able to go home and write the book about Jackie's life. The two men got on famously. Kenny even cracked jokes about some of McGeachy's escapades. The book would be a sensation. It would explain why Jackie did the things he did. Why he had no choice. Once it was written, God would have to forgive him.

* * *

Kenny Scott was barely holding it together. He'd now been at this house for over forty-eight hours and what a strange set up it was. The curtains were permanently closed, the heating was always on and you could cut the cigarette smoke with a knife. He understood the dynamic now, but it didn't make it any easier. Jackie McGeachy was in charge of everything. None of his men took a piss, without his permission. Second in command was Alec Keys, a nasty, muscular, man, covered in tattoos and sporting a shaved head and a mouth full of bad teeth. Others came and went at all times of the day and night. They didn't even acknowledge Kenny. While McGeachy was around, he was invisible to them and he made damn sure he didn't stare at any of them. He didn't want to catch their eyes. When he was released from this place, he didn't want any of them remembering him. In the meantime, his position, as biographer to their boss, meant that he was being fed and watered and generally taken care of. This was evidenced by someone straightening his bed in the morning, probably checking it for illicit notes, and refilling the bedside mini fridge with beers.

Kenny couldn't imagine what Caitlin and Ben were going through. Maybe they feared he was dead. Whenever he thought about them and about his home he came close to tears. If he got out of this situation unscathed, he'd never take a risk again. Please God, just let him finish his work and get out of here he prayed.

McGeachy was narrating his life story year by year, beginning with his first and only jail time when he was eighteen, in 1978. One thing about Jackie McGeachy, he'd learnt from his mistakes and he didn't get caught a second time. Not for any crime that led to conviction anyway. His crimes were shocking, horrifying. Kenny had taken notes, up to and including 2008 so far. Some of what he'd been told was so awful, so unbelievable, that he could imagine someone, sometime in the future, making a horror story out of it.

Kenny had been making good progress. He'd tried to appear interested and impressed, appealing to the madman's ego, and it had been working, he'd felt relatively safe, that was until McGeachy had left the house. He'd now been gone for several hours and Kenny was like a lone swimmer surrounded by sharks. One of the men in particular, kept staring at him, while playing with a flick knife, releasing the blade then clicking it shut, over and over again, until Kenny could stand it no longer and sought refuge in his room.

He wondered if the police were searching for him. Was he now the subject of a sensational headline? He hoped nobody would come knocking on the door looking for him, because the house was full of weapons and explosives. In a shoot-out, he might be injured or worse. If he could just hold it together for another couple of days, he'd finish taking notes and McGeachy would let him go. The gangster was confident that his wishes would be carried out and Kenny would write his story then have it published as a book, because he was sure there would be a demand for it. And, when people heard the story about the conditions in which it was written, with the journalist holed up in McGeachy's house, collaborating with him, the publicity would be enormous.

From his bedroom, Kenny heard the front door slam shut. "Clarky, I'm home," McGeachy called in a sing song, cheerful voice. "I've brought you a wee present," he added.

Kenny was extremely apprehensive about receiving a gift. What if it was a prostitute to share his bed, or a jar containing a body part? McGeachy had two gruesome looking, jars, filled with clear liquid, probably formaldehyde, standing on a shelf in an alcove in the lounge. One jar held eye balls the other a human hand. The ghastly horde came from people who'd crossed McGeachy. Sickeningly, they amused the madman. From time to time he'd make jokes, saying things like 'Are you looking at me, Falco? Don't you look at me now,' or 'Get your dirty, thieving hands off my woman O'Brien'. Then he'd laugh until a bout of coughing choked the voice from him, forcing him to stop. Kenny knew that whatever he was offered, if he wanted to stay in one piece and remain alive long enough to get out of this place, he had to accept the gift graciously and show enthusiasm for it. Taking a deep breath, he fixed a smile on his face and descended the stairs. McGeachy and Alec Keys stood in the dimly lit hallway.

"What's all this then, Jackie?" Kenny said, smiling, trying to act like his friend. "You didn't need to get me anything. Sharing your story is enough of a gift for me."

"See, Alec," McGeachy said to his sidekick, triumphantly. "That's why I chose Clarky for this job. The man appreciates what I'm doing for him. He knows I'll make him famous."

Kenny was relieved when McGeachy proffered a small, narrow box with 'Mont blanc' embossed on the lid. Thank God, he thought, it's not anything ghastly, it's just a pen and, not for the first time, his eyes welled up with emotion.

* * *

Caitlin Scott was in bits, she couldn't function, imagining all sorts of terrible things happening to her husband. She went from being frightened to deeply sad then to angry, in a matter of minutes. She'd warned Kenny not to get too close to McGeachy, but did he listen? Now they were all suffering. The terrified look in her son's eyes broke her heart. The police had sent a family liaison officer to sit with her, but instead of taking comfort from this, she felt vulnerable. Were they expecting to find Kenny dead? Would their lives ever be the same again? How could they be?

The police had taken the decision not to inform anyone of the situation. They felt they had a better chance of recovering Kenny safe and well if nobody knew he was missing. She'd had to phone in sick to work and keep Ben off school and they were both becoming stir crazy. If it hadn't been for Bobby Murphy coming round to visit, bringing his dog, Rex, for Ben to play with, she would have gone mad. By the third day of her enforced imprisonment, she practically threw herself at the door when he arrived, so happy for human company.

"Oh, Bobby, I'm so pleased to see you. I'm going mad stuck in here. I feel so helpless," she said with an exhausted catch in her voice.

When Ben took Rex to play with a ball in the garden, she broke down into loud sobs.

"I'm sorry, I'm sorry," she said, apologising for something that was clearly out of her control.

Bobby placed protective arms around her and drew her towards him, holding her close, trying to ease her pain. Her face was pressed against his chest and her tears wet his shirt. She felt like a fragile bird fluttering in his hands. Bobby felt a familiar stirring in his loins. He tried to fill his mind with boring thoughts, tried to quell his obvious ardour, but it was difficult. He could smell Caitlin's perfume and, as he inhaled deeply, he could taste the scent of her.

Suddenly realising what he was doing, he pulled away abruptly. Clearing his throat with embarrassment, he said, "I'd better check on Ben and Rex," then he left the claustrophobic confines of the room and made his way to the garden.

Chapter 29

John arrived fifteen minutes early for his rendezvous with McGeachy. He'd slept rough the night before and he was tired and chilled to the bone. He stood outside the red sandstone tenement building, not certain, but pretty sure, he knew what the set-up would be. Being a Christian, and a preacher for the Lord, John wouldn't judge the girls he'd be employed to protect, but that didn't mean he approved of their profession. Mary Magdalene was considered by many to have been a whore. Did not Jesus cleanse her of seven demons and save her soul? Perhaps, he, John, would save the lost souls who worked for McGeachy.

At five past six Alec Keys drew up in a shiny BMW car. John was disappointed to see that he was alone. He wondered if the job would still be available to him when McGeachy wasn't there, but he needn't have worried.

"Hello, big man," Alec said. "So you still want the job then?"

"Yes, Sir, thank you, Sir, I'll work hard," he assured.

Alec laughed. No one had called him 'Sir' before, a number of other names perhaps, but never, 'Sir'.

"Well then, we'd better go inside," he said, leading the way into a dingy, dimly-lit close.

First Alec walked John up the stairs to the top of the building. Then, as they descended again, he pointed out each flat's door and told John who and what they contained. Beginning with the two, top floor flats which John was informed were worked by a couple of eastern European girls.

"On this third floor we have Tina and Terry, they do straight sex, hand and blow jobs and they service paedophiles. The girls look about twelve," Alec explained. They moved on to the floor below. "On this floor, we have Mary and Molly, they do girl on girl, group games, and the usual straight sex, hand and blow jobs." They kept descending the stairs. "On the first floor, there's Jill and Jean, they take care of sadists and sickos, bondage and canings. These two girls are junkies. We use them, but they won't last long. You'll particularly have to keep an eye on them. They're the ones most likely to be hurt by punters. And, just so you know, none of these names are real. It's better if you don't know too much about them. I wouldn't tell them any of your shit either. You can't trust them," he stated. They moved on down, "And finally, here on the ground floor, Phoebe, she does dressing-up, humiliation, anything unusual, she's a specialist and she makes Jackie a shed load of dosh. There's a lot of weirdo's out there, and many of them earn big money. We get all sorts, judges, doctors, bankers and wankers," he said, laughing. "This other flat," he added, pointing to the remaining door on the ground floor, "Will be yours." Alec turned a key in the lock and pushed the door. It opened with a creak. "In you go," he said and John entered a narrow hallway.

The flat was a traditional room and kitchen with a long narrow shower room. The kitchen was very large and it housed two washing machines, two tumble dryers, a four ring electric hob and a small larder fridge.

"A lot of washing gets done here, but not much cooking," John observed.

"Aye, that's right," Alec replied. "One of your jobs will be to wash the bed sheets from all the flats. That will keep you busy for quite a lot of the day, seven days a week. In fact, it's what most of your work will be. Have you any problem with that?"

"No, Sir, no problem at all."

Alec then took John into the front room. There was a bed settee and a small coffee table, but the rest of the room was filled with storage furniture. As Alec walked around the room, he opened the various cupboards to show John piles of freshly laundered sheets, towels and boxes of condoms. One large wardrobe was stuffed full of costumes and sex toys.

"Tools of the trade," he explained.

John was overwhelmed. He hadn't realised the scale of the operation.

"Is everything okay then? Do you want the job?"

"Yes, yes Sir, I want the job."

"My name's Alec, Pal. Not Sir, or anything else, just Alec, okay."

"Yes, S…, Alec," John replied.

"The pay is free board and lodgings and a hundred pounds a week cash in hand. You'll be given money and a shopping list every Monday and you'll be able to buy whatever food you need for yourself. Just food, mind you, anything else like beer or clothes comes out of your pay, understand?"

"Yes Alec, I understand."

"Now then, although you'll live at the flat and it will be your responsibility to look after the place, there's another bloke working here too. His name is Chen and he's Chinese. He hardly ever smiles, he's built like a brick shithouse and he's got a scar running down one side of his face. He reminds me of the bloke who played Oddjob in the film Goldfinger. Chen's job is to fill in when you're not here. No one can be on call 24/7, so when you're out or sleeping, he'll be here. He'll only work three nights in any one week because he covers another establishment as well. So sometimes you'll have to sleep during the day. Any questions?"

"How do I know which times Chen will work?"

"Get your phone out and I'll give you his number. You can arrange things with him."

"I don't have a phone," John replied.

Alec stared at him incredulously. "How do you live without a phone?" he asked.

John shrugged.

"Wait here, I'll get you one from my car. You don't have a phone?" he muttered, shaking his head. "I've never heard of such a thing."

Alec left the flat returning a couple of minutes later with a mobile. "I've put Chen's number on it. My number's there too. Do you know how to operate this?" he asked, proffering the phone.

"Yes," John replied. "I know how it works I just didn't own one."

"Righteo, here are your keys then. Oh, and in the hall cupboard is a rack with keys to all the other flats, just in case you have to get inside in a hurry."

Alec handed over a set of keys together with a twenty pound note. "A wee advance," he said. "There's food in the fridge and in the kitchen cupboards. The girls will bring down their washing each day and exchange it for clean stuff and they'll pick up tins and packets of food. They usually do that at about eleven o'clock in the morning so make sure you're here at that time every day. I'll leave you to it then."

John was tempted to ask what had happened to the previous holder of the job, but thought better of it, probably safer not to know. As Alec turned to leave he said, "If any of the girls are willing to give you a free fuck, then that's okay, just so long as it doesn't use up time that could be earning money. I'd give the junkies a miss though, just in case they give you something more than you'd want, a wee extra like syphilis or herpes. Junkies are always getting diseases. Weak immune systems, you see."

The very thought of touching any of the girls sickened John, but he said nothing. When Alec left John closed the door. So many damaged people, he thought. So many souls to save.

* * *

Angela and Paul had been doing considerable leg work in their search for Kenny Scott. Jack and Tony too, had been shaking up every known thug to see if a name or a location dropped out, although, where Jackie McGeachy was concerned, nobody wanted to risk telling tales. The detectives used everything from threats to bribes, but to no avail. It was now seven in the evening and they were finishing up for the night.

"I'm thoroughly fed up," Paul said to Angela. "All this work, all this fuss, just because that stupid sod, Scott, can't keep his nose out of other people's business."

"You really don't like him, do you?" Angela replied. "What's he ever done to you?"

"I hate all reporters, not just him. They're like parasites, feeding off other people's misery. When did you ever read good news in a paper? They push their way into people's lives, asking questions when they're vulnerable, poking away, paying no attention to their feelings, anything to get at the truth."

"I'm sorry Paul, but you've just described our job. We get paid to ask questions when people are vulnerable too."

"Maybe so, but we try to ease their pain, Kenny Scott sensationalises it."

Angela could see she wasn't going to be able to lift his mood so she changed the subject.

"How's the house hunting coming along?" she asked.

"Pretty good, actually," he replied, his face brightening. "We think we've found one. It's in Ormonde Avenue and it has four bedrooms and a huge garden. It needs a bit of work, nothing major, just decorating, but we can do that ourselves. We've talked over the price with the current owner and it looks like we've reached an agreement."

"That's fantastic news, Paul. When would the entry date be?"

"In a couple of months, the exact date is negotiable. It'll take a while for Brigit's estate to be wound up, but the lawyer says he can arrange a bridging loan. We've got a buyer for our house, so it's all looking good."

"Wow, you don't hang around. I'm really pleased for you."

They sat chatting for a few minutes more then, once again, Paul brought up the subject of Kenny Scott.

"I don't know what we're going to do. Nothing is working out. We've got a journalist who seems to have vanished into thin air. Nobody knows anything, or if they do, they're saying nothing. John Baptiste could be in Glasgow or perhaps Timbuktu, anywhere, for all we know. He could have changed his appearance and be calling himself Fred Flintstone or Mickey Mouse and no one would be any the wiser. As for Jackie McGeachy and his gang of thugs, everyone's heard of him, but nobody's talking."

He sat up and rubbed his face with his open palms, looked at his watch, then stood and put on his jacket before continuing.

"The boss is depressed. When someone comes into the office he leaps to his feet, trying to look alert and busy, in case it's God paying us a visit, to read us the riot act. He's stopped yelling orders, always a bad sign. And we're all running out of things to do and people to see. I feel like I'm sitting on a ticking bomb. I know from speaking to Jack and Tony, they feel the same, all this work, work, work, and nothing to show for it."

"But we have to keep going, Paul. We can't avoid the problem, we can't just give up. We can only keep our heads down for so long before someone starts moaning for results. Why don't we go right back to the beginning, back to Rachel Stone's murder, and review the case again? We might just notice something we missed before."

"I think we should forget about Baptiste for the time being and concentrate on finding Jackie McGeachy," Paul replied.

"But technically, Baptiste is our case and McGeachy is Jack's."

"I'm not disputing that for one moment, but Kenny Scott is a victim and he's your friend. What's more, we all think McGeachy has him. Rachel Stone is dead. We can't save her. We have to believe Scott is still alive, so he should be our priority. I don't like the man, but if we find him, we'll probably also find McGeachy, and kill two birds with one stone. If you'll pardon the phrase."

"So what do you suggest?"

"Well, so far we've been interviewing known villains. I think instead we should go back to Davy Hughes' place and speak to the neighbours again. Let's shake them up a bit, harass them, somebody knows something, we just need to break them down."

"Should we tell the boss what we're planning to do?" Angela asked, glancing towards his office.

"No, leave him alone, his door's shut. It's not our job to look after him. He'll have to deal with his demons in his own way. We'll head over to Maryhill first thing tomorrow morning and see how we get on. I don't really want to talk to Frank unless I've got some good news to report."

* * *

Ann-Marie Fitzherbert had been hiding out since Davy Hughes was murdered, praying Jackie McGeachy didn't find her. She'd never had to look after herself before. Davy had done everything for her. She'd loved the man, all his girls had loved him, but Davy only had eyes for Ann-Marie. He was forever telling her that she was special. 'My special princess', he would call her, and he proved his love by giving her pocket money from her earnings. The other two girls worked for their board and lodgings only, but Davy made sure she had cash so she could visit the hairdresser or to buy nice clothes. Now he was dead and she was terrified.

Everything she'd owned was in the flat, but she couldn't return because the police had it taped off. The first day she went into the city centre and pulled a couple of punters for some ready cash. She wasn't used to giving blow jobs in dingy back lanes, but needs must. She'd booked into a cheap hostel for the night, when she couldn't go back to the flat, paying cash in advance. But she knew she'd have to lie low, hide out for a few weeks at least. If Willie Harkness hadn't taken her in, she didn't know what she would have done.

She hardly knew the man, apart from giving him a hand job a couple of times when Davy told her to do it. They had to keep the neighbours sweet, he'd said. When she'd subsequently knocked on Willie's door, at eight in the morning, she wasn't sure if she'd be welcome, but he invited her in like a long lost friend. The deal was that he'd let her live with him, and he'd provide for her, in exchange for sex. The first couple of days it was a quick hand job, but that progressed to a blow job sometimes twice in one day. Now he wanted more. His tastes were becoming more and more perverted, but what could she do? She had nowhere else to go. She was trapped.

When Inga and Katya turned up dead she was even more scared. Willie might be a perverted old lecher, with dubious washing habits, but she was relatively safe with him. He never hit her or hurt her and this was the last place McGeachy's gang would think of looking for her.

Chapter 30

The phone rang at seven in the morning when Bobby was still in the shower. Angela was sitting at her dressing table, applying her make-up, but she ran to answer it. Her immediate thought was, something's wrong. Surely, no one would call this early unless there was a problem.

"Thank goodness, a voice instead of the machine. Good morning Angie, it's Jake. Is Bobby in, or is he swanning off somewhere again, like he did yesterday?"

"He's in the shower," Angela replied with mild irritation in her voice.

Jake was Bobby's business partner. He and his wife used to socialise with her and Bobby at least once a week, but things had changed. Over a year ago, Angela discovered that Jake was a serial womaniser. She could no longer stand the stress of the rows that blew up between him and his wife. She didn't want to be drawn into their marital problems and neither did she want Bobby to accept their appalling behaviour as normal.

"As far as I know he was working here, apart from when he took Rex for a walk of course," Angela said. "What makes you think he was swanning off?"

"Well, I phoned four times looking for information and the machine answered each time. I even left a message in the morning asking for a call back, and I'm still waiting. Maybe he's just not talking to me," Jake replied laughing. "I've probably offended him in some way. Although it's usually you I offend, rather than Bobby, isn't it?"

Angela didn't reply. She didn't rise to the bait. Jake irritated the hell out of her, but Bobby worked with him and Jake was the senior partner in the business. Indeed, if it wasn't for Jake, Bobby would still be teaching maths instead of having his own business, doing a job he loved.

"I'll get him to phone you back when he's out of the shower. I really must go now or I'll be late for work. Bye now," she said, hanging up before he could reply.

She felt hot and bothered. Where had Bobby been yesterday? And why hadn't he returned Jake's calls?

After a couple of minutes Bobby emerged from the shower and entered the bedroom.

"I thought I heard the phone," he said. "Was it anything important?"

"It was your business partner. He'd like you to phone him."

"Jake, I wonder what he wants."

"If you'd answered any of the four calls he made yesterday or listened to the message he left, then you'd know. Where were you all day? I thought you were working here."

Bobby stared at his feet. He hesitated as if he was trying to think of a suitable reply. Angela felt apprehensive.

"If you must know, I drove Caitlin and Ben to the coast for the day. We had lunch there and we took Rex for a run on the beach. Ben needed to get out of the house. He misses his dad and he's got no idea what's going on. I cleared it with the family liaison officer first. I didn't think I had to report to you every time I left the house," he added defensively.

"Of course you don't have to report to me, but why hide it? Unless you thought I'd disapprove. Was there more to this day out that you don't want me to know about?"

"Of course not. There was nothing to it," he answered angrily. "Do you think I'm having some torrid affair with Caitlin while her husband's missing, maybe dead? While her son is playing with our dog? Don't be ridiculous, Angela."

Fuelled by his retort, suddenly all Angela's senses sharpened. He fancies Caitlin, she thought. He's angry because he's been caught out.

"I haven't time to discuss this at the moment, but I want to talk about it tonight. Phone Jake," she said. "Remember you have a business to run. I wish I had time to take a day off to socialise," she added sharply.

With that said Angela stomped downstairs, grabbed her handbag, car keys and jacket and strode to the front door. She hesitated for a couple of moments to see if Bobby would come after her to see her out, but he didn't appear. She felt sad and empty as she shut the door behind her. Is Bobby unhappy with our marriage, she wondered? Maybe she'd been so caught up with her job she hadn't given enough of herself to their relationship.

By the time Angela arrived at Maryhill to meet up with Paul, she was feeling very low. Driving from the south side of the city to the west end, first thing in the morning, was tedious. When she got out of her car and climbed into Paul's, having first inhaled the fishy, putrid smell which heralded bin day, her face was grim. Eventually, after being faced by five minutes of stony silence while he prattled on, Paul said, "Wassup, Ange? You're awfy quiet. Cat got your tongue?"

She'd been deep in thought, but the direct question made her realise how rude she was being. She sat up straight, fixed a smile on her face and turned to Paul, "No problem, pardner," she replied in a southern drawl. "I'm just tired, that's all. Let's go and rattle some chains. Shake up a few witnesses."

It was only eight-twenty a.m. when Angela began to press the door buzzers on the security entry pad.

"They'll probably all still be in their beds," Paul said. "It's a school holiday today and I don't suppose any of the adults will be awake. I don't think many of the people living in this tenement will have a job. This whole area seems to be full of students and idlers."

"I don't think you can generalise, Paul. Some of the folk living round here are the salt of the earth."

"Maybe one or two," he agreed, reluctantly. "Press the buzzers again, Angie. They're dead to the world in there."

A split second before she leaned on the buzzers again, Angela thought she saw the curtains of Willie Harkness' ground floor flat, twitch. "He's in," she said to Paul, pointing to the flat. "I'm sure the curtains moved."

Paul stepped over to the window and banged on it. "Now he can't say the buzzer wasn't working," he explained. "Keep pressing those buttons, Angie, lean on them. Let's get these lazy, good-for-nothings out of their pits."

Suddenly, a window above was noisily opened, the sash window screeching as it was lifted.

"Stop pressing my damned buzzer. Who the hell's down there?"

Angela and Paul looked up to see a very angry looking Mr Collins.

"What the fuck do you want?" he said. His face was contorted with anger. "Do you know what time it is? I've just come off my shift after doing twelve hours at the hospital. I'm shattered."

"Oops," Paul whispered to Angela. "I guess I got it wrong. This one is working."

"We're sorry, Mr Collins, but we have to ask you some more questions. It won't take very long. Just a few minutes of your time," Angela called up to him.

"You're damned right it won't take very long, no time at all, in fact. I'm going back to my kip. You two can fuck off," and with that said, he disappeared back inside and pulled the window shut with a bang.

"Maybe this wasn't such a good idea after all," Paul said.

"I know Willie Harkness is home, I definitely saw the curtains move. Let's go into the building and bang on his front door. We should be able to get in at this time of the morning using the service buzzer," Angela replied.

As soon as Paul thumped on the door of the flat, Angela put her ear to the letter box to listen for signs of life.

"Someone's definitely moving about in there," she reported.

"Mr Harkness, open up, it's the police," Paul called banging on the door again.

"Will you please stop making all that noise, you've woken my kids up," a woman's voice said.

Angela and Paul looked up to see Mrs Perry on the close stairs.

"Ah, Mrs Perry, we'd like a word with you too," Paul said.

"I'm still in my nightie, it's not even nine in the morning, I'm going back to bed," she replied. "This is a ridiculous time to be banging on doors on a school holiday. I'm going to report you two for police harassment," she threatened. "We're decent people in this close. We're not used to this sort of trouble. There's no point banging on Willie's door, either. He was going fishing at the canal with his pal, Jock Anderson, this morning. They always leave at about six in the morning. He won't be back until lunchtime. I heard the close door slam, so I know he definitely went." With that said, she turned and made her way back up the stairs, breathing heavily from her exertions, her flip-flop slippers slapping against the concrete as she went.

"If he's not home, then who's in his flat?" Paul asked.

"I have no idea, but someone's definitely there. I heard them moving about," Angela replied.

Paul pushed open the letter box and peered inside.

"It's no good, we'll have to come back. It's too dark, I can't see a thing. Let's go and get some breakfast. I'm starving."

"You're always starving, Paul. Are you sure you don't have a tape worm?"

Paul smiled, "Did I ever tell you about the time one of my kids got worms from eating unwashed fruit from the neighbour's garden?"

"No Paul, don't talk about it, the very thought makes me sick."

Really, it wasn't so bad, just a few little wiggly worms," he said grinning wickedly.

He kept talking so Angela covered her ears. "La, la la la, la," she sang, trying to blot out his words as she ran towards the safety of the car.

* * *

Ann-Marie Fitzherbert was startled by the banging on the window. Willie had switched off the security buzzer when he'd left to go fishing, so her sleep wouldn't be disturbed by anyone calling round. She sat on the bed, hugging her knees, her eyes flashing with fear. When she heard the banging at the door, she was petrified and jumped off the bed to hastily throw on her clothes. It was a relief when the callers identified themselves as the police.

She didn't venture into the hall, but waited until she thought they'd gone before peering out of the spy hole on the front door, to check. She hoped they'd thought it was Willie who'd been home and just not answering. She wished now she hadn't moved the curtains to look out. What if it hadn't been the cops? What if instead, it had been one of McGeachy's men? She'd really be in trouble if it had been one of them.

Time for her to move on, Ann-Marie thought, it was no longer safe for her here. But where could she go? And who could she turn to for help?

Chapter 31

John very quickly learned how to perform the tasks that were required for his job. The other man, Chen, was happy to show him the ropes, but John disliked him intensely. Chen never smiled. When he spoke, which was infrequently, he yelled orders, staccato style at him.

"Quickly, quickly," he would shout. "Don't be lazy, no time, no time. My uncle Mr Wu. He expects much work for your pay. Mr Wu, he is big boss, bigger than Alec. Bigger than McGeachy."

John wasn't exactly sure of the hierarchy, but as far as he was concerned, Alec was his employer and he was the only one to be concerned about.

The working girls paid the two men little heed. Barely saying a word when they came to exchange their soiled sheets for fresh linen, or to pick up their shopping. The only one who chatted with John, was Phoebe. She was a bit older than the other girls and when she came to his flat and met him for the first time, she introduced herself very formally and shook his hand. This time, when she banged on his door, she explained that she needed an item from the cupboard that held the sex toys.

"I need handcuffs, John," she said. "I don't want the bugger running away. Not when he's paying by the hour," she joked.

John laughed, then immediately, he felt ashamed. "Why are you doing this kind of work, Phoebe? Why are you forced to sell your body? This work is stealing your soul from God and offering it to the devil."

Phoebe stared at John, quizzically, "Do you really believe that, John?" she replied. "Do you think I'm forced to do this? Let me be perfectly clear, nobody is making me work. I haven't time at the moment. I'm a bit tied up just now, or rather my client is," she added, smiling. "But when we've both got half an hour to spare, for a proper chat, I'll tell you my story. Then perhaps you'll understand how I'm in this situation, and why I'll be forever grateful to Jackie McGeachy."

"So is Mr McGeachy the boss?" John asked. "Chen said his uncle, Mr Wu, was in charge."

"Both statements are true. Jackie runs the area from the city centre, west to Clydebank. He takes care of everything, girls, drugs, security, guns, gambling everything. Mickey Wu is like the Godfather. He runs the whole shooting match, all of Greater Glasgow and beyond. Everyone gives Mr Wu a cut from their takings. He's a very dangerous man, a mean bugger, you cross him and you're dead, no second chances. But don't worry, John, the likes of you and I will never meet Mr Wu, we're small fry."

"I see, I see," John replied. "So if there was no Mr Wu, there would be no crime."

"No, John, that's not the case. If there was no Mr Wu, there would be another dangerous bugger to take his place. There will always be someone like Mickey Wu. Anyway, enough chit chat, I've got to get back to work." And with that said, she was out of the door, leaving the sweet scent of lavender in her wake.

* * *

Kenny Scott sat back on the hard, wooden, dining-room chair and sighed deeply. He closed his notebook, put the cover on his pen and laid it down on the table. At last, his note taking was finished. Now he'd heard every secret, every ghastly detail, described in technicolor. Kenny now knew who torched the Silver Machine nightclub in 1999, he knew who was responsible for pouring acid over a car and driver of Flynn's Taxis in 2001, and who'd carried out the recent rapes and murders of Inga Bartock and Katya Cresslar.

If he'd known this information at the time the events had taken place, if he'd had scoops on even a couple of McGeachy's stories, he'd have been jumping for joy, but not now. The weight of this knowledge shocked and saddened him, it crushed him. It broke his spirit.

How could he return to his wife and child and be the same man he was before? How could he play with Ben without seeing David Miller's family, who were gunned down in their beds as they slept? They'd had a young son about Ben's age. He'd been shown no mercy. He too, had been shot to death. How could Kenny make love to Caitlin without his mind being flooded with the horror of Inga and Katya's last moments? His life had been changed forever. The phrase, be careful what you wish for, popped into his head and he smiled wryly. How true, he thought.

Jackie McGeachy reached for the whisky bottle and poured the last of its contents into the two tumblers on the table in front of him. Then he pushed one glass towards Kenny.

"Cheers, Clarky," he said as he held up his glass to clink it against Kenny's. "Good job done my man. Good job."

Kenny obliged by banging his glass against Jackie's. "I can't wait to get home and write this up properly," he said. "This is going to be the book of the year. Heck, it's going to be the book of the decade. Thanks, Mr McGeachy."

He would have said or done anything to get out of that house and back to his life, back to the people he loved.

"No rush, Clarky," McGeachy replied. "I thought I'd wait a day or two before I send you home. In case I remember something else. We can spend the time going over everything you already have. Just to be sure you've written everything down. It's lucky you like my company, isn't it?" he said. "And my whisky," he added, clinking the glasses again.

Kenny felt his heart sink to his boots. "I've been very diligent about my note taking," he replied trying to keep his voice from breaking. "Much as I like you're company my friend, I miss my wife and son. I'd really like to get home, if it's all the same to you. We're going to have to meet up again anyway, once I've written the first draft."

"I hear what you're saying, Clarky, but a couple of days isn't much in a lifetime and, if you do as you're told, you'll probably have a long and productive life. As you know, my life is coming to an end. You wouldn't deny me a couple of days, would you?"

The warning and menace in his words wasn't lost on Kenny. "Of course not, Mr McGeachy, a couple of days it is then," he replied.

"Good. Good man. Mickey Wu will be coming here on Friday afternoon to go over the books and pick up his money. I'll get Alec to drop you at your house or your office on Friday morning so you're out of here before he arrives. There's no sense in him knowing what we're up to with the book. I don't want him to find out until the time is right. Can I get you anything, Clarky? Maybe a girl, booze or drugs? Name it and it's yours."

"No, thanks, I'm okay at the minute. I'm rather tired. I think I'll take my scotch and have a lie down for an hour or two, if that's all right."

"Aye, fair enough, Clarky. You go and have a wee sleep, while the rest of us work," McGeachy said. "Office boy," he added with a chuckle, "What an easy life you have."

Kenny climbed the stairs, entered the dimly lit bedroom, lay down on the bed and wept. He'd expected to be on his way home. He'd counted on it to keep him from falling apart. Now he'd have to wait another two days and he wondered if he could stand it. And what about Mickey Wu? When he found out about the book would he be angry with him? Would his life and the lives of his family then be at risk? Kenny knew he'd have to make sure there was no mention of Wu when the book finally came to be published.

* * *

When Kenny's editor at the Gazette answered the phone to Caitlin, he was delighted to finally have some contact. His reporter had disappeared for days without as much as a word. It was not acceptable.

"Mrs Scott, hello, Chris McCall speaking," was all he managed to say before Caitlin's words tumbled out amidst sobs.

"Kenny's been kidnapped. We think he's being held by a murderer called Jackie McGeachy. The police can't find him. They said I shouldn't speak to you, but I don't know what else to do. Please help me. Please help me to find my husband before they hurt him."

Chris McCall felt a rush of excitement course through his veins. "Try to stay calm, Mrs Scott. I'm coming over. We'll help you all we can. Don't worry. We'll make Kenny front page news. Someone will know something I'm sure."

"Don't come here," Caitlin replied with panic in her voice. "The police will be angry with me. They might stop looking for him. They told me not to talk. I've been keeping my son out of school. Oh, God, it's all such a mess," she sobbed.

"Okay. It's okay, don't upset yourself. The police won't know you've spoken to me. I'll present it as breaking news. I won't let on where the source of the story came from. Tell me everything you know and I'll be careful what I say. Can you scan some photos of Kenny and email them to me? It would help the public to find him. A photograph is so much more powerful than mere words."

As soon as she ended the call to the Gazette, Caitlin phoned Bobby. "Please come round," she begged. "I've done something. It might have been a mistake, I don't know, but I was desperate. Please come round. I need you."

Bobby knew Angela would disapprove. The atmosphere between them recently had been uncomfortable to say the least, but he wanted to help Caitlin, he wanted to be in her company. He liked spending time with her and Ben. If Angela wasn't happy about it then too bad, she wasn't the boss of him.

Bobby couldn't understand why Angela didn't want to have a baby. They'd been married for quite a while now. It wasn't as if she'd have to stay at home and raise the child. He worked from home and would be happy to be the nurturing parent. Angela's life wouldn't have to change. If Caitlin and Kenny Scott could make family life work then why couldn't they? Bobby loved kids and he wanted his own family. Maybe that was the reason their relationship had been strained recently. Maybe she was jealous of Caitlin Scott's abilities.

By the time Angela crawled through the door exhausted after work, Bobby was home. He'd spent the entire day with Caitlin and Ben. There was no meal cooked and no food in the house. He hadn't had time to shop, and besides, he'd already eaten earlier in the day when he'd taken Caitlin and Ben for lunch at a country pub. Angela was already angry because the evening paper carried the story of Kenny's abduction. She was enraged when Bobby proceeded to tell her about his day.

"So let me get this straight," she began, struggling to keep the fury out of her voice. "I've been working under tremendous pressure. I come home after putting in a twelve hour day to nothing to eat. You've taken yet another day off work, spending it with another man's wife and child. You've made sure that they've been fed, at a country pub, no less, and you can't understand why I'm upset? Are you stupid or just thoughtless?"

Bobby's face stiffened with anger. "I am not your servant," he said. "Neither am I at your beck and call whenever it suits you. Yes, you've worked a twelve hour shift, but that was your choice. If I choose to take a week off then that's up to me. I'm still bringing in the money. You're right, I do enjoy spending time with Caitlin and Ben and I am aware they're someone else's family, but then we don't have any children of our own for me to spoil, do we?"

Now it was all coming out, Angela thought. They were back to the subject of children. It was family life Bobby craved, not Caitlin. Although still annoyed, Angela felt slightly relieved at this revelation. Her voice softened.

"You know I want to have a family one day, Bobby. Just not at this precise moment."

"You've been saying the same thing for over two years. When exactly will the precise moment be?" he replied bitterly.

"By the middle of next year, I'll have sat my exams and I'll be in line for a promotion. I promise you, Bobby, whatever happens after that, Christmas next year, we'll try for a baby. Just so long as we're agreed that you become a stay-at-home dad and I return to work. I'll want it in writing, by the way, no changing your mind after baby arrives."

Bobby smiled. He placed his arms around Angela and held her close and the tension between them slipped away.

"Thanks, Pet," he said. "I'm sorry about dinner. I was feeling sorry for myself and jealous of Kenny. Ben's a great kid. Can we have one like him, please?" he joked. "I know you're exhausted. Why don't you go and get changed while I order a carry-out? Then I'll go and collect it so you won't have to wait."

By the time Bobby returned with Chinese food, Angela had showered and changed into her towelling robe. She was already sipping a glass of robust red wine and she felt better. When seated, eating, she began to tell Bobby about the article in the evening paper.

"I know about this already," he interrupted, "Caitlin told me what she'd done. She was desperate to find Kenny and the paper was happy to help."

"I'll bet they were delighted to get the story," Angela replied. "We were trying to keep Kenny's disappearance quiet, so we didn't spook the people who are holding him. We didn't want to squeeze them in case they felt he'd become too hot to handle. We were trying to keep him alive while we attempted to find him. We've no idea why he was taken in the first place. And to think Frank's gone round to speak to Caitlin to try and reassure her about the story breaking, when all the time she was the one who'd spilled the beans."

"She was desperate, Pet. She was frightened and alone and she didn't know what to do for the best."

"I can understand how she felt, but I hope she's not made a terrible mistake and Kenny pays the ultimate price for it. I just hope we find him alive."

Chapter 32

Angela woke the next day feeling rather numb. She couldn't believe she'd made such a promise to Bobby. Maybe she would want to get pregnant next year, but what if she didn't? What then? She drove to work in a daze, negotiating the traffic on auto pilot. When she arrived a copy of the morning paper was on her desk and a photo of Kenny stared back at her.

"Mornin'," Paul said. "Boss is furious with Mrs Scott for undermining him. Seems that God phoned him yesterday evening for an update. Now Frank's really miserable. He's sitting in his room and the whisky bottle's been moved off the floor and onto his desk. You might want to take him a coffee and console him before he opens it and downs the lot."

"Why me?" she whined. "What's wrong with you consoling him?"

"He's already blown me out of the water and all I said was 'good morning'. We've got to do something. Otherwise, if he starts drinking, you'll have to drive him home. I haven't got my car, it's in for a service, Gemma dropped me off," Paul explained.

"Shit, I'll get it in the neck. He'll blame me for Kenny's picture being on the front page. Why don't we just find a reason to get out of the office and leave him to it? We're not his babysitters."

Paul stared at Angela. He raised his eyebrows and pursed his lips.

"Shit, shit, shit, I hate you Costello. I hate Frank. Hell, I hate all men," Angela replied vehemently.

She marched over to the coffee machine and collected a coffee for Frank, then made her way to his office.

"Enter, if you must," he replied when she rapped on the glass window of his door.

"Coffee for you, boss," she said and she stared pointedly at the bottle of whisky. The room smelled of body odour.

Following her gaze, he replied, "Don't worry, Murphy, I'm not stupid enough to drink it, not this morning anyway. I'm just reminding myself what it's like to slide into oblivion. That's what will happen, you see, if we don't start solving some cases. At the very least, we need some leads, something positive. God has spoken. He's told me, in no uncertain terms, that if nothing develops by the end of next week, I'll be replaced on every case. I'll be sent on holiday and someone will step in and take over. He's watching me like a hawk."

"But that's so unfair. Is he as hard on the other senior detectives?"

"No, I don't suppose he is, but then the others are much younger men and, as far as I know, they haven't had a drink problem. Added to that, God doesn't like me. I'm not the right sort. I wasn't born with a silver spoon in my mouth. I call a spade a fucking shovel."

Angela said nothing. She didn't know how to reply.

"Hell, maybe I should just throw in the towel," Frank said, hanging his head, clearly feeling sorry for himself. "I could go off on the sick and wait till they offer me a deal to retire. You might get someone more dynamic, a high flyer perhaps, maybe someone polite," he added, grimacing. Frank rested his elbows on the desk and held his head in his hands.

Angela was shocked. "Don't even think like that, boss," she said.

"You're being kind, Murphy, but I'm grumpy, I'm old and I think I'm fucked."

Angela couldn't stand it, she had to shake him out of this mood or they'd all be fucked.

"You might be a grumpy, old bastard, but you're our grumpy, old bastard, and we're used to you."

Frank began to laugh. "Eloquently put, Murphy, I don't know whether to be delighted or outraged," he replied. "Get back to work, you cheeky besom. Find me something to work with, for God's sake. You can report back to Costello. Tell him I said you're my favourite child. Shake him up a bit. He can be a right lazy sod. Let's focus all our energy today on trying to find Kenny Scott. Maybe we can save him and save ourselves from trial by media."

Paul had a shifty look in his eyes when Angela returned to her desk, as if he was trying to avoid looking at her directly.

"And so you should be ashamed," she said, "Sending me to face the wrath of Frank."

Paul said nothing. He still couldn't look her in the eye.

"Well, don't you want to know how I got on?" she goaded.

Paul shrugged.

Angela continued, "Frank said I'm his favourite child, even though I'm a cheeky besom. And you're a lazy sod."

"What," Paul protested. "How can he say I'm lazy? I've only had two unscheduled days off in a year, one, when we had a burst pipe and the other when Brigit died."

"I'm only reporting what he said."

"Well, stuff it. From now on I'll work to rule. See how he likes that."

"If we don't get some results soon, he won't care because he won't be here. God's given him till the end of next week."

"Shit, is that what he told you? Bloody Hell."

"Bloody Hell, indeed. We'd better find something soon or who knows what will happen. We might get landed with Cecil Prentice and he's a right royal pain in the arse," Angela replied.

"I just don't see what else we can do," Paul said mournfully. "Jack and Tony have been all over the cases linked to McGeachy and so have we. Half the country is searching for Baptiste. The uniform boys have been banging on every door for information and, as for Kenny Scott, Christ knows where he is."

"I feel if we can find Kenny Scott, we'll have a link to McGeachy. I just don't know where to begin looking," Angela replied.

* * *

Ann-Marie had been awake for most of the night, lying beside Willie who slept deeply, snoring and farting without a care in the world. She, on the other hand, was wracked with worry and fear. When she'd told Willie that she was planning to leave, he'd talked her out of it.

"You've nothing to fear from the police, Hen," he'd said. "They were looking for me. They didn't know you were here. They want me to point the finger at McGeachy. But don't worry. I know when to keep my mouth shut. As long as I don't talk to them, McGeachy has no reason to be interested in the likes of me."

But Ann-Marie wasn't convinced. If word got out that the police wanted to question Willie, then that could be enough to bring the gangster to his door.

By six a.m., she'd made her decision. She'd have breakfast with Willie then she'd go and call on her mum in Scotstoun. See if she'd take her in for a few days. Harland Street was a distance from Maryhill so neither McGeachy nor the police had any reason to look for her there. Not now that some time had passed since Davy's death. Anyone who'd thought she might have run to her mum's would have already checked out the address. She would tell Willie she was going to the bus station in the city centre. Then, if he was questioned, he could tell McGeachy she'd left town. Besides, if things didn't work out, she could always return here.

* * *

"Put the kettle on, John. Make Phoebe a strong cup of tea, please. I'm so ready for it. If I've had one drunken bugger visiting me, I had half a dozen last night. It's harder to get them finished when they've had a few. I feel shattered this morning."

Phoebe, still dressed in her dressing gown and slippers, plonked herself down at the table and lit a cigarette. John poured strong tea from the pot into the best china mug he could find.

"I love roses," Phoebe said, commenting on the overblown pink blooms emblazoned on the mug. I haven't been bought flowers for years, not since I was engaged, in fact."

"I didn't know you'd been engaged. Were you married? Do you have children?" John asked.

Phoebe's face fell. Her normally plump cheeks sagged.

"I was married for five years to the love of my life, my darling Eddie. We had a son. Liam we called him."

"But you're not with them now," John stated. "What happened?"

Phoebe's eyes filled with tears and her face was engulfed by such sadness her grief was palpable.

"They're both dead, John," she replied in barely a whisper. "They were killed in an accident. Eddie had put Liam in his buggy and gone to buy milk. A 4x4 mounted the pavement and hit them. They died instantly. It was nobody's fault. The driver had a heart attack. I felt as if I'd died too that day. I wish I had died with them. The girl I was, the wife and mother, was gone. My wonderful, happy life was over."

A sob escaped from her throat and she sipped her tea and wiped her eyes with her sleeve.

"There's not a day goes by that I don't miss them. My heart breaks for what I've lost. That's why I can do this sort of work. I don't care you see. If I get murdered by a client, so what? He'd probably be doing me a favour. If I wasn't so scared I'd kill myself. I'm not frightened of death, but I'm a Catholic. Suicide is a sin. I want to be with Eddie and Liam in heaven. So I can't take the chance of having the pearly gates slammed in my face."

"You still trust in God even after being faced with such adversity?" John asked. His voice was full of admiration.

"Of course, when everything else is gone, God is all we have left. I pray every day for deliverance."

"You are a true believer, Phoebe. I too have unshakeable faith. I pity the unbelievers because they will never find peace."

"You're a good man, John. It's not easy when you're surrounded by evil. Sometimes, I visit the Glasgow Cathedral, in the city centre, just to be in a holy place. Next time I'm going you can come with me if you'd like."

"I'd like to see the cathedral," he replied.

John stood to put on the kettle while Phoebe remained deep in thought. She had her back to him and didn't notice when he came and stood behind her. She couldn't hear his silent prayer seeking guidance, didn't see him grit his teeth. When he grabbed her head and snapped her neck, it happened so quickly, she had no time to feel fear or pain.

"Accept this good woman, Lord. Welcome her into the kingdom of heaven. Open the gates for her Peter. Reunite her with Eddie and Liam," John beseeched.

Then he dragged Phoebe's dead body to his bed and carefully laid her out, closing her lifeless eyes and crossing her arms over her chest. She looked as if she were sleeping. After a while he left the flat locking the door behind him. Stepping into the cold air, he walked to the small cafe where he'd first met Jackie McGeachy and Alec Keys. He would wait there for a while until God told him what to do next. He was exhausted. It was hard work saving souls for the Lord.

Chapter 33

Willie Harkness was upset when Ann-Marie left. The flat felt empty without her. He was used to having the waif-like creature around. She'd been undemanding and accepting of anything and everything he'd asked of her. He worried what would become of her. The streets were dangerous for a girl working on her own and unprotected. There was a vast difference between servicing punters in a warm flat with a strong man looking out for you, to meeting strangers in a dark alleyway, and what about Jackie McGeachy's gang? On the streets she was vulnerable. Anyone could see her and report back to McGeachy. Then what would happen to him? McGeachy wouldn't be pleased to learn that Willie had been hiding the girl.

As he paced the floor of his flat, all sorts of awful thoughts coursed through his mind. He imagined Ann-Marie being forced into a car or dragged into a derelict flat. Vivid pictures of Inga and Katya flashed through his brain. In his mind's eye he could see their shadowy images, passing through the corridor of the close on the way to their flat. This was suddenly and shockingly superimposed by ghastly visions, as he imagined how they'd looked in death, tortured, raped and murdered.

He fished Angela Murphy's business card out of his inside jacket pocket, turning it over and over in his hands. "What should I do?" he said aloud. "What should I do?"

He took a near empty whisky bottle from the kitchen cupboard and poured himself a wee dram. It was still morning, but he needed it to steady his nerves and to stay his shaking hands. Willie took his mobile from his pocket and began to dial the number on the card. He needed protection. If McGeachy found

Ann-Marie it wouldn't be long before one of his minions would be knocking at his door.

* * *

"Show me a lead. Show me a lead."

Paul waved his hands over his computer like a magician before pulling a rabbit out of a hat. Angela grimaced.

"Well I've got to try something," he said, "And so far praying hasn't worked."

"If only the phone would ring," Angela replied. "We haven't even had a crank or a wrong number this morning. Has the rest of the world vanished into thin air, and we haven't heard anything about it?"

As if on cue, her mobile began to ring.

"There is a God," she said as she reached for it.

"Detective Murphy, is that you? It's Willie Harkness here," a voice said, "Remember me?"

Angela quickly caught Paul's attention and mouthed Willie's name. Paul raised his eyebrows then gave her call his full attention.

"Yes, Mr Harkness, what can I do for you?" she asked.

"I think I might be able to do something for you," he replied. "But if I tell you what I know it could put me at risk. Can you keep me safe? Can you protect me from Jackie McGeachy?"

"Why don't you tell me what you have then I'll see what I can do. Are you home? I could come over and see you right away."

She glanced at Paul who nodded and gave her a 'thumbs up'.

"I don't want you turning up here. You might be seen. I might be seen. I'll meet you somewhere else, somewhere away from the west end."

"How about meeting me in the city centre, maybe outside BHS at the St Enoch Centre, say in about half an hour? Then we can go and have a coffee. Once I hear what you have to say, my partner and I will be in a better position to decide what to do to help you."

"Okay, yes that's fine. I'll leave here in five minutes. I'm taking a big risk you know," he stressed. "You'd better not be stringing me along. You'd better not let me down."

Before she could reply, he'd hung up.

"Bingo," Angela said punching the air. "At last, at long last, a possible lead."

They took Paul's car and, when they arrived at the car park, Angela suggested she went alone to rendezvous with Willie.

"If you stay here, I'll bring him back to the car. Then we can decide where to have our chat. If he sees us both coming to meet him, he might feel intimidated and bolt," Angela explained.

"Just make sure you do come back here. Don't go anywhere with him on your own, in case he's setting you up. Remember what happened to Kenny Scott."

"Paul," she replied, "When you see this guy, you'll realise he's not smart enough for subterfuge. He's got the brains of a lemon."

Angela climbed out of the car and made her way to the entrance. Before she reached the stairs in front of the building, she could see Willie skulking just inside the glass doors and she signalled for him to come to her.

"Let's not hang around here," he said, looking about nervously.

"My colleague has his car in the car park," Angela replied. "We can take a drive and find somewhere quiet to talk."

"I don't know much. It'll just take me a few minutes to tell you what I have. We could park near Glasgow Green, outside the People's Palace," he suggested. "I can make my own way home from there."

As suggested, Paul drove the short distance then pulled in. The car park was fairly empty, but still offered the privacy they desired.

"Dear green place," Willie quoted. "We're lucky living in Glasgow because there're so many parks."

He was chatting away nervously, obviously needing to fill the silence.

"Well now, Willie, why don't you tell us what's troubling you?" Paul suggested.

"Aye, okay then. It's Ann-Marie, I'm worried about Ann-Marie," he said.

"Ann-Marie Fitzherbert, the girl who worked for Davy Hughes?" Angela asked.

Willie nodded.

"What about her? Do you know where she is?"

"I know where she's been," he said. "She's been living with me."

Angela and Paul exchanged glances.

"She left my place because your lot came banging on the door and it scared her. She thought McGeachy was coming to get her. She told me she was going to Buchanan Street bus station, but I don't believe she'll leave Glasgow. It's all she knows. I don't think she'll work on the streets either and that's why I'm scared. She's more likely to try to find a house to work from, with a pimp to look after her. I'm frightened she'll come in contact with one of Jackie McGeachy's men. Her mum lives in Scotstoun, in Harland Street, so she knows that area. McGeachy runs a whole close of flats just round the corner from where her mum stays."

"So you're scared she'll inadvertently place herself in danger. Right into the hands of the man she's trying to avoid," Angela said. "And where do you come into all of this? Why are you scared?"

"Well, if McGeachy finds Ann-Marie he's going to want to know where she's been staying. He won't be too happy when he finds out I've been hiding her."

"I see. So you think he might come after you?"

"Exactomundo," Willie replied. "Look what happened to Inga and Katya and they could earn him money. He'd have no use for me."

"How do you know about this close full of prostitutes?" Paul asked. "Have you had dealings with McGeachy in the past?"

"In a way. I don't know him personally, but I visited his girls occasionally, when I didn't have a girlfriend, if you know what I mean. Begging your pardon, Officer," he said to Angela, clearly embarrassed by this admission.

"You'd better give us the address," Angela replied. "We'll check the bus station and the surrounding area then we'll pay Mrs Fitzherbert a visit. One of my colleagues has spoken to the mother before, but of course we now know Ann-Marie was staying with you at that time. If there's no sign of her at her mother's, we'll check out the brothel."

"And what about me? What should I do?"

"You're in no immediate danger, Mr Harkness. I suggest you keep your head down for a few days. When we find Ann-Marie we'll call you. But, in the meantime, if she returns to your flat, you call us and we'll help you both."

"Do you think you'll manage to find her?"

"Definitely, rest assured," Angela replied, hoping her words would prove to be true. "We're one step ahead of her now instead of being one step behind. And, when we do catch up with her, she'll have you to thank for her wellbeing."

Satisfied with the reply, Willie opened the car door. "I've sat here long enough," he said. "I'll be off now. Remember to call me when you find her. Tell her she's got a home with me whenever she wants." He was about to close the door when he bent down and peered back in. "Tell her Willie sends his love." His eyes were pleading. "Tell her I love her," he said softly.

Then he shut the door and he was gone. They watched as he hurried away through the park towards the city centre.

"Poor bugger," Paul said. "What a life."

"He likes his life," Angela replied. "He doesn't know any better."

Chapter 34

When two of McGeachy's girls came down with their washing and to pick up their shopping, they found the door to John's flat locked. They rang the bell and banged on the door, but there was no reply.

"I'll try phoning John," Tina volunteered. "Maybe he's asleep."

When there was no answer, Molly knocked on Phoebe's door.

"Phoebe will know what to do," she said.

There was no response.

"This is ridiculous," Molly complained, "I'm starving and there's no food in my flat."

"And I haven't anything I can give you," Tina said. "Much as I hate to do it, because I can't stand him, I'd better call Chen. He'll come over and he's got a key. The boss is going to go nuts," she added with a hint of excitement in her voice. "He's only just hired John."

"Never mind him," Molly said, "I'm going nuts. I'm so hungry I could eat a scabby horse."

Tina dialled Chen's number, pulling a face as she did, as if she had a bad smell under her nose.

"Well what the fuck do you want me to do, Chen," Tina said when the call was answered. "No, I don't know where he is. If I knew I wouldn't be calling you, would I? Yes, you have to come right away. Well, if you'd rather tell the boss we're not able to work? No, I thought not. Twenty minutes? Yes, yes, okay, bye."

"I take it you heard all that, Molly? Twenty minutes he said."

Still moaning and complaining, the girls returned to their flats to await the arrival of Chen.

* * *

Angela and Paul drew a blank at the bus station. Nobody remembered seeing a girl answering Ann-Marie's description.

"I suppose it was a long shot," Paul said. "It would have been too easy if we found her waiting for a bus."

"Yeah," Angela agreed, "Far too easy. But I had hoped someone might have remembered selling her a ticket. She probably didn't come here at all. Hopefully we'll have better luck with her mother."

"I hope so, but who knows, this case has been a bitch right from the start. Have you got the mother's address in Harland Street?"

"Yeah, and I called Jack to see what he knew. He said the mother's a right tough cow, a real hard ticket. I suspect Ann-Marie won't be there either. Seemingly, her mother didn't have a good word to say about her."

"How do you want to handle it?" Paul asked.

"I'm not sure, we'll have to play it by ear, but I don't want her to think we're pushovers, so let's not put up with any nonsense from her. I think, if we seem weak, she'll slam the door in our faces."

The drive from the city centre to the west end took them nearly twenty minutes because of heavy traffic. Paul cursed and swore the entire journey. He hated driving through the town at the best of times and today was particularly bad.

"Are you any further on with your house purchase and sale?" Angela asked trying to calm him down.

"Yes," he said brightening up. "It's a done deal. Our lawyers have received a written offer for our house and we've had our offer accepted on the Ormonde Avenue house. Gemma's been to both the primary and secondary schools for a visit and she was very impressed."

"That's fabulous news. We'll soon be neighbours then."

"Not soon enough. We didn't realise just how cramped we were until we saw what we could have. Now we're desperate to move. If you don't mind, can I pick your brains about where's the best place to buy carpets and furniture. Do you know anywhere that gives a deal to cops? We're going to have to replace some of our stuff because it's worn out and, besides, you could fit all our belongings into two rooms of the new house, so we'll have to get some more bits and pieces."

"Sure thing," Angela replied. "The place you want is called 'Allans' in Wallace Street. The prices are good and the quality is first rate. Whatever you need, be it carpets or furniture, they'll have it. Just mention my name and say you're my colleague and you'll get a discount. Bobby and I have used them many times and we sent Liz Brown there when she moved to Kilmarnock."

"Thanks Angela, all this is new to me. We've struggled financially for so long, we've lost touch when it comes to buying things. Not that it's stopped the kids. They've already found the local bicycle shop and the pet shop!"

When they turned into Harland Street, Angela directed Paul to the Fitzherbert residence. He pulled up outside the tenement, behind a battered, old Ford.

"Every car in this street has a bash in it," he observed, as they alighted the car. "I hope mine's okay parked here."

"We'll not be very long," Angela reassured.

They banged on the door of the ground floor flat and within seconds, it was wrenched open by a large, red-faced woman brandishing a ladle.

"Whit are ya wantin'?" she shouted. And before either of them could reply, "Come oan, come oan, I'm burnin ma soup."

Angela proffered her warrant card and identified herself.

"Ave spoken to your lot already. Ave nae idea where Ann-Marie is. A sent her packin. Wee hoor isnae welcome here. Ma man won't have her in the hoose."

"So you've seen her recently," Paul stated.

"Aye, she were here the day, but as a said, a sent her packin. Away ye get, noo. Ave nithing mare tae say to yoos," and with that, she slammed the door.

"She was eloquent," Paul said.

"And charming too," Angela added.

"What a difference from the good people I'll be rubbing shoulders with when I move."

"Oh yes," Angela agreed, laughing. "Nether twee is very posh."

"So far, we're not doing very well," Paul said. "Get in the car and we'll drive round the corner to the brothel. We could walk, but I'm worried that if I leave my car, by the time we get back, it'll be up on bricks."

"I'm afraid if you leave it, there'll be nothing here when we get back. Someone will have stripped it down and sold it for scrap," Angela replied.

* * *

"Ayeee! Ayeee! Ayeee!" Chen's screams filled the close.

"Jesus Christ, what's going on?" Molly shouted, as she ran down the stairs to the door of John's flat.

Within seconds, she was joined by Tina, Mary and Terry.

"She dead, Phoebe dead," he wailed. "She in John's bed and she dead."

"Oh, Christ, are you sure Chen? Are you sure she's dead?" Mary asked. "Let me see her," she added pushing her way past him into the flat.

"She dead. She dead. I know dead," he replied. "John do this. Not me. John do this. I tell Mr McGeachy. He know what to do. Go back to rooms now. Go back to rooms."

"I'm staying right here, Chen. We're all staying here," Tina said.

Chen took out his mobile and called Mickey Wu speaking for only seconds, then immediately afterwards he called Jackie McGeachy.

Angela and Paul witnessed the commotion as soon as they entered the building. "Police," Paul shouted. "Police. What's happened here?"

"Police here now, boss," Chen said into the phone. "Police here. I no call them. I just phone Uncle Mickey. He speak to you, boss. He get in touch with you."

Chen ended the call. Before Angela or Paul could say anything he said, "Girl dead. I find her. I no kill her, just find. I think John do this."

"What's the girl's name," Angela demanded, expecting that they'd found Ann-Marie.

"Phoebe, her name's Phoebe," Tina answered.

"Do you all live in this close?" Paul asked.

The girls exchanged glances.

"We had nothing to do with this," Molly said. "Speak to the Chinaman. He found her."

While Paul phoned for back up, Angela said. "Nobody is to leave this building. You'll all be questioned. You can return to your homes, but no one is going anywhere until we say you can leave, understand?"

Used to obeying orders, the girls meekly headed back upstairs.

"Right, Sir," Angela said directing her conversation to Chen. "Why don't you tell me what's happened here. What do you know? And who is this John you spoke of?"

It took Angela and Paul only moments of speaking to Chen to reach the same conclusion.

"Oh, sweet Jesus," Paul said. "John George is John Baptiste and he's killed again."

Angela nodded slowly. "We might have missed him by only a couple of hours. I'll play you for this one, Paul. Rock, paper, scissors. The loser tells big Frank."

Chapter 35

McGeachy began to tremble. This is it, he thought. I didn't expect it so soon. I didn't expect to die today. He shut the lounge door, signalling that no one should enter, and then opened a new bottle and poured himself a tumbler of whisky to steady his nerves. His hand shook as he raised the glass to his lips.

A dead whore and the police at the door. A whorehouse run by him raided and the Chinaman's nephew blabbing to the cops. He should never have agreed to take on that half-wit Chen, but Mickey Wu pressured him. Now Wu's nephew was in the hands of the police. God knows what he'd tell them. McGeachy knew he was meant to keep Chen out of the way because the young man wasn't quite right in the head. But how could he have predicted that something like this would happen?

McGeachy knew that Wu didn't like him and would have preferred to replace him with one of his own men, but he'd had no reason to take him on. Besides, the other bosses wouldn't have stood for it. They would have joined forces to protect him. They wouldn't have let Wu step in, for fear the same thing might happen to them. But now Wu had every reason to crush him. This kind of incident, this kind of mistake could threaten the whole organisation.

He should have just killed Chen, made up some excuse to tell Wu. He should have got rid of the weak link when he'd had the chance. Now he was in trouble. Nobody would support him. None of the others would help him. He was well and truly fucked.

McGeachy knew what he had to do. He was pleased Clarky had all the information for the book. Just one final chapter and his story would be over. McGeachy opened the lounge door.

"Clarky, Alec, come here. I need you," he called.

When they entered the room, McGeachy drew Alec aside and spoke to him softly. Kenny Scott sat slumped in a chair. He was despondent. He wanted to go home. As he stared at the other men, he could see Alec's demeanour change. He seemed to deflate, as if all the stuffing had been sucked out of him.

"Gather up your stuff, Kenny," Alec said. "Then quickly write down what Jackie tells you. There's very little time. We're clearing everyone out of this building. I'll have one of the men drive you to the Gazette office. Jackie wants you to run with the story he's about to give you. Then I'll be expecting to see his whole story published."

Kenny could tell that something was seriously wrong. He ran to his room and gathered up his meagre belongings placing the notebooks in a polythene bag, before returning to the lounge. When he entered the room, he could see that an envelope stuffed with cash and a revolver had been placed on the table in front of McGeachy alongside his phone.

"This is for you, Clarky," McGeachy said, proffering the phone and the envelope. "And this is for me," he added, taking the gun in his hand.

It took Kenny a mere fifteen minutes to take notes on Jackie McGeachy's additional chapter. When he closed his notebook the three men stood. McGeachy embraced Kenny, then Alec ushered him out of the door and into the hallway where he was met by a monster of a man with a tattooed head.

"Craig, here, is going to drive you to your office. Make sure that article appears in the next available paper. When Jackie's story is published in a book or, at the very least, serialised in a newspaper, you'll receive another envelope. If it doesn't get printed you'll receive something else, something less pleasant. Do you understand?" Alec said.

"Don't worry, it will be published," Kenny replied. "This is the scoop of my life. This is Pulitzer prize stuff," he assured. He'd have said anything to make the man happy so he'd let him go.

When Kenny stepped out of the stifling house into the cold air, he shivered. His eyes blinked at the natural light. He sucked in air like a drowning man. Was he really free? Would McGeachy really let him go, he wondered? It seemed too quick, too easy. He didn't dare use his phone, or indeed say a word until the car pulled up outside the Gazette's office and he'd alighted. Then, as it drove off with a screech of tires and in a cloud of exhaust fumes, he broke down in tears of relief and sobbed his heart out.

Jackie McGeachy drained his glass of whisky then ran his fingers through his thinning hair.

"Well, Alec, my friend," he said. "It's time you hit the road. You've overstayed your welcome. All I have to do now is empty the safe. There's over twenty grand in cash, a carrier bag full of drugs and two guns, easily enough for you to start over somewhere else. You know you can't stay in Glasgow, don't you?"

Alec's eyes were downcast, he nodded solemnly.

McGeachy walked over to a cupboard at the corner of the room and unlocked the heavy wooden door to expose the safe. He keyed in the code. Alec heard the barrels whirring then the satisfying click as the safe door sprung open. He stood a few feet away from McGeachy when he fired the gun, so he didn't get his friend's blood on his clothes. He managed to get off two shots before McGeachy fell backwards onto the floor. The next two pulls of the trigger ensured that he was dead. Then Alec picked up a holdall he found on the sofa and emptied it, tipping out McGeachy's gym kit.

"You won't be needing this again, Pal," he said aloud. Then, stepping over his friend's lifeless body, "Or this," he added, as he filled the bag with the contents of the safe.

Alec ran to his car and threw the bag onto the back seat. As he drove away, he looked in the rear view mirror and saw the distinctive top-of-the range Mercedes, owned by Mickey Wu. It pulled up outside the house and a dark coloured van parked behind it.

"Too late, Mate," Alec muttered as he sped away.

* * *

Ann-Marie was distraught. She'd expected her mum to give her a hard time, but she was unprepared for such vitriol. She'd begged her mother for help, explained her life was in danger, but instead of sympathy, she was met with a tirade of scorn and abuse.

"Serves you right," her mother spat. "You've made yer bed. Yer no bringin yer hooring to ma door."

As Ann-Marie stared in disbelief, her mother folded her arms stubbornly.

"Can you give me any money, Mum?" Ann-Marie begged, "Just a few pounds to tide me over."

Reluctantly, her mother handed her a ten pound note before the door was shut in her face.

Ann-Marie didn't know what to do. She had been sure her mum would help her. She knew her mum's partner hated her, but blood was thicker than water, wasn't it? Ann-Marie felt weak, she hadn't eaten much and she could do with a cup of tea to steady her nerves so she made her way round the corner to the cafe. She was shivering and it was warm inside, comforting. She ordered a mug of tea and a sausage roll. There was one man sitting at the lone table in the room.

"Do you mind if I sit here?" Ann-Marie asked.

"Of course, sit down," the man replied, smiling at her. "There's plenty of room."

The man stood and pulled out a chair for her. He took the mug and the plate from her cold hands and placed them on the table. "Let me help you," he said.

Ann-Marie stared into the gentle eyes of the stranger. She was overwhelmed by his kindness and promptly burst into tears.

"Sister, sister, what's wrong? Have I offended you in some way?"

"No, not at all, I'm just having a bad day," she replied. "You're very kind. What's your name? I'm called Ann-Marie."

"Well, Ann-Marie, hello. My name is John. Talk to me about your bad day. Perhaps I can help you."

The large, black man was soft spoken. He had an air of calm about him as if he had all the time in the world to listen. He looked strong and able to defend himself. Maybe she could hook up with him, for a short while anyway, maybe he'd protect her.

In the space of twenty minutes Ann-Marie poured her heart out to John. He listened patiently. When she told him about her mother's rejection, he felt deep sadness. The fragile, waif-like creature reminded him of his mother. She'd had the same desperate look on her face when John had helped her. When he'd rescued her soul from the devil's clutches.

After Ann-Marie finished speaking he said, "I too, know this man. And I think Mr McGeachy will be searching for me as well. We have to find somewhere to hide from him until we have a plan. I can save you, but I need time to think."

"I have an idea," Ann-Marie said. "I've been staying with a friend for a few days. I still have a set of his keys in my pocket. We can go to his place for just now. He helped me before, I'm pretty sure he'd help me again. We'd have to leave before tonight though, but at least, for the time being, we'd be off the streets and have some time to think and make plans."

As they left the cafe Ann-Marie slipped her slim hand into John's meaty paw. He smiled down at her. She felt that she could trust him and would be safe in his company. Perhaps this man would save her from McGeachy.

John gazed into the hopeful eyes of the young woman. Don't worry, Mum, he thought. I, your good son John, will save you from the devil. I will protect you until I can deliver you safely into the hands of our Lord.

* * *

After he'd left the detectives, Willie had walked into the city centre from Glasgow Green and hung about in town, reluctant to return to his empty flat. Even though the cops told him he'd be safe, he wasn't so sure. If only he'd thought about it sooner, he could have taken Ann-Marie away for a few days, perhaps down the coast to Ayr. They could have stayed in a B&B. It wouldn't have cost much as it was out of season and, besides, he had a little money saved for emergencies.

It was late afternoon now and the sky was darkening ominously. There was no point walking around aimlessly in the rain. He had to go home sometime. Feeling very low, Willie queued at the stop and waited for his bus to arrive. He'd feel better once he got into the heat and had something to eat and drink. He would go to Tesco when he got off the bus and pick up a ready meal and a six pack of beer. Then he could settle down and watch 'Casualty' on the telly later. He liked that programme. Suddenly, Jackie McGeachy's menacing face flashed into his mind. Willie shuddered involuntarily, maybe 'Casualty' wouldn't be such a good choice of viewing after all, he thought.

Chapter 36

Paul's mobile began to ring and he answered it on the hands free.

"DS Costello," he said.

"Paul, it's Frank, is Angela with you?"

"Yes, Frank, we're in my car. I'm on hands free so she can hear you."

"Where are you at the moment?"

"We've just left Scotstoun and we're on our way back to the office. We've been checking out a couple of leads."

"We got a call about gun shots being heard coming from a house in Scotstoun. The armed response unit is there now and Jack and Tony are at the scene. I'm just on my way over."

"Do you want us to swing round and join you, boss?"

"No, you two return to the office and man the fort. I'll call you if you're needed. If you have to leave the office to attend anything, phone me and let me know where you are. I'll keep in touch. I just hope this shooting has something to do with a current case. I don't think we could handle anything new. We're already drowning under work," he said, before doing the usual, and hanging up abruptly.

"Damn," Paul said. "So near and yet so far. I wish we'd got that shout. Now we'll most likely be stuck in the office for the rest of our shift."

"At least we'll get home tonight," Angela said. "Jack and Tony will probably be there for hours, particularly if it's something ongoing. Anything involving firearms can drag on and on."

"I suppose you're right," Paul replied, but he didn't sound convinced. He'd much rather have been at an incident than stuck indoors.

* * *

Willie splashed out, treating himself to an Indian meal at Tesco's. He bought a whole range of tasty delights, vegetable pakoras, papadoms, naan bread and a packet of chicken jalfrezi with basmati rice. He even purchased tinned mangoes for his dessert. And not for him a six pack of regular beer, instead he'd bought Carlsberg Special Brew. His stomach was rumbling at the very thought of eating. So far it hadn't rained. Another five minutes and he'd be home.

As Willie turned into his street and hurried along it, toting his bags, the first few spots of rain hit his face. I'll just make it, he thought. When he neared his flat, he noticed that the light was on in the front room. Willie was sure he'd switched it off. He stopped in his tracks and stared. Through the net curtains he could make out a woman's shape.

"Ann-Marie," he muttered, his face breaking into a grin. "You've come back to me, Doll."

He was about to run across the road to enter the close when the curtain was pulled aside and a man's face appeared, looking out of the window.

"Oh, fuck," Willie said aloud. It must be one of McGeachy's men, he thought. They've caught up with Ann-Marie and they've come for me.

He quickly walked on past his flat then made his way to the main road. Standing in a doorway, he took his mobile and Angela Murphy's card from his pocket and dialled her number.

Paul was watching some inane rubbish on his lap top when Willie's call came in. He was laughing out loud when Angela patted him on the arm to tell him to shut up and pay attention.

"You're absolutely sure there was a man in your house? And it wasn't anybody you recognised? I see, yes, I see, the man was black and you don't know any black men."

Angela felt a rush of adrenalin.

"Could you tell if he was a big built man, Mr Harkness?"

She turned to Paul and nodded then wrote on a notepad, John Baptiste???

Paul's face froze. Then he stood and grabbed his jacket.

"Tell him we're on our way," he said. "Warn him not to go near the flat."

They were half way to Maryhill when both of their mobiles rang only moments apart. Angela just had time to say to Paul, "Kenny Scott's back. He's at the paper. He's okay. McGeachy had him," when Paul took a call from Frank.

"McGeachy's dead," Frank said. It was relayed over the hands free. "He's been shot. The house is empty. Whoever killed him is gone, but my money's on Mickey Wu."

"I've just heard from Kenny Scott, boss. He's at the Gazette. He said he'd been held by McGeachy," Angela replied. "I'm so relieved. I thought he was a goner after all this time."

"Jesus Christ," Frank said. "I want you two to go and pick Scott up. Let's see what he knows."

"Can't, boss. Sorry," Paul cut in. "We're on our way to Maryhill, Davy Hughes' old place. We've had a reported sighting of Baptiste."

"Shit, no buses for hours then they all arrive at the same time," Frank replied. "Phone me when you reach the address. Don't enter the flat alone. Once you've gauged the situation, you can let me know if you need any help. Remember, don't take any chances. Baptiste is a big bugger, and he's mad, completely off his trolley. Okay? Understand? No heroics."

* * *

For all her previous confidence, Ann-Marie had been apprehensive about letting herself in to Willie's flat when he was out, more so because she'd brought John with her. She was worried about how he'd react. She knew Willie liked her and would help her all he could, but when he saw her with another man, would he still be happy about letting her stay?

John seemed to be okay, it was hard to judge him though as she'd known him for only a couple of hours. He seemed gentle and calm, rather eerily calm, and he spoke about God quite a lot. Maybe he was actually a guardian angel, sent to protect her, Ann-Marie speculated. Then she immediately chastised herself for having frivolous thoughts when she should have been concentrating on where to go next.

"Your friend is a good, Christian man," John stated, breaking her chain of thought.

"What makes you say that?" Ann-Marie asked, she was unaware of Willie having any religious belief, Christian or otherwise.

"This picture of Mary, above the bureau, it celebrates her holiness."

Ann-Marie hadn't even noticed the picture before. It was small and in a plain wooden frame, but as John gazed at it, he smiled benignly.

"Yes," he said, "Your friend is a good man. He will help us, Mother."

He'd called her that a couple of times now, even though she'd pointed out that she had no children. Ann-Marie glanced out of the window through the net curtain, where on earth could Willie be, she wondered.

"Do you want some tea, John?" she asked. "There's a packet of digestive biscuits. I could open them if you'd like."

"No, Mother, we have taken the man's shelter without his knowledge. We cannot take his food. We will await his return then break bread with him if food is offered."

Ann-Marie was beginning to feel rather uneasy. John's conversation was becoming increasingly strange. All this religious babble and references to God and why did he keep calling her mother?

"John," she said, "I think maybe, you should leave the flat. Go along to Tesco and wait for me there. I'll come and get you when Willie comes home. He might be upset to find I've let a stranger into his house."

"No, Mother, I will remain here with you. When Dad comes home I will deal with him. Don't worry, Mother, he will never hurt us again."

A jag of fear hit Ann-Marie square in the chest. John had changed. His expression was determined and hard. What was he talking about? Who did he think she was?

"John, John, what's going on?" she said grabbing his sleeve and tugging at his arm. "What's happened to you? Why are you saying these things?"

"Say your prayers, Mother. Beg God for forgiveness. Repent your sins. It won't be long now. When your husband returns, I will save you. I will save you both. Soon you'll be in our Father's house."

He's mad, Ann-Marie thought, I've let a madman into this house.

"You won't hurt me John, will you? I'll do anything you want, but please don't hurt me," she begged. "Let me help you to relax."

She reached out and began to unzip his trousers, rubbing and caressing him, trying to turn him on. She felt his penis stiffen.

"No," he roared, grabbing her by the shoulders. "Get thee behind me Satan," he screamed and he pushed her away from him, propelling her across the room.

John towered over the terrified young woman. He began to preach.

"And the Lord said," he started. "I will see you again, and your hearts will rejoice, and no one will take your joy from you. Be patient, Mother," he added,

"The time will soon be right. Soon you will be able to throw off your mortal coil."

* * *

"There he is," Angela said to Paul when she spotted Willie standing near the entrance to a clothes shop. "Pull in and we'll get him into the car."

As soon as Willie saw them, he wrenched open the back door and got in, throwing his shopping onto the seat beside him.

"Have you sent a cop car round to the flat? Do you think they'll be there yet?"

"We are it, Mr Harkness," Paul said. "We're responding to your call. Once we see what's going on, we'll decide if we need more officers."

"But McGeachy will probably have a weapon. His men will be tooled up as well. You two on your own wouldn't stand a chance against the likes of him."

"It's not McGeachy," Angela stated.

"What do you mean? Of course it's him. Who else would be at my flat with Ann-Marie? She wouldn't take a punter there."

"McGeachy's dead," Paul said. "His men will have more important things to think about than your friend."

"Dead? Are you sure? Then who's the big, black guy. Who's in my flat?"

Angela and Paul exchanged glances.

Willie leaned forward between the front seats and grabbed Angela's arm. "Tell me, what's going on," he said. "You know something, tell me who you think's in there."

Angela lifted Willie's hand from her arm.

"Calm down, Mr Harkness. We won't know anything for sure till we get inside your flat."

"But you have your suspicions," he persisted.

Paul parked a short distance from Willie's door. "Wait here," he said. "We'll try to see in through the window. Then we'll come straight back here and decide what to do."

"But what if you don't come back? Am I just expected to stay here knowing Ann-Marie's in trouble? I'm coming with you. I won't go near my house, but I'm not waiting in the car."

"We can't force you to remain in the car, but I warn you, if you get in our way, I'll arrest you for obstruction. Do you understand?" Angela said.

Willie nodded, "Aye, I understand," he replied reluctantly.

Paul edged along until he was standing to the side of the front window. He peered in, trying to see through the net curtains. He could make out John standing, his hands clasped in front of him, as if in prayer. There was no sign of Ann-Marie.

Quickly, he returned to the others.

"It's him, I could see him clearly, but I couldn't make out the girl. It's hard to see anything much through the net curtains. We'd better phone for back up."

Willie was alarmed. "Who did you see? Who's in my flat? Is Ann-Marie in trouble?"

Once again Angela and Paul exchanged glances.

"Tell me," Willie screamed.

"We're not a hundred per cent sure, but we think that it's John Baptiste," Angela said. "That's why we have to wait for assistance."

Paul was already on the phone calling for help.

"John Baptiste? The serial killer? And he's in the flat with my Ann-Marie? Well you can wait for assistance. I'm going to help my girlfriend."

Before they could stop him, Willie ran from them. By the time they'd caught up he had his key in the lock of his front door. Paul grabbed him and pulled him back. Then they heard Ann-Marie scream.

"Shit," Paul said, "We'll have to go in."

They could hear Ann-Marie begging, "Don't hurt me, John. Please don't hurt me."

"If she's talking, she's still alive," Paul said.

In the distance they could hear the sounds of approaching emergency vehicles.

"Help her," Willie beseeched. "She's just a wee lassie."

"You stay back," Angela said to Willie. "If you enter the flat, I'm leaving and you'll be on your own. Understand? Go outside and guide the emergency vehicles to the door. That will speed things up."

Without further question, Willie did as he was told.

Angela turned the key in the lock and opened the door then she and Paul quietly and cautiously entered the hallway. They could hear John preaching and Ann-Marie whimpering.

"I'm fucking terrified, by the way," Paul whispered.

"Me too," Angela replied.

"This is stupid and dangerous," Paul said.

"The boss is going to kill us," Angela replied.

"That's the least of our worries," Paul hissed.

They stood outside the door to the front room and listened.

"We cannot wait any longer for your husband to return," they heard John say. "The time is now, Mother. Now I will set you free. Let not your heart be troubled. You believe in God, believe also in me."

"Fuck, he thinks she's his mother and look what happened to her," Paul said.

Angela threw open the door and she and Paul rushed into the room. John was holding Ann-Marie by her hair. She was in a state of near faint. He held a narrow-bladed kitchen knife in front of her face.

He repeated for the benefit of the detectives, "Let not your heart be troubled. You believe in God, believe also in me."

He raised the knife.

"No, wait," Angela screamed. "Jesus said, I am the way, and the truth and the life. No one comes to the Father except through me."

John hesitated. "What are you saying, Sister?" he asked.

"Ann-Marie hasn't been baptised. She can't go to God without being baptised," Angela said, trying to play for time.

Paul stared at Angela in disbelief. He raised his eyebrows, clearly impressed.

"Is this true? You have not been baptised?" John asked the terrified girl.

"Nnno," Ann-Marie stammered, playing along. Her voice was little more than a whisper.

John released his grip slightly and the girl slid to her knees. He still held the knife. Nobody moved. They could all hear the emergency vehicles arriving outside.

"I cannot save you," John said sadly, releasing Ann-Marie from his grasp. "Father, forgive them for they know not what they do," he preached. Turning to Angela, he said, "You have killed me, but I will rise again."

Without warning or hesitation, John drew the blade across his throat, his blood spraying the room. Ann-Marie screamed hysterically as she was showered in gore.

"Noooo," Angela shouted, too late.

"Oh, fuck, no," Paul said.

John was dead before his body hit the floor.

Suddenly, the room was full of people. Ann-Marie had fainted clean away and was carried outside to be reunited with a very relieved, Willie Harkness. Angela and Paul were deeply shocked. They would later be taken to hospital to be checked over, but for the time being, they were ushered to one of the waiting ambulances.

"Where did you learn all that religious guff?" Paul asked. "I couldn't believe it when you started spouting it."

"Sunday school," Angela answered. "I can't believe I remembered it. It's amazing what you remember when you're stressed.

"You know you saved that girl's life. You should get a commendation or something."

"It's the something I'm worried about," Angela replied. "Frank told us not to go in without back-up. One of us is going to have to tell him what we did."

They sat in silence for a couple of minutes.

"Rock, paper, scissors," Paul said, "The loser tells Frank."

Angela won.

"Best out of three," Paul suggested.

"Not a chance, loser," Angela replied laughing. "Not a snowball's chance in Hell."

Chapter 37

It wasn't even a nine day wonder. After the deaths of Baptiste and McGeachy, the detectives basked in their glory for only a couple of days, before the media and the public lost interest. Good news didn't sell papers. However, Kenny Scott did become front page news. The Gazette ran with his personal story, 'My life amongst the Glasgow Gangs', for several days, before serialising his account of the Jackie McGeachy tale. Of course, Kenny carefully ignored the involvement of Mickey Wu. He had gained street smart and a strong sense of survival during his days in captivity. Kenny never received the second envelope of money he'd been promised. Alec Keys was long gone taking all the cash with him. But Kenny didn't care, he didn't want any contact with him ever again.

When God came to the office to congratulate the detectives on solving the cases, only Angela was there. Frank was off sick, having drunk himself into a stupor the night before after a blow up with his wife. Paul was at lunch. And Jack and Tony had been called to an incident of road rage which had culminated in a stabbing. So God congratulated Angela. And she alone was credited with the solving of the crimes. Angela was delighted and she shamelessly accepted all the praise.

"I'll remember you, Murphy," God said as he patted her on the shoulder. "I'll watch your career closely. You'll go far."

Angela smiled to herself. She was fiercely ambitious. She'd make sure she'd keep the Chief Inspector in the loop. His support could fast track her career.

Paul and Gemma moved house a few weeks after the furore died down. Bobby and Angela helped them by looking after their children and their dog for several hours. It was a nightmare. The noise level was unimaginable and the children's demands, constant. By the time Paul came to collect his brood,

Bobby and Angela weren't worth a button. The only good thing to come out of the experience, as far as Angela was concerned, was that Bobby stopped talking about babies.

On the gangster scene, nothing much changed. Mickey Wu was still in charge. One of his men took over Jackie McGeachy's patch. The police knew the gangs were operating, still running their illegal businesses, but they were powerless to do much about them. Until a major incident occurred, or someone made a complaint, there was nothing to go on. And of course no one could make a complaint then live to see it through.

Within a month everything was back to normal. Frank was sober. The detectives were working their usual shifts without overtime being required, and nothing of the previous month's magnitude had landed on Angela's desk. That was until her phone rang.

"Where did you say? Give me that address again," she said.

Her face was pale and strained with shock, she tapped the desk to gain Paul's attention.

"A major incident," she said. "And it's nasty, very nasty."

"Damnation," Paul replied. "And I've almost finished this Sudoku."

The End

About Elly Grant's books

From the Death in the Pyrenees series

'Palm Trees in the Pyrenees' is the first book in Elly Grant's series 'Death in the Pyrenees'.

The story unfolds, told by Danielle a single, downtrodden , thirty year old, who is the only cop in the small Pyrenean town. She feels unappreciated and unnoticed, having been passed over for promotion in favour of her male colleagues working in the region. But everything is about to change. The sudden and mysterious death of a much hated locally based Englishman will have far reaching affects.

'Grass Grows in the Pyrenees' is the second book in Elly Grant's series 'Death in the Pyrenees'.

The story unfolds, told by Danielle, a single, thirty year old, recently promoted cop. The sudden and mysterious death of a local farmer suspected of growing cannabis, opens a 'Pandora's' box of trouble. It's a race against time to stop the gangsters before the town, and everyone in it, is damaged beyond repair

Sample chapter enclosed - see the end of the book

'Red light in the Pyrenees' is the third book in Elly Grant's series 'Death in the Pyrenees'.

The story unfolds, told by Danielle, a single, thirty-something, respected, female cop. The sudden and violent death of a local Madame brings fear to her working girls and unsettles the town. But doesn't every cloud have a silver lining? Danielle follows the twists and turns of events until a surprising truth is revealed. Hold your breath, it's a bumpy ride.

'Dead End in the Pyrenees' is the fourth book in Elly Grant's series 'Death in the Pyrenees'.

The story unfolds, told by Danielle, a single, thirty-something, highly-respected, female cop. A sudden and unexpected death at the local spa brings to light other mysterious deaths. Important local people are involved, people who Danielle respects. She must quickly solve the case before things get out of control

'Deadly Degrees in the Pyrenees' is the fifth book in Elly Grant's series 'Death in the Pyrenees'.

The story unfolds, told by Danielle, a single, thirty-something, senior, female cop. The ghastly murder of a local estate agent reveals unscrupulous business deals. Danielle's friends may be in danger. She must catch the killer before anyone else is harmed

All these stories are about life in a small French town, local events, colourful characters, prejudice and of course, death.

Also by Elly Grant

The Unravelling of Thomas Malone

The mutilated corpse of a young prostitute is discovered in a squalid apartment.

Angela Murphy has recently started working as a detective on the mean streets of Glasgow. Just days into the job she's called to attend this grisly murder. She is shocked by the horror of the scene. It's a ghastly sight of blood and despair.

To her boss, Frank Martin, there's something horribly familiar about the scene.

Is this the work of a copycat killer?

Will he strike again?

With limited resources and practically no experience, Angela is desperate to prove herself.

But is her enthusiasm sufficient?

Can she succeed before the killer strikes again?

Massacre at Presley Park

It is 29th September on a hot, sunny day. Presley Park, in the centre of a leafy suburb, is the setting for a family charity picnic event. Most of the district has turned out and everyone is having fun until the unthinkable happens. Amongst the families, many of whom are in fancy dress, strides a lone man, he is clothed in combat gear and he's carrying an AK-47. He walks into the middle of the picnic ground seemingly unnoticed, but he is not taking part in the event. Without any warning, he opens fire indiscriminately into the startled crowd. People collapse wounded and dying. Those who can run, flee for their lives. Who is this madman and why is he here? What made him turn into a murderer?

The story takes us back to two weeks before the awful event, into the lives of the people involved. Who lives and who dies? Who amongst them become heroes, which cowards abandon their friends and where did everything go wrong?

Never Ever Leave Me

'Never Ever Leave Me' is a modern romance

Katy Bradley had a perfect life, or so she thought. Perfect husband, perfect job and a perfect home until one day, one awful day when everything fell apart.

Full of fear and dread, Katy had no choice but to run, but would her split-second decision carry her forward to safety or back to the depths of despair? A chance encounter with a handsome stranger gives her hope.

Never ever leave me, sees Katy trapped between two worlds, her future and her past. Will she have the strength to survive? Will she ever find happiness again?

Twists and Turns Released by Elly Grant Together with Zach Abrams With fear, horror, death and despair, these stories will surprise you, scare you and occasionally make you smile. Twists & Turns offer the reader thought provoking tales. Whether you have a minute to spare or an hour or more, open Twists & Turns for a world full of mystery, murder, revenge and intrigue. A unique collaboration from the authors Elly Grant and Zach Abrams.

A selection of stories by Elly Grant and Zach Abrams ranging in length across flash fiction (under 250 words), short (under 1000 words) medium (under 5000 words) and long (approx. 16,000 words)

Waiting for Martha

(released as a novelette but also included within Twists and Turns)

It is Halloween night. Four teenage friends spend their evening having fun and scaring younger children then suddenly, quite unexpectedly, one of the four, Martha goes missing. The fifteen year old simply vanishes without a trace leaving her friends and family anxiously searching for her. They are all waiting for Martha to come home, but as the night goes on they come to realise that they might be waiting for a very long time.

But Billy Can't Fly Released by Elly Grant Together with Angi Fox

At over six feet tall, blonde and blue-eyed, Billy looks like an Adonis, but he is simple minded, not the full shilling, one slice less than a sandwich, not quite right in the head. When you meet him you might not notice at first, but after a couple of minutes it becomes apparent. The lights are on but nobody's home. In Billy's mind, he's Superman, a righter of wrongs, a saver of souls and that's where it all goes wrong. He interacts with the people he meets at a bus stop, Jez, a rich public schoolboy, Melanie the office slut, Bella Worthington, the leader of the local W.I. and David, a gay, Jewish teacher. This book moves quickly along as each character tells their part of the tale. Billy's story is darkly funny, poignant and tragic. Full of stereotypical prejudices, it offends on every level, but is difficult to put down.

Chapter 1 of Grass Grows in the Pyrenees

For a moment he flew horizontally as if launched like a paper aeroplane from the mountain top then an elegant swan dive carried him over the craggy stone face of the mountainside. There was no thrashing of limbs or clawing at air, he fell silently and gracefully until a sickening crack echoed through the valley as bone and flesh crunched and crumpled on a rocky outcrop. The impact bounced him into the air and flipped him in a perfect somersault, knocking the shoes from his feet. Then he continued his descent until he came into contact with the grassy slope near the bottom of the mountain, where he skidded and rolled before coming to a halt against a rock.

His body lay on its back in an untidy heap with arms and legs and shoulders and hips smashed and broken. The bones stuck out at impossible angles and blood pooled around him. He lay like that for almost three days. During that time the vultures had a feast. There are several species of these birds in the mountains of the Pyrenees and all had their fill of him. Rodents and insects had also taken their toll on the body and, by the time he was discovered, he was unrecognisable.

A hunter found him while walking with his dog and, although he was used to seeing death, the sight of this man's ravaged face, with black holes where his eyes should have been, made him vomit.

Jean-Luc still wore the suit that he'd carefully dressed in for his meeting three days before. It looked incongruous on him in his present condition and in these surroundings. His wallet was still in his pocket and his wedding ring was still on his finger, nothing had been stolen.

The alarm had been raised by his business partner when he failed to turn up for their meeting but of course no one had searched for him in this place. This valley was outside of town and on the other side of the mountain from where he'd lived. He wasn't meant to be anywhere near to this place.

His wife hadn't been overly concerned when he didn't return because he often went on drinking binges with his cronies and he'd disappeared for several days on other occasions. She was just pleased if he eventually came home sober because he had a foul temper and he was a very nasty drunk. Indeed she knew how to make herself scarce when he was drunk, as more often than not, she would feel the impact of a well -aimed punch or a kick. Drunk or sober he lashed out with deadly accuracy and he was quick on his feet.

When he was finally discovered all the emergency services were called into action. The pompiers, who were firemen and trained paramedics, the police and the doctor, all arrived at the scene and an ambulance was summoned to remove the body to the morgue.

Everyone assumed he'd died as a result of his rapid descent from the mountain top and the subsequent impact on the ground below. But what they all wanted to know was whether his death was a tragic accident, or suicide, or perhaps something darker and more sinister, and why was he in this place so far from his home or from town? Many questions had to be answered and, being the most senior police officer in this area, meant that I was the person who'd be asking the questions.

About the Author

Hi, my name is Elly Grant and I like to kill people. I use a variety of methods. Some I drop from a great height, others I drown, but I've nothing against suffocation, stabbing, poisoning or simply battering a person to death. As long as it grabs my reader's attention, I'm satisfied.

I've written several novels and short stories. My series 'Death in the Pyrenees' comprises, 'Palm Trees in the Pyrenees,' 'Grass Grows in the Pyrenees,' 'Red Light in the Pyrenees,' 'Dead End in the Pyrenees,' and 'Deadly Degrees in the Pyrenees'. They are all set in a small town in France. These novels are published by Creativia. Creativia has also published, 'The Unravelling of Thomas Malone' - the first book of The Angela Murphy series, as well as 'Death at Presley Park.' 'Never Ever Leave Me,' 'But Billy Can't Fly' (co-written with Angie Fox) and a collaboration of short stories called 'Twists and Turns' (along with Zach Abrams) are also published.

As I live much of my life in a small French town in the Eastern Pyrenees, I get inspiration from the way of life and the colourful characters I come across. I don't have to search very hard to find things to write about and living in the most prolific wine producing region in France makes the task so much more delightful.

Perhaps you will visit my town one day. Perhaps you will sit near me in a café or return my smile as I walk past you in the street. Perhaps you will hold my interest for a while, and maybe, just maybe, you will be my next victim. But don't concern yourself too much, because, at least for the time being, I always manage to confine my murderous ways to paper.

Read books from the 'Death in the Pyrenees' series, enter my small French town and meet some of the people who live there –– and die there.

Alternatively read about life on some of the toughest streets in Glasgow or for something more varied delve into my other stories.

To contact Elly ellygrant@authorway.net

CPSIA information can be obtained
at www.ICGtesting.com
Printed in the USA
LVHW031447261120
672639LV00003B/246